IN THE ARMS OF AN ANGEL

"I didn't know angels danced so well."

"I've taken a few lessons in my time," he admitted with a grin. "Have I told you how beautiful you are?"

She blushed with pleasure. "No, but perhaps you shouldn't."

"Oh? Why not?"

"Well . . . I may come to think you regard me with . . . special favor."

His hand tightened on hers. "If you don't know that by now, you're blind."

"Oh, Simon." Disturbed, she locked gazes with him, then, caring nothing for what anyone might think, pressed closer to his chest. *He loved her. Her angel loved her!*

And so far, lightning had not struck.

Praise for *LORD MERLYN'S MAGIC*:

WATCH FOR THESE ZEBRA REGENCIES

LADY STEPHANIE   (0-8217-5341-X, $4.50)
by Jeanne Savery
Lady Stephanie Morris has only one true love: the family estate she has
managed ever since her mother died. But then Lord Anthony Rider
arrives on her estate, claiming he has plans for both the land and the
woman. Stephanie soon realizes she's fallen in love with a man whose
sensual caresses will plunge her into a world of peril and intrigue . . .
a man as dangerous as he is irresistible.

BRIGHTON BEAUTY   (0-8217-5340-1, $4.50)
by Marilyn Clay
Chelsea Grant, pretty and poor, naively takes school friend Alayna
Marchmont's place and spends a month in the country. The devastating
man had sailed from Honduras to claim his promised bride, Miss
Marchmont. An affair of the heart may lead to disaster . . . unless a
resourceful Brighton beauty finds a way to stop a masquerade and keep
a lord's love.

LORD DIABLO'S DEMISE   (0-8217-5338-X, $4.50)
by Meg-Lynn Roberts
The sinfully handsome Lord Harry Glendower was a gambler and the
black sheep of his family. About to be forced into a marriage of con-
venience, the devilish fellow engineered his own demise, never having
dreamed that faking his death would lead him to the heavenly refuge
of spirited heiress Gwyn Morgan, the daughter of a physician.

A PERILOUS ATTRACTION   (0-8217-5339-8, $4.50)
by Dawn Aldridge Poore
Alissa Morgan is stunned when a frantic passenger thrusts her baby into
Alissa's arms and flees, having heard rumors that a notorious highwayman posed a threat to their coach. Handsome stranger Hugh Sebastian
secretly possesses the treasured necklace the highwayman seeks and
volunteers to pose as Alissa's husband to save her reputation. With a
lost baby and missing necklace in their care, the couple embarks on a
journey into peril—and passion.

*Available wherever paperbacks are sold, or order direct from the
Publisher. Send cover price plus 50¢ per copy for mailing and
handling to Penguin USA, P.O. Box 999, c/o Dept. 17109, Ber-
genfield, NJ 07621. Residents of New York and Tennessee must
include sales tax. DO NOT SEND CASH.*

Darby's Angel

Marcy Stewart

ZEBRA BOOKS
KENSINGTON PUBLISHING CORP.

ZEBRA BOOKS are published by

Kensington Publishing Corp.
850 Third Avenue
New York, NY 10022

First Printing: July, 1996

Printed in the United States of America

10 9 8 7 6 5 4 3 2 1

*In memory of a real angel
and a beloved niece*

*KELLI DENISE FROEMKE
1975–1995*

Chapter One

She was the portrait come to life.

Beneath the arch of whispering ash leaves, Simon Garrett stared at her, hollow-eyed, disbelieving. It was impossible. The brown-haired beauty in the painting had lived and died nearly two centuries before.

He had spent too many days brooding in the library of Elena's ancestral home, that was all; too much time tracing resemblances of his late wife and son in the wall of fading British images. What a waste of time it had been, for none of the stiff-faced reproductions captured a glimmer of Elena's irrepressible spirit, of Tay's sense of mischief—none, that is, save the one of the brother and sister, the twins. And now it seemed the woman of that portrait stood before him, trembling at his presence in this lonely wood, her grey eyes sweeping his wild appearance from head to foot with wonder and fear.

Although he knew she must be a ghost born of his imagination and sorrow, he could not resist speaking the name he had seen inscribed in bronze beneath the portrait.

"Darby? Darby Brightings?"

"You speak rightly, sir," she answered. There was a tremor in her voice. Her lips pressed together at the sound of it, and when she spoke again it was gone. "And what— who might you be, and why do you trespass in my wood?"

His eyes widened. He had not expected this lovely delusion to answer him, and he felt afraid. This was beyond all sanity, all reason. Dell had warned him that his grief was spiralling out of control, and here was the evidence.

But she seemed so *real.* Her voice hinted of a nature sweet yet self-assured; the blood rushed and fled beneath seamless skin that revealed her emotions as transparently as the mood rings he had seen in his childhood.

She was waiting. The alarm he felt seemed to augment her own, or perhaps it was only his lengthening silence that increased her caution. She began to back away. Hallucination or not, he didn't want her to leave; not before this mystery was solved. She *must* be flesh-and-blood. Perhaps she was the troubled one, she of the long dress and upswept hair, thinking to call herself Darby Brightings.

"Wait," he said, reaching his fingers toward her, meaning to touch her face or sleeve or arm, anything to convince himself she lived.

"Do not dare to lay a hand upon me!" she declared immediately, taking another backward step. "I shall call my brother, and he will run you through with his sword!"

He almost smiled at this archaic threat, and the burst of humor startled him more than its cause. He'd never thought to laugh again. How could he?

The lightness drained away as quickly as it had come.

"I won't hurt you," he said.

But she was continuing to move backward, her gaze pinned to his face as if fearing he would attack her if she looked away.

Intent on demonstrating his harmlessness, he spread his

hands outward and stepped back between the ash trees, blinking when a wave of dizziness swept over him.

She vanished instantly. There was no noisy flight through the woods, no dash to hide behind a tree, not even the vapory dissolution one might expect at the disappearance of a ghost. She was simply . . . gone. And had that been her scream he heard, or was it only the echo of his ruined heart?

For many long minutes, he stared at the place she had been standing, allowing the horror to rise within him, almost enjoying it. It had been months since he felt anything. When he turned homeward at last, his steps were no longer aimless through the dense wood.

"Well, what think you of my new designs?" Alexander Brightings asked his sister impatiently. "You look to be dozing over them. Are they so dull?"

Darby turned from the wall of windows that broke the daylight into little squares across her hands, the sheaf of papers she held, and onto the marble floor of the conservatory. She blinked away her contemplation of the ridge of woods behind the house and focused her gaze on the sketches.

"They are only preliminary, of course," he added, an anxious note creeping in. "I can refine them, make them more detailed if you think I should."

She paged slowly through the ink drawings, pausing now and then to look closer when something caught her interest. Her eyebrows lifted at one, her lips curled upward at another. Alexander, studying her face intently from his chair across the room, gradually relaxed and crossed one long leg over the other. A similar smile curved his mouth as he began to pluck pieces of lint from his pantaloons and flick them to the floor.

"This is your finest work to date," she said. "John Flaxman himself could not have done better when he was working for Mr. Wedgwood.''

''That's going it too strong,'' Alexander protested, but his face betrayed delight. ''You saw his sculpture of Sir Joshua Reynolds at St. Paul's. I haven't one fraction of his talent.''

''Perhaps not in sculpting, but I know of no one who surpasses you in design. I've never seen such striking interpretations of Greek myths. Our name will become as well known as Wedgwood or Spode.''

With an answering enthusiasm, he leaned forward, arms dangling over his legs, his grey eyes twinkling. ''A single place setting shall be thought cheap at fifty pounds.''

She joined in the old game, the game their father had begun with them as children. ''Daughters will treasure their mother's Brightingsware and add to their collection every generation.''

He scowled abruptly and leaned back.

''If only Uncle Richard would allow us to take the pottery into the nineteenth century. How can we hope to compete using old methods while a few miles away, Staffordshire employs tens of thousands using modern equipment? Had Father not purchased a steam engine before he died, we would still be grinding flint and pigments by hand.''

''I know it well, but we shan't have to endure our uncle much longer.''

The young man brightened at this. ''Yes, thank God.'' He sprang to his feet and stood beside her. Darting a stealthy look toward the hall, he lowered his voice and added, ''I think our esteemed relation is overdue a measure of justice, do you not?''

She did not answer, did not appear to have heard him. Again her gaze had drifted to the landscape beyond the window; his carefully-prepared artwork lowering as if forgotten.

A twinge of annoyance crossing his brow, Alexander

took the papers from her fingers, meeting no resistance. After replacing the sketches in his portfolio, he returned to her side and observed her with increasing worry. Her strong profile, so much a feminine version of his own, remained unmarked by anxiety or any other emotion, yet tension emanated from her like ripples of heat from an inferno.

Slipping an arm around her waist, he forced a chuckle into his voice and said, "Oh, come now, old girl. It has been weeks since we plagued him last. You remember how good it felt, don't you?"

Although she continued to stare at the wood, her lips twitched. "You were inspired in your choice of blue."

Alexander laughed. "But it was your notion to paint the interior of his hat. His hair shone with indigo highlights for weeks. We make an incomparable pair, do we not?"

She looked at him at last, a little sideways glance that sparkled with affection. "A pair of terrors, more like. We have been called so often enough."

"Only by those who do not matter."

Her eyebrows arched. "The servants and our relatives do not matter?"

"I have spoken too hastily," he conceded with a grin. "Of course the servants' opinions matter."

"But not those of our relatives."

"You have said it, not I."

Darby's smile remained in place, though her eyes grew serious. "Not even the opinion of our golden-haired cousin, then? She does not concern you?"

Displaying sudden absorption in a butterfly seeking entrance through the glass, Alexander withdrew a step, his arm drifting away from his sister's waist.

"Lenora is not really our cousin," he said carefully.

"Oh, I see," Darby said quietly, returning her attention to the window. "Poor Evelyn."

"Don't be an idiot, twin. You are making too much of

it. My affections are not engaged by anyone. I'm too young to be leg-shackled, don't you think?"

"I think you won't be able to say that much longer. Not if Lenora has her way."

His eyes widened. "Oh, come now. Surely you don't believe—"

Without turning her head, she asked softly, "You think I'm wrong about the attractiveness of the heir to Brightings?"

He regarded her in silence, his eyes stormy. Slowly the fire bled from his veins. In gentle tones he said, "You're not yourself. What troubles you, Darby? For days you've acted strangely, taking long walks and looking out windows. Tell me."

She lowered her eyes. "There is nothing to tell, Alex."

Stepping closer, he patted her cheek lightly. "You're lying, old girl. Don't you know you can't hide anything from me?"

Evading his eyes, she turned from the window and strolled away, pausing at a collection of potted plants gathered near the window but placed out of the direct rays of the sun.

Fingering a fern frond absently, she inquired in an off-hand voice, "Have you seen any strangers hereabouts, Alex? Recently, I mean?"

"No," he answered, joining her, standing so closely she had to look at him. "Have you? Is this what is wrong? Has someone troubled you? I shall kill him."

She laughed suddenly, but her eyes were bright and her cheeks scarlet. "Oh, Alex, did anyone hear you they would think a hot-headed child was speaking. Of course I haven't seen anyone. Everyone knows there are no strangers at Brightings!"

* * *

Simon returned to the wood every day for a week, always searching for her but too afraid to admit it to himself. That he didn't see her again confirmed his fears: she had been a figment of his imagination. Of course he had known it all along; ghosts did not exist.

But no, unless he was totally insane, he *had* seen her, and she seemed so alive! If only he could see her once more, help her. Maybe she was earthbound, waiting for someone to release her soul. Perhaps she needed to understand how it was she died. He could tell her that, now that he'd read the family history. Where was she?

Just listen to him. Had he really come to believe in ghosts?

Well, why not? Apparitions were easier to explain than the evil which had befallen his family. Evil in the guise of love.

He had told no one of his sighting, though he did ask the housekeeper a few questions that made her view him in alarm. The cheery, middle-aged lady half-spooked him with her answers.

"Be careful, Mr. Garrett," she warned. "Be careful of them woods. My family's lived here for centuries, and the old name for that forest is Witchwood. People have wandered in there never to return. There are legends that the wood swallows the desolate in heart. It happened to a great-uncle of mine. After his love married another, he entered the trees and was never seen again."

"That seems easily explained. He probably killed himself, if you'll forgive me for saying so."

"My father's uncles searched the entire wood and never found his bones."

"Well, then," he said, exasperated, "he walked out the other side when no one was looking."

"Yes." She nodded wisely. "But what was on the other side?"

He snorted. "Mrs. Greene, you should have been a screenwriter."

But in spite of his amusement, he continued to hear her words as he searched. *The wood swallows the desolate in heart.* If that was the requirement, he must look very appetizing to every oak, beech and ash tree springing from this ancient earth.

Ash trees . . . Hadn't he walked between a pair of ash trees when he saw Darby? Childhood rituals sprang to his mind. *Step on a crack, break your mother's back. It's all right to lie if you cross your fingers behind your back. Put your tooth beneath the pillow and the tooth fairy will come.* Everything magical had to be done in a certain way or the spell wouldn't work. Maybe he should find those trees and walk through them again.

He laughed at himself and walked on. But his eyes moved restlessly, scanning the treetops. He wasn't looking for anything in particular, of course; but he wanted to find those ash trees, just to see if he could.

It was a beautiful wood; haunting, really. Little undergrowth marred the soil, almost as if the earth had been swept clean of the tangled vines and rotting logs he expected. Were English forests as refined as their people were reputed to be? Didn't their woods grow as thick and wild as American ones?

As he neared the heart of the forest, the little noises of birds chattering, branches rustling and his Reeboks crackling over fallen leaves and pine needles grew quieter, as though muted. He remembered that preternatural hush from his other excursions, but today the silence seemed fraught with meaning. Where were those ash trees?

And then he saw them, two widely-spaced towers whose upper branches interlocked as if one reached to embrace the other. Without hesitation, he plunged beneath the arch.

For a moment he felt disoriented, the ground sliding

beneath him as if his shoes had suddenly sprouted wheels. When the world righted itself, he felt a surge of hope. Hadn't he experienced this strange imbalance just before he sighted her?

"Darby?" he called tentatively.

Silence met his ears. Feeling increasingly foolish, he cried her name again and again.

The forest remained stubbornly quiet, mocking him with moist, dark smells that hinted of growing things, of unrestricted life burrowing beneath the earth and scurrying among the leaves. *No room here for ghostly dead things*, it said.

He breathed in disappointment. She wasn't here. Of course she wasn't. Had he really expected her to be?

He should go home, fly back to Los Angeles and plunge into work. That was what Dell wanted him to do, and he'd asked as a friend, not an agent, wasn't that what he'd said? Dell's concern had nothing to do with Mel Luther wanting him for his next film.

Right.

He shrugged his shoulders and turned back, avoiding the ash trees as he would a besotted fan. His old sorrow, for days held at bay because of the mystery which had now proved to be nothing, again branded horrible images into his brain.

Tasting bitterness, he retraced his steps for a long time, the puzzling configuration of trees hardly capturing his notice. No matter how often he walked here, nothing ever became familiar. He could almost begin to think himself lost were it not for the gradual thinning of the trees.

When he cleared the forest, he stopped, paralyzed.

Before him lay Brightings, but it was not the Brightings he had inherited from Elena's estate.

The west wing was completely gone, as though removed with a scalpel; yet the surgery had left no scars. What remained of the house looked cleaner; the stones shone brighter with no traces of rust around the outside spigots—there *were* no spigots—and the grounds were different, with orderly rows of flowers and shrubs set in squares, and a high hedge in front.

Could someone in the neighborhood have built a newer, more compact version of Brightings? But, other than the differences in the garden, the layout of the road and forest looked the same.

As he watched, a boy emerged from the back of the house carrying a pail of something which he dumped into a pile of dirt and leaves. He raked the foul-looking mess into a heap, drew a bucket of water from the well—*from the well?*—rinsed the pail, and returned inside, whistling all the while.

Simon stood on the edge of the forest, alarm clanging within. The boy had been wearing kneepants, stockings, a peasant blouse of some sort, a vest to match the pants, and shoes with buckles.

The house and the child were not alone in their wrongness. In the time he had been standing here—five minutes at least—not one car had passed on the highway at the end of the long drive. And, unless his eyes deceived him, the highway was no longer paved.

How could the road not be paved? Where was this place? *What is on the other side?* Mrs. Greene had asked him.

This was crazy. He should go down there and ask to use the phone. He would call Mrs. Greene and demand she pick him up, because he was lost.

But he did not move for a long while, not until he saw Darby Brightings riding toward him from the vast park in back of the house. She appeared to be headed toward the garages—stables?—and her path would take her directly past him.

Stomach lurching, he turned from the inexplicable scene, leaned his back against an oak tree and bent over, bracing his hands on his knees. He had not really expected to see her again, and certainly not like this, painted into her background, not his.

Life as he knew it was over. He'd end his days in an asylum.

"That is not Darby Brightings," he panted, repeating it like a mantra, covering his ears to shut out the sound of hoofbeats approaching. "Not. Not. Not Darby Brightings."

"But it is," came that clear voice he remembered, though it wavered with an emotion similar to his own. "Have I not told you before? And you have returned, I see."

He lowered his hands slowly, pushed away from the tree, and turned around. His heart beat like a jackhammer, pumping all the way into his eyes, making the woman seated sidesaddle on the beautiful grey horse appear to jump up and down. Well, he'd wanted to find her and there she was, wearing a black velvet riding habit, not more than ten feet away from where he stood, and he couldn't think of anything to say. His senses were overloading. If he were a computer, smoke would be pouring from his microchips.

While he continued to regard her with silent awe, she spoke again. "Perhaps now you will answer the question I asked then. Who, or ... what ... are you?"

"To tell you the truth," he said finally, his voice cracking like a boy's, "right now I'm not sure what I am."

She appeared startled by his answer, but curiosity blended with the fear in her eyes. "When I met you several days ago, you ... vanished from sight." She chuckled nervously. "It was almost as if you were a—a spirit of some sort."

He stared. It was what he'd feared about *her*. He didn't verbalize the thought but made a sound that would have been a laugh if he were not so dumbfounded.

"Oh, that. It must have been a trick of the light."

A feeble explanation to be sure, but he didn't want her

thinking he was a tree nymph or something worse. But why should he care what she thought? She was an illusion. Still, he couldn't just ignore her until she went away, could he? What *were* the rules of etiquette for conversing with a hallucination?

She was eyeing him skeptically. "Truly? I could not find you anywhere."

"I'm very fast." The explanation rolled off his tongue without premeditation. Maybe he was beginning to relax. Now, if only he could enjoy his madness.

"I see," she said thoughtfully. The fear faded from her expression. She appeared to be gaining confidence, looking down at him from her proud seat, and sparks flew into her eyes. "Then, if you are merely a man, you must tell me why you have chosen to trespass again. Perhaps you are a thief or a poacher. If you have heard we do not hang such misdoers at Brightings, do not think we pardon them. If that is your intent, you will not go unpunished."

"No, I'm not—I don't—I'm not a thief."

"Then you won't mind telling me your name."

Hesitating only briefly, he told her.

"You are an American, aren't you?" she accused.

He swallowed dryly and admitted it.

"Perhaps that explains the strangeness of your raiment," she said softly, as if to herself. "Although even the Americans I have known do not dress themselves so."

He glanced down at his jeans and sweatshirt which was emblazoned with three lightning bolts, one beneath the other, each boasting the title of his latest film, *Assassin from Hell.* He smiled briefly and apologetically, folding his arms across his chest.

And then the unreality of the situation fell over him again, shocking as an icy shower. The young lady glaring down at him was no ghost. Somehow—no, he could not think it; that was sheer insanity, but yes, yes, it *had* to be!— in some unbelievable way, he had stepped through a pair of trees and walked into the past. And if that were so, if he did not sit screaming in a padded cell somewhere, he could prevent this girl's untimely death, *for he knew her future.*

But should he? Every movie he'd seen, every science fiction novel he had read on the subject during his fantasy-prone youth, had cautioned against changing the past. Step on a worm out of time, and you could wipe out an entire nation.

He didn't care if he did. Looking at Darby now, seeing her lean forward to pat her horse's neck while her suspicious gaze never left Simon's face, he could only think: *What if someone had warned Elena?*

But Darby was speaking again. "Perhaps it would be prudent for you to come inside and explain yourself to my brother. He prefers to be apprised of strangers on our land."

"What? Oh, no, I don't think so." One person from the past was enough for his brain to deal with. Two, if he counted the boy with the pail.

"If your intentions are as harmless as you say, there should be no objection."

Things were spinning out of control. He had better get on with it before she called the police, or whatever law enforcement they had in these times.

"What's today's date?" he blurted.

She frowned. "I beg your pardon?"

"The date," he said, impatient to be done now that he had started. "You know—the month, the day, the year."

"Surely you jest. And your tone offends me."

"I'm sorry, but I'm in a hurry. Please answer my question. I—I hit my head and can't remember."

She glanced doubtfully at his unblemished forehead. In a skeptical voice she murmured, "It is the fifth day of April, eighteen eighteen, and if you have truly injured your head, you should come inside. My housekeeper can attend to it."

"That's all right; it doesn't hurt anymore."

He stepped closer, lifting his hand toward her in a rush of earnestness. Although he meant only to touch the horse's neck or his reins as if making some connection would make his next words more believable, she flinched. He lowered his arm but did not back away.

Fastening his gaze on hers, calling upon all his power as an actor to deliver his lines with sincerity and conviction, he said, "Darby, I've come here for a reason." He grimaced at the pretentiousness of his words, but he was an actor, not a writer, and he pressed on, "I've come to warn you about something that will happen in "—he calculated, then said wonderingly—" in three days."

Her eyes narrowed as she waited.

"You and your brother are planning a visit to an abandoned house somewhere in the neighborhood, aren't you?"

"I know of no such plans."

He sighed. "Well, if you haven't thought of it yet, you will."

"How can you possibly know that?" Her voice rang with anger.

He felt a corresponding irritation rising. Two hundred years he'd traveled to help her, and she wouldn't listen to him.

"It doesn't matter how I know. The point is, the two of you *will* go, and there'll be a fire. You'll both be trapped. Alexander will escape with a few burns, but you'll die, Darby. That's why I'm warning you. Don't go to that house."

"You are mad!"

Simon grabbed the horse's reins. "Listen to me! I have no reason to tell you this except to save you!"

"Release me at once!" she cried. Her hand moved suddenly to seize her whip. Not taking time to unfurl it, she banged the handle against his head.

"Ow! Stop it!" He jerked the whip from her hands, half-pulling her from the saddle as he did so.

"Help!" she screamed. "Someone help me! Alexander!"

Dear God. They were far enough from the house that no one should be able to hear her, but if anyone looked out the window and saw them flailing at each other, he was a dead man. An interesting thought, that. Born in the twentieth century, executed in the nineteenth.

Ducking the open-palmed blows she rained on his skull, he said, "I'm sorry, Darby, for what I'm about to do." And he pulled her from the saddle, clutched her around the waist, placed a hand over her mouth, and dragged her toward the trees.

Whether she wanted him to or not, he was going to rescue her.

She kicked and fought like a wildcat and about as effectively, her riding boots hammering bruises into his shins. Amid his pain he saw the stallion turn toward home. When the stableboys saw the riderless horse, they would search for her. Hopefully the servants wouldn't look in the woods for awhile.

As soon as they were out of sight of the house, Simon released her mouth—she had bitten his palm in several places—and was rewarded with a piercing scream.

"Will you stop?" he yelled, wrapping both arms around her waist to keep her from wriggling away. "I'm not going to hurt you, I promise! I just want to convince you I'm telling the truth!"

"Indeed?" She took a few heaving breaths. "You have an unusual way of showing it!"

"I did apologize, but you weren't listening to what I said."

"I heard every word," she said acidly.

"But you didn't believe me. I'm going to prove it to you." *I hope.* Surely his trip wouldn't be one-way. *The wood swallows . . .*

He didn't want to be marooned in the past. Days ago he had evidently gone back and forth between the centuries by walking under the ash trees. Surely he could return again to Elena's home, and surely he could take Darby with him.

It would be no kindness to shatter her world with time travel. But once she saw the future Brightings and read the family history, she could not deny the evidence of her own eyes. There would be no untimely tragedy, no shriveling fire to transform a vital life into ashes. Such things should never happen, especially not to the young. Not to anyone.

Not to Elena and Tay, either, but no one had warned them.

Then, after he returned Darby to her own time, he'd chop down the ash trees. Easy passage between centuries couldn't be a good thing. The world might tilt off its axis or something.

"And how do you propose to do that?" Darby snapped.

He released her waist carefully, grabbing her hand in a tight grip at the same time.

"Come with me. You'll see."

He tugged gently, then harder as her boots remained planted on the soil. She came with him grudgingly, her fiery eyes becoming guarded and, he thought with a lifting of spirits, a little interested.

"What you are about to experience may seem frightening at first, but don't be afraid," he said, trying to sound encouraging. "Nothing will harm you."

He put on his most appealing expression, lifting his brows, forcing an entreating twinkle into his eyes. It was the look even his critics called *irresistibly charming,* but she was having none of it, would not so much as meet his eyes.

They trudged on in silence for some time, he darting

looks at her, she staring resolutely ahead, her mouth set in a thin, tight line.

"How far away is this . . . proof?" she asked finally, in scornful tones.

"We're almost there," he answered, his heart pounding as he spotted the ash trees. What if he went through and nothing happened? A fitting end it would be for him, to be trapped in a world without television or movies. He had lost everything else; why not his profession, too?

He stopped before walking beneath the interlocking branches and contemplated her. Darby's indignant eyes darkened to a stormy grey-blue, swimming with questions and caution.

"You have to understand," he said at last, "I've never done this with anyone before. I don't know if you'll be able to go with me."

"Go with you where?" she asked, looking at him dubiously, then glancing past his shoulder at the endless procession of trees.

"To the place where truth lives," he whispered, thinking to make the future sound magical. Maybe she'd believe an enchantment had fallen over her and afterwards remember her experience as a dream. It might save her from madness.

"To the place where truth lives?" she whispered back, caught in his spell. But then her eyebrows lowered.

"Hold on tight," he said quickly, before she could change her mind and back away. He pulled her toward the arch.

The disorientation, the dizziness, swept through him with nauseating strength. A hurling wind buffeted his hair backward. He pressed on, pushing against a force that willed him back. He squinted and lowered his head. Windy tears swept from his eyes. The maelstrom stung his face with sandy pellets. How long was it, this arch? It hadn't been like this before. And then, while his cries echoed

Darby's screams, her hand whipped backward from his; and he plunged to the leaf-covered earth on the other side of the trees, alone.

"No!" he shouted, struggling to his feet, looking around frantically for any signs of Darby. She was not on the other side of the trees; she did not run from him through the forest. She had not come through.

He leaned his hand against one of the ashes, shaking in reaction. His eyes burned with frustrated tears. He could not save her. He could not make this one little difference in all the tragedies of the world.

A sudden, feeble hope came to him then. Pushing away from the tree, he stared into the arch with resolution and licked his lips. He cupped his hands around his eyes and stepped back through the trees.

There was no hurricane this time, only that slight tilting of the ground he'd felt before. And there, sprawled in a dead faint at his feet, lay Darby. He knelt beside her immediately, his soul singing with relief and regret. Poor girl. What had he done to her?

He slipped his arm beneath her head and cradled her against him. There was not a flutter from her lashes when he did so. Her hat had fallen off, and golden brown hair trailed across her shoulders. Despite her faint, her cheeks glowed pink against ivory skin. Hesitantly, surprised at the rush of tenderness he felt for this unconscious creature, he patted her face lightly.

"Darby, wake up. It's all right. You're okay."

Her lids opened slowly. Blinking several times, she lifted her gaze to his. Immediately, her eyes widened in fright, and she struggled from his arms to sit several feet away.

He was glad she did. Holding her made him uneasy.

"What are you?" she whispered. "A mighty wind pushed against me; then you vanished again, and it was no trick of the light." She scanned his face, the silvery-blond hair falling dishevelled against his neck, the words embedded on his shirt. With trembling lips, she asked, "Be you angel or demon?"

She was making him laugh. Before he could deny being one or the other—indeed, before he disclaimed his belief in the existence of either—the thought struck him forcefully: *this is the way to convince her. She has given you the means of saving her.*

Religion would be real to Darby. People in this age surely weren't disillusioned, at least not to the extent of twentieth-century man. Darby would believe those old stories, the ones he hadn't given credence to since he sat as a child in Sunday School.

Were he to start babbling about being from the future, now *that* she wouldn't believe. But if he told her he had a message from God . . . True inspiration!

He called upon his talent, gathering sincerity from every corner of his soul. Rising to his feet, he looked down at her kindly.

"Yes, Darby," he said, his voice throbbing with truth. "I wasn't supposed to tell you, but you've guessed it, and I can't lie to you. I—I'm an angel."

If Dell could hear him, how he would howl!

Darby's mouth dropped, her eyes searching his. She wasn't entirely convinced, he could see that.

Her gaze lowered. "But, your clothing—"

His cursed shirt; why hadn't he thrown it out?

"Oh, this?" He laughed lightly. "It's not mine. I had to borrow it after—after I waged war with some demons."

That was right, wasn't it? Angels fought wars. He thought he recalled something about Michael or Gabriel fighting with bad spirits; a dragon, if he wasn't mistaken. Yes, he remembered being enraptured by that image as a boy.

"But . . . you are an American, you said. I didn't know angels were Americans."

"Angels come in all nationalities," he said heartily.

"And you have a first and last name. I thought angels had a single appellation."

He cleared his throat. "Well, some do, but not all. The famous angels only need one name because everybody knows them. You've heard of Gabriel, of course, but have you ever heard of me?"

"I certainly have not." She frowned. "And you say you have come to warn me ..."

"Yes. You can't go to that house. What I've told you is true. You'll die."

She lowered her eyes and blinked rapidly, sorting through an inner confusion. "Why have you told me this? I know of no one else who has received such a warning."

His thoughts sped. "That's because dealings between people and angels have to remain secret. You can't ever tell anyone you saw me, or they might"—*put you away*—"um, become jealous of you, since you're one of those who merit individual attention."

"But why me? Why do I deserve notice?" Her expression grew pensive. "No one warned my father not to take the long walk that caused his heart to fail. My mother might be alive now had an angel stopped her from crossing an old footbridge when she visited her friend."

Why, indeed? It was a question that had been nibbling at his own mind. How was it the passage linked him to this century, this time? Why not carry him back only a year, so he could warn Elena? What strange alignment of dimensions kept him returning to Darby again and again?

Were he superstitious, he could almost think the situation smacked of destiny. But life had taught him differently. There was no supernatural guidance, only random events, and sometimes, cause and effect.

"Don't worry about it," he said. "Leave the reasons to God."

He sounded as mysterious as his dotty old Sunday School

teacher had when one of the children asked a question she couldn't answer.

Uncertainty warred with hope in her eyes. "If you truly are an angel," she said slowly, "can you do something to prove yourself to me?"

"A miracle, you mean?" He forced sternness into his voice. "Wasn't vanishing through the trees enough for you?"

She bowed her head. "I'm sorry. Yes, of course it was."

Sunlight laced through the trees, kissing the top of her head with crimson sparks. Pity pierced him. She was struggling so hard to believe, and no wonder. To think how he appeared to her—hair uncombed, face unshaven, clothes ragged. He must look like a bum.

Slipping a hand into his back pocket, he pulled out his Walkman, turned it on, and held it to his ear, hoping time travel hadn't affected the batteries. He grinned at the sound of joyous strings, turned it off, then pulled her to her feet and draped the earphones over her head—not without a tussle, because plainly she didn't trust him to touch her.

"Listen, Darby," he whispered. "Listen to the music of heaven."

He pushed the on button and thanked himself for craving Baroque music today and not heavy metal; otherwise, she *would* think he was from hell.

At the first sounds, her hands flew to her ears, and she jerked at the headphones as if to fling them away. Immediately he covered her fingers, stilling them, forcing her to listen. Gradually her fright faded to wonder, and the eyes that met his brimmed with delight and tears.

"Vivaldi?" she breathed. "Vivaldi is played in heaven?"

"Naturally. You know *The Four Seasons?*"

"I have heard it performed in London, but never so beautifully as this. Oh, how wonderful."

He smiled and lowered his fingers, but she kept hers

over her ears, as if dropping her hands would take away the magical sounds. She stood that way for a long time, her expression intent and faraway, lost in the music.

Finally she came to herself, pulled the headphones from her head and gave them to him. Her glance moved upward from his hands, flickered over the words on his chest, and settled at his throat. Breathing in suddenly, she sank to her knees and lowered her head.

"Forgive me for doubting you," she said.

Shame and dismay washed over him. Seizing her arms, he pulled her to her feet.

"Never do that, Darby. Don't you know better than to worship an angel?"

"I'm sorry," she said humbly. "I meant no offense."

He tugged her chin upwards so she would look at him. "You haven't offended me. Just promise you'll heed my warning."

"I will, sir."

Mission accomplished. He breathed the clear air of relief.

"That's all I ask," he said. "Except, don't call me sir."

"No, I won't, my lord—my angel—you *are* my guardian angel, are you not?"

"Yes, yes," he said, exasperated. "But call me Simon."

"Simon," she repeated obediently.

It was his turn to view her with uncertainty. He did not know what to make of this suddenly pious young woman.

The thing to do now was go back to his time and read the family history, see if he'd been able to change the past. He could hardly wait to find out. Yet still he stood there, hating the way she regarded him with awe. He'd set her straight if he could, but it was best she felt this way, best she feared him, because now surely she wouldn't go into that house.

Go on. Go back. You've done all you can.

Still he remained there, watching her watch him with nervous glances that continued to hold questions.

"I must go back," he said at last.

"Back to heaven?" she asked in a shaking voice. "Was that where you were trying to take me moments ago?"

"Heaven?" Scalding memories sifted through his mind. Reporters pushing microphones in his face. Paparazzi flashing their cameras behind every corner, everywhere he went, feeding off his sorrow like parasites, splattering his grief in their tabloids for all the world to see. "Hardly."

"Oh," she said in some relief. "I thought perhaps that was where you wanted me to go when you offered proof, as John was taken to heaven for awhile in a vision. When the gale prevented me, I feared it meant I was unworthy."

He could not resist touching her cheek. This time, she didn't flinch away. He felt lower than a snake for inspiring such fear in her. If there existed a God to strike him dead, this was His opportunity.

"You're as worthy as anyone I know," he said gently. "No, I'm not returning to heaven. There are other places on earth that need me."

"Oh, certainly. Well . . . thank you, Simon."

"You're welcome." He turned to the ash trees, moving slowly, reluctantly. Before going through he paused again, looking at her once more. "Remember my warning, now. You've promised."

"I will," she said solemnly, raising her hand in a wave. "Farewell, Simon. Shall I—shall I see you again?"

"No, Darby. It's best that guardian angels remain invisible."

He heard the regret in his voice with surprise. A sad kind of spell was weaving itself into the leaves and branches surrounding them. Before he allowed it to sink into his bones, he returned her wave and stepped beneath the trees.

Chapter Two

"Oh, darling!" sang Aunt Gacia in her fluttery, high-pitched voice as she descended the hall stairway of Brightings Manor, her gauzy shawl caressing the handrail behind her like a train. "Where is my darling Mr. Lightner?"

Ensconced within a deep winged chair by the parlor fire, a book of sermons opened on her lap, Darby looked up and met her brother's agonized gaze. Alexander, who was seated a few feet away on the sofa flanking the fireplace, dropped his newspaper to the floor, pressed his hand to his heart, rolled his eyes, turned sideways on the couch, and fell backward as if dead. His legs rose to plummet the air, then dropped in an ungainly sprawl across the sofa's arm.

For the first time in the weeks which had passed since her guardian angel disappeared, Darby laughed unrestrainedly.

"Where are you, my darling?" Aunt Gacia persisted gaily from the hall, drawing nearer. "Remember, guests are coming this evening, and you must dress for dinner. And though they are only our neighbors, the good souls are none the less important for that, for they cannot help where they live. Where are you, Mr. Lightner?"

"Not here!" cried Alex, stirred from his funereal pose. "He is not in the parlor, so look somewhere else, I beg you!"

With the unerring direction of an arrow, Aunt Gacia turned into the room, her head swiveling right and left. "He is not here?" she asked woefully, clasping her hands beneath her thin bosom.

"No, he isn't," Alexander said peevishly. "Did I not tell you?"

"Well, you are always so busy with your painting, dear; I thought you might have overlooked him."

"Not possible," Darby commented quietly, having recovered her composure. She turned the page of her book.

"Oh, I don't know," the older lady said. "He can be most unassuming at times; one hardly notices him."

Darby stared at her aunt, wondering how anyone could delude herself so. But her mother's sister had ever held to her own opinions, opinions formed of logic unknown to the world in general.

If Aunt Gacia was trying in her speech and thoughts, at least she was not embarrassing to behold. Her thin, sharp-boned face still held traces of her former beauty; the beauty Rosemary, Darby and Alexander's mother, had shared, for the sisters had also been twins. Although the skin sagged now at Aunt Gacia's neck and beneath her blue eyes, Darby often envisioned her mother's youthful face overlaying her aunt's.

All the more reason to view her relative with pain, especially when the woman spouted nonsense as she was wont to do. How Gacia could be twin to the sensible Rosemary, Darby could not understand. She and Alexander were of different sexes, yet their minds were never so far apart.

"Perhaps Mr. Lightner is in the stables," Aunt Gacia said thoughtfully.

"Wherever he is, he's asleep," Alexander said. "And why must you persist in calling him by his surname? It is ridiculously formal and drives me mad everytime you do it."

"Oh, Alexander," Aunt Gacia said, laughing piercingly. "I have always done so, for such little formalities preserve the romance in a marriage. I did the same for my first beloved husband. Even while he lay on his deathbed, I addressed him as *my dear Mr. Fothswalling*. It was, in fact, the last thing he heard on this plane before he took a final rattling gasp, and his dear eyes closed in death. Oh, how early comes *mortus coilus* to the good. But you could not have known, and how you delight in teasing me! Everything drives you to madness, but that is because of your gift, your delightful artistic soul."

To his obvious dismay, she tapped his shoulder with her fan, forcing him to move aside to allow her room to sit. After settling her flowing yellow skirts across the sofa cushions, she folded her hands on her lap and gave a delicate shiver.

"You remind me, in fact, of Lord Byron with your stormy ways and dark good looks—though it is a pity your hair is not black as the night, then you would truly be dashing as that poor, exiled hero." She appeared to ponder for a moment, then added, "Although not so scandalous as he, of course. Rosemary would haunt me had I raised you so shoddily."

"You haven't raised me," he said, annoyed.

Her brow creased in hurt. "I'm certain you don't mean to disregard the past five years when my dear Mr. Lightner dropped his promising career in banking to flee to your aid, and without a backward look or complaint, I might add. And though my hand in your upbringing can surely be dismissed as unimportant—for Rosemary would have raised Mr. Lightner's Lenora, I'm sure of it, should I have snuffed my candle carelessly early as she did—you cannot deny *his* unselfish sacrifice."

"Sacrifice!" Alexander sputtered. "Better to say he bled every farthing his guardianship allowed him to—"

"Alex," Darby interjected, stopping him with a cool look.

"Never mind, dear," Aunt Gacia said, patting his knee. "I understand how you miss your own parents. We never thought to replace them in your heart, you know that. And just imagine! Soon you will reach your majority, and my dear husband will be able to hand the heavy burden of the—the plateries—"

"Potteries," supplied Alexander, grinding his teeth.

"Er, yes, though I cannot fathom why they are called *that,* because you do not make pots, do you? Or at least, not many. But nevertheless, you will soon have to shoulder the business yourself, and *then* you will appreciate his goodness to you and Darby, his priceless guidance in the financial aspects of all of it."

She frowned and waved the fringe of her shawl against her face. "I do not doubt you will miss his advice. We shall remain as long as you need us, be it months or years. Nothing is more important to us than family."

Alexander barely restrained a shudder. "Darby will continue to direct the business side of things as she always has, since she has the head for figures. Father began training us when we were barely out of childhood, you will recall."

Aunt Gacia laughed indulgently and tried to pinch Alexander's cheek, but he dodged her fingers with the expertise of long practice.

"I shall tell you what I recall, precious boy," she said. "Mr. Lightner has tolerated her interference all these years with the patience of a saint."

Perceiving two pairs of grey eyes regarding her unkindly, she added, "Not that you are unbrilliant, Darby. It is only

that your ideas are so—how is it Mr. Lightner puts it?—
slip pocket, I think he says. It is all very well to be forward-
thinking, but when profits are endlessly thrown back into
the business, it leaves very little for your family's comfort."

"Hadn't you best continue your search for uncle?"
Darby asked sweetly. "The guests will be arriving soon."

"What an excellent notion!" Aunt Gacia said with a
start, and rose rapidly. "I had almost forgotten with all
this talk of business." She paused at the doorway. "Anytime
you desire further advice, my dears, you have only to say."

Rustling her skirts importantly, she swept into the hall.

"Damnation," Alexander breathed when the sound of
her footsteps faded.

"Alex," chided Darby gently.

"Well, the woman is an idiot."

"That goes without saying. But I wish you would not . . .
you know."

"Are you scolding me for my language again? I've known
you to say much worse. You have become too nice of late,
my sister."

Darby worriedly scanned the corners of the room. Was
her angel watching her at this moment?

"I'm only trying to be better," she said.

"You are becoming deuced stuffy," Alexander refuted.

She threw another glance toward the ceiling, then
looked sadly down at her book. She turned another page.

"I don't know what is happening to you, Darby." Her
brother's voice betrayed his perplexity and concern. "Why
do you read those dry old sermons day after day? I'm
certain you don't comprehend one word in five."

"I try," she said. Loudly, she added, "I try very hard to
understand what learned men have gleaned from their
spiritual studies."

"Balderdash. And why do you shout? You are not on
the stage, I tell you."

"I only mean to improve myself. I desire to be as good as I can."

"What a load of cabbages. You are good enough already. Too good, in fact. I liked you better before you started trying so much."

Darby sighed dispiritedly. She, too, had liked herself better before her angelic encounter, or at any rate had enjoyed herself more. But it seemed to her that a certain responsibility came with being singled out for a heavenly visitation, even if she could not speak about it. Surely there was a reason for Simon's interference in her destiny. To be spared a fiery fate must mean she should accomplish something worthy with her life, and she was determined to find out what. Hence her endless studies.

She had no doubts now that Simon had prevented her death.

Not five hours after she returned, pale and shaking, from her meeting with the angel, Alexander had proposed his latest plan to torture their uncle.

"You know the Holley estate has been on the market this age," he said after dinner while they strolled along the grounds.

She murmured some little sound of assent, though truly she hardly heard her brother, so lost was she in the stunning memory of her angel. Everytime she closed her eyes, she saw Simon again: hair so fair it was almost white, and unfashionably long, hanging to his shoulders; strangely dark brows and lashes, and eyes of such a pale blue they appeared almost silver; his astonishing height and powerful shoulders and chest, the taut waist and long, muscular legs.

How could she have doubted he was an angel? No mere mortal could look so. Yet his expression had been achingly sad . . .

"Are you listening?" Alexander had asked irritably.

"Yes, the Holley estate," she mumbled.

He smacked a fist against his open palm. "I've had the

most excellent idea. We can tell Uncle Richard we're considering buying it after our birthday.''

"But that old place is terribly ramshackle," she protested, suddenly attentive now that their finances were in question.

"I've no real intention of purchasing it, silly. But it will give us an excuse to have uncle view it. Before he does, however, we shall prepare the place beforehand. You've heard the gossip about it being haunted. Well," he became loud in his amusement, "with a few wires and sheets, we can rig up a jolly ghost—"

She had begun to scream then, babbling that they would be burned if they tried, she would die, no jest was worth the risk, had he not thought what a firebox was that horrible old house, and similar protestations until he, eyes wild and fearful at her outburst, had squeezed her mouth shut and promised never to mention the notion again.

When the house burned down three days later, she was not in the least surprised.

From that time onward, she had tried to be worthy. Each day was more difficult than the last. Especially when her favorite companion sat across from her as he now did, eyeing her with disapproval and a degree of alarm.

"Are we gathering already?" inquired a sweet voice from the doorway. "I feared I might be too early."

Darby's confusion faded to scorn as she watched her brother, his cheeks blazing crimson, jump to his feet and rush toward their visitor, banging his knee against the sofa as he passed. If he felt any pain, he gave no sign of it.

"Of course you aren't too early, Lenora," he assured her, bringing her hand to his lips. "You look lovely, as always."

That is the truth, more's the pity, Darby thought, her glance passing lightly over the diminutive form of her aunt's stepdaughter. Lenora wore a satin gown with puffed sleeves trimmed in rows of Alencon lace; similar rows decorated the seam beneath her bust and at the hem. The neckline plunged toward the lace as if looking for it, and a diamond pendant rested smugly upon her plump cleavage. Her long curls, wound intricately around a modest diamond tiara, gleamed red-gold in the candlelight.

The gown, as always, was pink. Lenora seldom wore any other color. Darby wondered if she imagined the shade brought a needed blush to her cheeks. In the five months Lenora had lived with them since her husband's demise, Darby had not seen her lose composure once.

Perhaps marriage stole the blushes from one's face, Darby thought uncharitably, then lowered her eyes and shook her head to rattle the bad thoughts from her brain.

"How kind you are," Lenora piped. "You make me feel a girl again."

"You *are* a girl, or hardly more than that," Alexander protested, leading her to the sofa with the care of one handling glass.

"And *you* are gallant," Lenora said, smiling when he pulled a footstool to her feet, then sat beside her attentively. "I'm fully a year or two older than you and Darby, as you well know."

"I believe it is four years," Darby corrected, laying her sermons on the floor beside her chair, raising her eyes in time to meet her brother's fierce stare.

"Is it? I vow I can never keep the numbers straight, but how thoughtful of you to remind me." Lenora's limpid brown eyes glanced over Darby. "Oh, cousin, had you not best hurry and dress for dinner? Our guests will be arriving shortly."

"I *am* dressed for dinner," Darby said with a tight smile.

"Oh," Lenora said in apologetic tones, tapping her chin with her closed fan. "Forgive me, I had not meant to imply anything was lacking in your toilette. You look charming as usual in your blue gown." She bent forward to finger the fabric at Darby's knee, the diamond pendant at her

bust swinging perilously in mid-air, then returning home
as she scooted back; Darby noted cynically that Alexander
observed the jewel's journey with fascination. "Now what
is this fabric called again?"

"Lawn. You yourself have a dozen dresses made of the
material."

"Oh, yes. I had only thought since it is evening you
might want to put on something more . . . formal. In truth,
I hoped you'd wear the ivory silk Rena and I stitched for
you."

There was a brief silence before Alexander, his voice
rising with incredulity, cried, "Darby, has Lenora made a
dress for you, and you haven't worn it?"

"It's too short, Alex," Darby said, her eyes remaining
on Lenora's. *And so tight I cannot breathe without popping
seams.* "Quite strangely so, since Rena measured me several
times."

"I'm to blame for that," Lenora said. "As she laid it on
the form, I kept disputing her, saying the measurements
could not be right. You do not give the impression of being
a large girl, and I insisted she cut it more closely."

Even Alexander could not fail to note the message
behind this, and he met his sister's glare with amusement.
"Perhaps—perhaps Rena can add a flounce to the bottom," he choked.

Lenora's tiny fingers flew to her face. "Oh, dear," she
said, and burst into apologetic giggles. "I have just heard
myself. You must both think me the veriest cat. Forgive
me, Darby. Of course you are *not* large, only larger than I
am, but then, who is not?"

"You *are* a most petite creature," Alexander said fondly,
then, catching his sister's expression from the corner of
his eye, sent her a look that said, *What's wrong now?*

Lenora looked from one to the other of them, then said
in confidential tones, "I suppose I am small, but it's horrid
to be so. One can never reach anything and must forever be

asking for help." She leaned toward Darby, her expression beseeching. "But say you are not angry, please? I meant no offense."

Looking into her sincere eyes, Darby felt doubts warring with her irritation. Lenora often inspired such inner battles. The woman's charm was undeniable, and Darby frequently received generous doses of it. Yet Lenora's tongue possessed two edges; one dripped honey, the other poison, leading Darby to a fundamental distrust. It did not help that Alexander seemed blind to her venomous side.

"You haven't offended me," she lied.

They began to talk of other things until the remaining three long-term residents of Brightings joined them. Aunt Gacia entered on the arm of her husband, who had been found in time to don his newest dark evening clothes. Claude Heathershaw, friend to Lenora's late husband, followed a moment later. Wearing his usual Brummel-blue frock coat, black pantaloons, white shirt and cravat, he eyed the inhabitants of the room lazily before pulling an armchair beside Darby.

"Stunning," he said in a private voice, casting her a lingering look that would have been offensive had it not been so comically overdrawn. "I can scarce bear to look at you, Miss Brightings. Your countenance does more than justice to your name."

"You are full of nonsense as usual," Darby said.

While he assured her of his sincerity, the sounds of a carriage drifted to their ears.

"The Wallaces," Uncle Richard announced, tweaking the front draperies back into place with his chubby fingers. "Where is Simbar when he's needed to answer the door? The servants in this house spend more time hiding than they do aught else. Gacia, my dear, you should do something about it."

"Oh, I have tried, Mr. Lightner," said his wife in a long-suffering voice. "But Darby would have it that she is mistress here, and the servants only listen to her anyway. Excepting my dear Persimone, of course."

"I shall answer the door myself," Darby said, rising.

"It is not seemly, dear child," said Uncle Richard, his soft brown eyes sorrowful within folds of puffy flesh. "And please don't think anyone was criticizing you just now."

"No, indeed not," agreed Aunt Gacia. "Your energy is a constant source of amazement to us all, though why one as tender in age as yourself would want to shoulder so many responsibilities when assistance is unselfishly offered on every side, I cannot fathom."

"Nevertheless, I will answer the door, since our guests are knocking," Darby said, one eyebrow raising ironically. "I'm certain neither Edward nor Evelyn will be shocked."

Thus called to his senses, Alexander sprang to his feet, declaring he would join her.

The siblings walked several paces in silence across the pink-swirled marble floor of the hall, then Darby whispered, more to herself than her twin, "Only one more month."

"Yes," Alexander returned, "but I fear they will be harder than paint to remove from these walls."

"Be honest, brother. There is one you don't wish to leave."

He gave her a telling look beneath his lashes but did not answer, only moved past her to open the door, which he flung wide. Jovial greetings were exchanged on either side as their life-long friends, Edward and Evelyn Wallace and their mother, were admitted.

As Darby stood aside to permit their entry, a flash of blue caught the corner of her eye. She looked away from her friends, past their carriage, and to the field which bordered the wood. A tall, fair-haired gentleman was walking toward the forest with the air of one who meant to visit but, having seen the visitors, had changed his mind, there being a certain downward slant to his shoulders and a pensive look to his face when he glanced back.

Upon seeing that face, Darby's fears were confirmed. She felt her knees go weak and groaned softly.

It was her angel.

Alexander caught her immediately. "What is it?" he cried, then, following the line of her vision, looked from her ashen face to the figure of the stranger, who had stopped now in evident confusion. "Are you afraid of that man?"

Darby's fluttering eyelashes opened wide, and she felt strength returning to her legs. "Do you mean to say that you can see him?" she asked hopefully, and slipped from her brother's arms to stand alone.

"What? Of course I can see him, silly. What's the matter with you? Do you think I need spectacles?"

At this, the Wallaces also began to stare at the stranger. Seeing four accusing faces and one beatific one regarding him steadily, Simon began to retreat once more.

"Hullo there!" Alexander called, none too friendly. "Who are you, and what are you doing here?"

"I'm sorry," Simon shouted across the distance. "I didn't realize you had company. I'll come back another time."

"You'll come here now or I'll send the dogs after you!" Alexander declared.

Simon stood very still for a moment, then turned his steps toward them.

"Alex!" Darby shrieked. "How could you? Mind your tongue! He is an—an—"

Four pairs of eyes watched her expectantly.

"What?" Alexander asked, finally. "He is an what?"

"An—a—a friend of mine," Darby said despairingly.

"A friend of yours?" Alexander inquired in tones of disbelief. "When could you have made such a friend and I not know him?"

"Yes, nor I," Edward said, somewhat belligerently. "I haven't seen this fellow in my life, and him I'd remember."

"Only look at how he is dressed," Mrs. Wallace whispered faintly. "Oh, my."

"You didn't tell us to costume ourselves tonight, Darby," Evelyn commented dryly. "I could have worn Great-Aunt Astrid's wig."

Darby watched Simon's approach with growing dismay. He wore a brilliant blue satin jacket with matching knee-pants. A froth of white lace bubbled at his neck and at the end of his sleeves, and white stockings stretched into a pair of high-heeled slippers with bows. His hair was caught into a ribbon at the nape of his neck.

He looked as if he had stepped from the last century, or had adorned himself in a servant's fancy livery. Why had he done such a thing? There must be a good reason for an angel to behave so.

Yet something was making Simon become more uncomfortable-looking as he drew nearer, and Darby could not miss the way his eyes scanned Alexander and Edward from head to toe. A look of comprehension entered his expression, and his crystalline eyes sparked resentfully even as a slow flush spread up his neck. Had she not been positive angels were above such things, she could almost imagine he was embarrassed.

But there was no apology in his stance when he came to a halt at the bottom of the steps and looked at them. He stood without awkwardness, his head tilted proudly, his powerful body betraying only grace.

Darby thought her heart might fly away, it was fluttering so. He had said she'd never see him again. What possible reason could there be for her angel to change his mind?

"Forgive me if I sounded rude earlier," Alexander said in a voice too strident for apology. "Darby tells me you're a friend of hers."

"Who is it?" called Aunt Gacia before Simon could

answer. She, along with Uncle Richard and Lenora, had come to see what was taking them so long. She squeezed a passage among the press of bodies gathered at the door to get a better look at the stranger. "Goodness gracious, what a big fellow it is!" she added. "Who is that, Alexander?"

"That's what I'm trying to find out," Alexander answered. "Who are you, sir, and why have you come to us dressed as Gainsborough's *Blue Boy?*"

Chapter Three

Gainesborough's Blue Boy! Simon thought furiously. *I told that puppy-eyed salesgirl in the costume shop early nineteenth-century, but this is obviously not it.*

To be fair, though, *he* had asked for the kneepants, since he'd seen the slop-boy wearing them on his previous visit; but apparently the servants dressed differently from the gentlemen. These men were wearing tight pants long enough to enter their boots, and the jackets didn't match the pants and were made of stiff cotton or something; whatever it was, it wasn't satin. Well, it was his own fault for not researching the period.

He should have taken more time, should have at least brought some old-fashioned English money, even though he was convinced he wouldn't need any. Now he saw he'd require new clothes, and who would pay for that?

But he couldn't blame himself too harshly; he'd been frantic with the need to hurry. The past weeks had been spent sorting out the tangled mess he'd made of his life. He'd even been to America and back, each moment bring-

ing one unwelcome discovery after another. How naive
he'd been, thinking he could change the past without
affecting the future. During his last time excursion, he
had done more than prevent Darby's death; he'd put into
motion an impossible number of changes that had resulted
in his not owning Brightings anymore. The house was no
longer even called Brightings. How surprised the present
owners had been to see him, sweating and dusted with
burrs and pine needles, burst through their back door
after his visit with Darby. He'd only been able to re-read
the family history by forcing his way into the library while
the owners dialed the police.

And that was the least of it.

Who would have dreamed a simple word of warning
could cause such havoc? But seeing Darby now, he knew
he'd done the only thing possible. He would rescue her
again. In fact, he *planned* to do so, and this time he'd put
everything right. He must.

Darby was looking at him with a face broadcasting wonder, fear, and curiosity in turns. At least she didn't look
hostile as did the crowd surrounding her. What luck, to
arrive when she was entertaining. Surely time was passing
at equal rates on either side of the ash trees, and it wasn't
the twins' birthday already.

An acting coach had once told him, "When in doubt,
bluff." His mistake would only require the slightest modifi-
cation in his planned story. He displayed his most disarm-
ing smile.

"I'm sorry," he said, bowing slightly. "I didn't mean to
bother you when you have guests, but my car—*carriage!*—
was robbed, and all I have left are the clothes on my back.
And the reason I'm wearing *this* instead of—of my regular
things, is because I was playing the part of *Blue Boy* on
stage, just before I was robbed."

"Save me," Uncle Richard exploded. "Is that an American accent I hear?"

"Yes, but what did he *say?*" Aunt Gacia asked in an annoyed voice. "What is he talking about?"

"It is no use asking me," Alexander replied. More loudly, he demanded, "Who the devil are you?"

"Alex, really!" Darby exclaimed, almost giggling in her nervousness. She clasped her hands together in a prayer-like gesture, then released them. "How rude you are being to our guest."

As Alexander murmured, "Our guest?" in scalding tones, she descended the stairs, extended her hand toward Simon's elbow, then dropped her fingers suddenly as if fearing to touch him. Simon felt a stab of guilt as fear deepened the colour of her eyes.

With her back turned to the others, she whispered, 'Shall I tell them your name, and that you are an angel?"

He started. "God—goodness, no. I mean, my name's okay, but don't ever tell them that other thing."

"Yes, sir—Simon." She swallowed, struggled to smooth her features into a placid expression, then faced her guests. "I should like to introduce Mr. Simon Garrett." Swiftly she pivoted back to him, saying under her breath, "Is *mister* suitable, or do angels have titles?"

"Mister is fine," he whispered back.

Her hands spasmed together again. He noted her fingers were long and graceful-looking, but he was making her awkward. It was too bad, because she'd seemed an elegant creature in the little time he'd known her.

"Do you wish to come inside?" she asked quietly.

"What are you whispering about down there?" Alexander called.

Simon gave him an irritated look, then smiled at Darby. "Yes, thank you."

She nodded and gestured for him to follow. As they ascended the few steps to the door, Simon saw no softening in the suspicious faces regarding him. Speaking more to them than Darby, he said jovially, "I'm glad you recognized me from my advertisement, Miss Brightings, and that you recalled inviting me. I was afraid you might have forgotten, since it's been awhile since you wrote."

They had reached the top step, and though several of the guests backed into the hall to allow him entrance, Alexander placed himself firmly in the doorway.

"What is this, Darby?" he asked, keeping his eyes on the stranger. "What invitation?"

"What invitation?" Darby echoed weakly, throwing a helpless look toward Simon.

"You remember," Simon prodded. "After seeing my advertisement and picture in a magazine, you wrote and asked me to entertain your guests at your birthday ball."

"Oh, yes!" Darby exclaimed. Beaming at her brother, she said, "I saw his advertisement and asked him to entertain on our birthday!" Immediately upon saying the words, her smile dissolved, and a look of confusion passed over her face.

"Did you now?" Alexander asked coldly. "And you never said a word to me."

Darby's questioning gaze flew to Simon's, whose face immediately became woeful. "Have I spoiled the surprise by arriving too early?"

"Yes," she answered slowly. Turning to Alexander, she said, as if reciting, "It was to be a surprise, but he has come too early."

Standing beyond the threshold, Edward proclaimed, "Early? I should think so. Alexander and Darby don't reach twenty-one until next month."

"So long as that?" Simon inquired, genuinely dismayed.

"I'm surprised my sister failed to mention the date," Alexander said grimly. "Now you'll have to go back to wherever you came from."

Simon shuddered. Only the most careful planning had allowed him to steal his way onto the property again. He might not have another opportunity.

"No, I can't," he said.

Blood rushed to Alexander's cheeks as he straightened in outrage. After exchanging an indignant look with Edward, he said, "You *can't?* What does that mean, *you can't?*"

Thinking rapidly, Simon looked from one face to another, then lowered his eyes. In a soft voice he said, "Everything I owned was in that carriage. All my clothes. My money that I'd saved to—to buy my mother a house. I'd promised her a beautiful little cottage."

He lifted his lashes, and there were feminine murmurs of sympathy as he blinked the wetness from them. "She's had a hard life, scrubbing floors and doing laundry from daylight to dusk, and all for me. The house was to be her reward, but now the money's gone, all of it. And I don't have any other acting engagements between now and next month. I must depend on your kindness, I'm afraid."

"Oh, dear," said Mrs. Wallace, whose expression had changed from doubt to heavy sympathy. "Your poor mother. Will she starve? Do you seek lodging for her as well, or is she still in America?"

"Um, no," Simon replied quickly. "She does laundry at—at a count's house in London. She's okay for now."

"What a sad, sad tale," sighed Aunt Gacia, dabbing at her eyes with her handkerchief while darting a comradely look at Mrs. Wallace. "Mr. Lightner, can we not do something?"

"Well, I don't know. That is—" blustered Uncle Richard, then fell silent.

"Don't you realize he's making this up?" Alexander demanded. "Has he not said he's an actor? Be off with you, fellow, I find your performance lacking in conviction."

There's always a critic, Simon thought angrily, then appealed silently to Darby, whose face, he saw with shock, was pale with some inner turmoil. What could be wrong? She looked more disturbed now than she had at the first sight of him. Nevertheless, she returned his glance with comprehension and stepped boldly to her brother, pushing her hand against his chest, forcing him either to give ground or look foolishly defiant.

"He is *my* guest, Alex," she said firmly. "I have invited him, and he shall stay as long as he needs."

Alexander glared into his sister's eyes. Darby met his gaze steadily and almost without expression. Certainly there was no appeal on her face, only steadfast will and resolution. After a moment of silent battle, Alexander shifted his smoldering glance to Simon. With a gesture of exaggerated politeness, he beckoned him inside.

"Welcome to Brightings," he said hatefully, as Simon passed by.

"Now here, here," rumbled Uncle Richard. "Should I not have some say in this matter?"

"Don't be unkind, Father," Lenora said, looking very far up into Simon's eyes and taking his arm. Pulling him down the hall, she added, "So you are an actor, are you? How delightfully scandalous. You must tell me all about it."

Simon glanced over his shoulder as they walked. Finding Darby at the end of what seemed a long line of people in various stages of fury and confusion, he smiled appealingly. Her lips moved in response, but fell short of true good humour, her large eyes remaining glassy and serious.

Feeling a growing disquiet despite his relief in having charmed his way into the house, Simon reluctantly turned his attention to the tiny beauty at his side and allowed her to lead him into the parlour.

Less than an hour later, Simon found himself seated at a long dining table between Lenora Ellison on his right, and Fiona White, the Methodist preacher's spinster daughter, on his left. The dining room was decorated in a simpler manner than he'd known in future times. Scarlet *fleur-de-lis* wallpaper did not climb the walls, only pale yellow paint. It was good to know that underneath the twentieth-century carpet he remembered, the same marble that floored the hall swirled beautifully in here; whoever changed it should have left it alone. The chandelier was different too, though just as striking, especially since this one twinkled with candles and not little decorative bulbs.

Since he'd entered the house, Darby had only spoken to him once, taking him aside to ask if he could partake of normal food. He'd responded in the affirmative, eagerly; the tension of the last few weeks had robbed him of his appetite, and now that he'd passed the first hurdles—returning to the past in time, and getting into this house—he was starving. That he'd been allowed to join the guests for their meal seemed to be another concession on Alexander's part, for a heated, whispered conversation had taken place between the twins before Simbar, the butler, had been instructed to set another place at table.

Apparently actors were regarded as something less than respectable. Simon vaguely recalled hearing this in some history class or other. All of his memories of history were vague; he'd never found the past interesting. What a cosmic joke that he should be the one allowed to travel backwards in time. There were probably a million history professors who would happily give their arms for a chance like this. He couldn't help wondering if they would've made the mess of things that he had, and in such a short time, too.

And his intentions had been so good.

"You will find the country folk here rather dull, I fear," Lenora said to him in an undervoice as a footman circled the table serving soup. "When my husband, Reece, was alive, we divided our time between London and Bath and enjoyed the company of many urbane, sophisticated people such as yourself. Poets, artists, as well as the cultured gentry—these were our friends and constant companions.

How difficult it was for me to join my father and step-mother in the industrial North. Here the conversations revolve around glazes and kilns and bone-ash, if you can imagine. Maddening!''

He smiled politely, since she was smiling at him. All her statements had been delivered with worldly amusement and sly, if not downright coquettish, glances beneath long, golden lashes. He was not unfamiliar with the workings of charm, and he felt its delicate strands spinning around him; though to be honest, Lenora did not exert herself only for him. Even so, he'd seen that look in women's eyes often enough to know she was strongly attracted to him. Her eyes lingered a fraction too long on his; she glanced more than once at his lips; her voice sparkled when she spoke to him. The signals had not changed in the past two hundred years, apparently.

But he didn't want her to fall for him. The complications could be tremendous. This was not what he'd come here to do. He needed to observe, to understand the relationships among this family, to rescue what he could of the future, *his* future. Not to mention saving Darby's life once more.

The footman placed a bowl of soup in front of him, something greyish-white with bits of meat floating in it. Simon looked at it doubtfully, then glanced at Darby, who sat to the left of her uncle, at the far end of the table. He wished again that she had sat by him, but Lenora had grabbed his arm, then the quiet young girl on his left had made a dash for the other chair.

Darby met his gaze solemnly, then looked at her aunt, who sat at the table's other end.

When all the guests had been served their soup, Aunt Gacia lifted her spoon companionably.

"Wait!" Darby cried. As over a dozen spoons paused in mid-air, she added in a shaking voice, "Had we not better say a blessing?"

"Oh!" Aunt Gacia dashed a look of confusion toward

her husband. "Why, yes, of course. We do have an unusual number of clergymen at our table, after all! Er, uh—which one of you reverend gentlemen would like to lead us, or shall I choose? I don't wish to hurt anyone's feelings." She gave a sharp peal of laughter.

"You do the honours, Mr. White," said the Reverend Victor Suttner, a dignified-looking gentleman with grey streaks in his dark hair and a rather flat nose. He was the vicar of St. Stephen's of Mirren and sat near the middle of the table with his wife and son, Eustace.

"No, you please, sir," urged Reverend Ralph White, minister of the Methodist chapel in Mirren. He was a thin, faded-looking man seated with his wife directly across from the vicar.

While the men of God argued politely, Lenora whispered to Simon, "This nonsense is all because Darby has become overly religious of late. She used to only attend St. Stephen's once a month like the rest of us, but now she has begun going every week, visiting St. Stephen's and the Methodist chapel on alternate Sundays, as if she cannot decide where her allegiance lies. Although she is a dear girl, it is really too vexing of her."

"Strange," Simon murmured, eyeing Darby with concern. Suddenly he realized the probable cause of her spiritual search, and currents of embarrassment passed through him.

To his further chagrin, Darby interrupted the clergymen's dispute by saying, "Why not have our guest pray?"

"Him!" declared Alexander scornfully. "Better to have Caesar ask the blessing. His barks are at least sincere."

"Alexander, you are behaving abominably!" she lashed. Turning again to Simon, she asked, "Would you mind, sir?"

Simon felt pinned like a butterfly in a display case by the eyes that turned to him. He didn't want to pray. He hadn't prayed in years. Of what use was it? All the prayer in the world could not bring back Elena or Tay. But Darby was waiting; all of them were waiting. He was trapped in a role—a fantasy part—he'd brought on himself. And he was going to have to pay for it, he could see that.

Slowly he stood to his feet, childhood prayers flying through his mind. *God is great, God is good*—no, couldn't do that. *For what we are about to receive, we are thankful*—too short. He'd have to improvise.

In the manner he was taught in acting class, he went into himself and breathed calmness. Squaring his shoulders, he bowed his head and closed his eyes.

"Heavenly Father," he began, and there was nothing else, nothing. Panicking, he searched the dark corners of his mind for words but could find none. As the pause lengthened, one of the men cleared his throat. Someone scraped his chair backwards. Eustace, a teenager just beginning to break his way into manhood, sighed heavily. Simon's lids flew open, and he saw Darby watching him intently, an expression of surprise and disappointment beginning to shine from her eyes. He closed his eyes again so he would not have to look at her.

"Heavenly Father," he repeated, forcing confidence into his voice. He could make something up, *he could*. Had to. "Thank you for this family and their friends gathered around the table." He coughed briefly. "Bless them with the goodness that shines from your heavenly light."

Still too short a prayer for an angel, surely, but *heavenly light* reminded him of old hymn titles.

It might work. He sucked in another breath.

"Thank you for your amazing grace . . . Lead on, oh King eternal . . . Blessed be the tie that binds." That was it; he couldn't think of anymore. "And, um, thanks for this food, of course. Amen."

"Amen," echoed several voices inquiringly.

Craving approval, Simon telegraphed a look of hope toward Darby as he sat down. She smiled at him uncertainly, bewilderment clouding her eyes. Ah, what was wrong with her tonight? Was she having doubts about him? He could not imagine why.

"Well done," Lenora whispered to him in an amused voice. "You have inspired me."

He gazed into her dancing eyes and suddenly felt sick. Without answering, he turned to his soup and brought a spoonful to his mouth.

"This is good," he said after a moment. "What is it?"

"Why turtle, of course," Lenora answered with a laugh. "Don't tell me you've never eaten it. Surely America is not so backward as that."

He choked a little as he swallowed a chunk of meat. "Oh, sure, we have it. I just forgot. What is this broth— some kind of white sauce?"

"I believe M. Donelle makes it with our heaviest cream. We do not stint on the finest ingredients in our foods, not at Brightings."

He smiled weakly and placed his spoon beside the bowl with care. Lenora glanced at him curiously, then shrugged and continued to eat.

Fearing he ignored the girl to his left, he looked at her and smiled. "Your name is Fiona, I believe?" he asked.

She was a plain girl, very pale, with thin brown hair pulled into a tight bun. At his question, her face grew even more ashen. "That's Miss White to you," she said in an unpleasant voice. "Don't be familiar. Don't know you."

"Sorry," said Simon, and turned away. A second later, he felt a fingertip prodding his shoulder with irritating persistence. He returned his attention to the minister's daughter.

"Don't mean to be short with you. Got to be careful of men, though. Mamma told me so." A smudge of soup gleamed whitely at the corner of her mouth.

"I'm sure she's right," he said with some distaste.

Even though he still looked at her, she prodded his

shoulder again. "You can call me Fiona if it means so much to you. I'll be home tomorrow, but I will not go in a carriage alone with you."

"Um, thank you, but I believe I'll be busy."

"All right, if I must, I'll go on a carriage ride with you, but not a closed carriage. 'Tain't seemly."

"Miss White, I can't take you anywhere. I don't have a carriage and couldn't drive one if I did."

"Very well, since you have your mind set on it, I'll drive. I shall be here at one tomorrow."

"No, please! I—"

"Fiona," Lenora said, leaning forward to speak around Simon, her voice shaking with laughter, "I'm afraid Mr. Garrett has duties here tomorrow. And the next few days after that."

"Oh, well," Miss White said. "You must ask Papa about next week. We are holding a revival and I may not be free."

Simon turned to Lenora in a blaze of relief. Her brown eyes warmed a little too much for comfort, however, and he glanced across the table at the man he'd learned was Claude Heathershaw. He'd already noticed Heathershaw occasionally watching him and Lenora with lazy interest in his heavily-lidded eyes, and now those eyes turned from Aunt Gacia's chattering face to meet his gaze.

Aunt Gacia's steady stream of talk broke off at the desertion of her companion's attention, and Simon seized his opportunity.

"What line are you in, Mr. Heathershaw?" he asked politely.

"I beg your pardon?" came the astonished reply.

"It is all right, Claude," Aunt Gacia said, misunderstanding. "You may speak with Mr. Garrett across the table. They have probably not taught him all his manners in America, and we are not formal here." In a louder voice she added, "Do not feel you must only speak to the person

on either side of you, dear ones. We are like family with
our guests." She breathed deeply, then screeched, "Aren't
we, Mr. Lightner?"

"Yes, yes!" Uncle Richard yelled, his deep voice echoing
off the candelabrum spaced down the long, long table.
"We are!"

Simon blinked. Apparently he was breaking all kinds of
rules. But what did that matter in the light of this unimaginable adventure? He was talking and eating and breathing
in the world of two hundred years ago. He did well to
remain conscious.

Currents of joy ran through him as he leaned back to
allow the footman to remove his unfinished soup. For a
full moment he forgot the heaviness that had become so
much a part of him.

Heathershaw continued to gaze at him with curiosity.
He had the kind of face Simon imagined could be called
aristocratic—a long, thin nose; high forehead; large, well-
shaped skull; thin lips and deep-set eyes. It could be a stern
face, yet wasn't; something about the tilt of the mouth,
the liveliness of the eyes, and the careless manner in which
his windblown hair tumbled across his forehead, gave him
an almost comical aspect. Everything about him, even his
slouching posture in the chair, looked likable and non-
threatening.

"I don't understand your question, I'm afraid," Heathershaw said. "What line am I in . . . is that an American
expression, or are you thinking in actor's terms?"

"Sorry. I only meant, what is it you do for a living?"

Simon heard muffled laughter at his side. Heathershaw
heard it, too, and lifted his brows at Lenora.

"What is it I do for a living?" the gentleman echoed,
bringing his wineglass before his eyes and contemplating
the liquid as he spun it in circles. "My dear fellow, as little
as possible."

Still chuckling, Lenora held her napkin before her lips

and whispered, "That is not regarded as a polite question, Mr. Garrett. Not to Claude, at any rate, who is something of a professional guest."

"Oh." Simon looked across the table in surprise. "Sorry if I spoke out of turn."

Heathershaw winked and lifted his glass higher in a salute. "No offense taken with you, sir, though Lenora has mightily offended me by whispering about me to you."

"And what makes you think I spoke of you?" she asked archly.

"Your beautiful brown eyes were on me the entire time, a thing I can well understand," Heathershaw answered. "And what else of interest is there to talk about?"

"You flatter yourself, Claude," Lenora said, the merry light in her eyes fading a little.

Simon turned to watch the servants enter carrying steaming platters. There were undercurrents here that he did not understand, and he wanted to be silent awhile and observe.

His gaze found Darby's as it had done repeatedly through the soup course. She seemed quiet, though her brother and the Wallace siblings often engaged her in conversation, conversations that seemed doomed to end quickly as her attention wandered. He knew the cause of that, of course.

Alexander sat at Darby's left, and Evelyn was seated next to him. Mrs. Wallace appeared to be tangled in an intent conversation with Richard Lightner, who gesticulated frequently and eagerly, sometimes waving his fork in the air with dangerous abandon. Beside his mother and across from Alexander sat Edward Wallace. The pairs of siblings seemed unusually close; when Alexander was not casting incensed looks down the table at Lenora and himself, he regarded Evelyn attentively; and Edward seldom looked away from Darby. Simon couldn't fault him for that.

While Simon continued to study the faces around the

table, the footman placed a dish of meat in thick sauce in front of him. Simon stared at it a moment before lifting his knife and fork.

"Calves' tongue in cream," Lenora whispered helpfully.

Simon blanched. "God help me, I'm going to starve."

"No, you should try it," Heathershaw said. "In the ordinary way of things, I don't enjoy tongue either, but the Brightings's chef could make leather taste well."

"His method appears to be cream sauce," Simon observed. Had these people never heard of cholesterol? No, of course not.

"Is something wrong, Mr. Garrett?" Alexander asked in disdainful tones, raising his voice to be heard over the others. "You are not eating. I suppose you're used to much better fare, traveling around in wagons and cooking over campfires."

"Nothing's wrong with the food," Simon answered. "I'm just waiting for the vegetable course. You *do* eat vegetables, don't you?"

"Of course we do—" Alexander began angrily.

"You do not eat meat, then?" Darby interrupted, her incisive voice cutting across her brother's and ringing with worry. She looked at the morsel of flesh caught in her fork and lowered it to her plate. "Is it wrong to eat meat?"

"Why do you ask him?" exclaimed Alexander. "He is an authority of nothing!"

"Meat is fine, especially for young women," Simon interjected rapidly, before Darby could spring again to his defense. "And the cream sauces are good for your bones. But men . . ."

Realizing that he now had the attention of everyone seated at the table, he stammered to a halt. Even the footman and maid stood frozen, dishes and serving spoons poised in their hands.

Alexander saw the actor's discomfort and smiled.

"Please, Mr. Garrett, do continue. We await your wisdom with breathless anticipation."

I'd like to wipe that sneer off your face, Simon thought. But he hadn't traveled through time to brawl. He stared furiously at a spot on the wall a fraction above Claude Heathershaw's head until he felt calmer, hardly noticing when that gentleman worriedly ran his fingers through his hair.

Should he tell these people what he knew about healthy eating, or would it cause more problems down the line? Maybe one of these men would live an extra year or two and sire a child that wasn't meant to be born. Maybe that child's great-great-something-grandchild would blow up the world. It wasn't impossible. Look at what had happened to *his* future, simply by delaying Darby's death.

Well, so what. He couldn't worry about everything.

"Too much meat and dairy products build fat inside your arteries and clog them up. In men and older women, it can cause heart attack and strokes."

"It causes the gout, too," said Reverend Mr. Suttner. "My physician warned me off rich foods because of it."

"But Mr. Garrett is no physician," Alexander said. "Perhaps he gathered this bizarre information from one of his comedic roles."

"As you mentioned, I'm no doctor; but what I'm saying is the truth."

"Well, if eating vegetables is responsible for your fine stature and physique, I say, bring on the carrots!" Uncle Richard quipped.

"Well said, Papa," agreed Lenora, laughing and raising her glass. Several others also raised theirs, and a general air of relaxation swept around the table.

Only Alexander and his friend Edward appeared unmoved, both of them eyeing Simon with hard expressions.

"What sort of roles do you perform, Mr. Garrett?"

Edward asked. He had a round, pleasant face with a ruddy complexion and eyes so bright they looked feverish. "You mentioned *Blue Boy*. I never knew the painting was also a play."

Simon slid his feet back and forth under the table. His shoes were pinching like the devil, and he wondered if he could get away with pushing them off. Probably not. He was getting away with very little this evening.

"*Blue Boy* is new; a comedy. Our performance wasn't too successful, I'm afraid, which is one reason I came here so early."

"I thought you were robbed," Edward said accusingly.

"I said it was *one* reason, not the only one."

"Where were you when it happened?" Edward persisted. "Did the magistrate offer you no hope for the recovery of your goods?"

"What? Oh no, he said there was no chance. And it happened in London."

"London? Good lord, do you expect us to believe you traveled over a hundred miles on foot with no money?"

"Did I say London?" Simon asked, laughing loudly. "What's wrong with me? I meant to say *outside* London, um, very far north of London, in fact." He frantically tried to recall a map of England and Wales that he'd glanced at during the flight over the Atlantic. In a hopeful voice he added, "Birmingham, that's where it was."

Edward scowled and narrowed his eyes. A look passed between him and Alexander.

"And you travel with which acting troupe?" inquired Darby's brother.

Darby brought her glass to the table with a crash, bringing every eye to her. "You are both grilling Mr. Garrett as if he were on trial. I have a different sort of question; a query for our clergymen, and anyone else who cares to offer an opinion." Her glance flickered toward Simon,

then lifted to her mother's portrait on the east wall. "Do
you believe in angels?"

Simon's heart immediately began to pound. Was she
going to give him away?

"What about you, Mr. Suttner?" she persisted, as no
one jumped to answer her question. "This is something I
have wondered about for awhile."

The vicar peered past Evelyn and Alexander to look at
her with interest. "Do you mean literal angels, Darby?
Wings, robes, haloes, all of it? Or do you mean symbolic
spirits, carriers of God's good will?"

"Oh, how you go on," Mr White said. His voice was
permanently hoarse, the result of too much loud preach-
ing. " Confusing the girl, ain't you? Yes, Miss Brightings,
there are angels. It is my belief we each have one or several
to help us through our earthly lives."

"There must be a vast number of them, then," Mr.
Suttner commented in an amused voice. "And surely they
have better things to do than watch us at all times."

Mrs. White and Mrs. Suttner looked at one another
across the table and exchanged feeble smiles.

"God can make as many angels as He needs," asserted
Mr. White, his face splotching, "and nothing is more pressing than guarding His greatest creation."

"There are many learned men who would argue with
your literalism," returned Mr. Suttner. "Men whose intel-
lects are strained to imagine myths, but who well understand the meaning behind the symbols."

The footmen had already removed the plates of calves'
tongue—many of them uneaten—and were now serving
poached salmon and side dishes of mushrooms, baked
apples, and garden greens. They moved with unusual quiet-
ness, glancing back and forth frequently between the two
theologians.

"Why are angels in the Bible at all, then?" asked Mr.
White, spearing a mushroom with his fork. "I tell you, sir,

your faith is a thin and wispy thing and no good to anybody. It may please you to tickle your mind with might-be's and symbol-this-and-that, but 'tis because you're high-minded and over-educated. What use are the philosophies of your Oxford professors to a widow-woman coughing out her life in a hovel, with five children to be cared for when she's gone?''

Mr. Suttner chewed a mouthful of salmon rapidly, swallowed, and directed a mildly condescending look at the other minister. ''I suppose she does better shouting and shaking in the aisles of a thin-walled, whitewashed chapel. Is that what you are saying?''

Pushing his plate aside angrily, the Methodist minister leaned his forearms on the table and glared at the man across from him. Uncomfortable looks were exchanged among a few of the guests, and for awhile the only sounds were of knives and forks scraping against plates.

Aunt Gacia broke the silence. ''Now then, Darby, this is your fault,'' she said cheerily. ''Discussing religion at the table. You should know better.''

''Hear, hear,'' Uncle Richard agreed.

Darby looked up from her plate and stared directly at Simon. ''I have but one further question. Saying that angels do exist, do you think it's possible they can lie?''

Simon grew very still, returning her gaze levelly, though inside he quaked. So that was it. Now her brooding silences were explained. She'd begun to doubt him when he claimed to be an actor, and since then he'd piled one story on top of another.

If only he could tell her the truth; but the chances were too great she would never believe him, especially now that he'd started with the angel fantasy. With a chill, he recalled her reaction when he first tried to warn her about the fire; she'd thought he was crazy before he convinced her he was from heaven. If he changed his story again, she'd throw him out, he was sure of it; and he had to stay here, had to be nearby to put things right.

"No," Mr. White was saying. "Angels never lie. They cannot."

"Don't be so hasty," said Mr. Suttner. "What of Satan, who was an angel? He is the Father of Lies."

Darby's eyes, still fastened on Simon's, widened in horror.

"Yes, that is true enough," conceded the Methodist minister. "But I meant the angels of today, the ones who haven't fallen. They are perfect creatures."

"But what if they aren't?" Simon blurted, hardly knowing what he was saying, but positive he had to prevent Darby from thinking he was the devil.

"Angels not perfect?" Reverend White asked, as if he could not believe his ears. "What can you mean? Explain yourself, sir."

"Yes, pray do, Mr. Garrett," Alexander said mockingly. "You appear to have an opinion on every subject."

A surge of resentment kept Simon from speaking for a moment. He played with his spoon as he gathered his thoughts, idly admiring the reflection of the table candelabrum in the silver.

"Of course angels are perfect," he said finally. "But what if there are degrees of perfection? Suppose an angel is in a situation where the only solution is to do something generally considered um, sinful?"

"Can't happen," Mr. White said with authority.

"No, think about it for a minute," Simon persuaded. "Imagine that a small child is trapped in an abandoned mine, and the air supply is short. The only ones who can bring help in time are a group of laborers repairing a nearby road. The angel asks the foreman to release his men to dig out the child. The foreman is regretful but says he can't; if the men don't meet their deadline, they'll lose their jobs, and their families will starve. What does the angel do?"

" 'Tis easy," said the Methodist clergyman. "The angel flies into the cave and frees the child himself."

"No, he can't; he's taken human form temporarily."

"Angels ain't limited by that," argued Mr. White. "They can do anything, anytime. Didn't those two angels strike the Sodomites blind—excuse me, ladies—when the townsmen tried to beat down Lot's door to er, get at them?"

A fist closed over Simon's heart. He'd forgotten that old story. Time to bluff again.

"But suppose this one angel can't," he said. "Maybe he doesn't have all his powers. Perhaps he's new at it."

"Faugh!" declared the preacher. "You're proposing things that don't happen. 'Tis no better than counting how many angels can dance on the head of a pin."

"What happens to the child?" Fiona demanded. "I want to know what happens to the child. Don't let it die, Mr. Garrett."

Simon wiped the moisture from his brow. Darby's unyielding eyes were drilling holes in his head, and Alexander's were filling the holes with heat.

"The child lives, Miss White," Simon replied quietly. "He lives because the angel lies, telling the foreman the little one is his son."

"I'm so glad," breathed Fiona. "You tell good stories, you really do."

"Unnecessary, I assure you!" shouted her father. "The angel could have sneezed the child out of that mine had he wanted!"

"Now hold on, Ralph," Mr. Suttner said, his expression lively, "what of Rahab and the two spies Joshua sent to Jericho? Did she not lie to protect them, and wasn't she rewarded for it?"

"The spies were men, not angels," growled Mr. White.

"Still, it is an interesting dilemma." The vicar leaned

forward. "You only see life in black and white, my friend. Things are not always wholly good, or wholly evil."

"Oh yes, they are," said Mr. White, an obstinate look crossing his face.

The vicar laughed. "If only life were so simple."

"It *is* that simple. There's no sense to this world if we can't tell what's right and wrong."

Simon turned to Darby once more, dreading to see her reaction. Her features remained expressionless, giving him little hope that his arguments had made a favorable impression. There was an air of despondency about her as she leaned toward Alexander to hear something he whispered in her ear.

But the ministers were not quite done with each other.

"Oh, my treasured friend, we are making our companions uncomfortable," the vicar was saying in a warm, yet slightly scornful, voice. He was slicing an apple, and popped a piece in his mouth before saying, juicily, "I suppose we will ever disagree, but I wish everyone at this table to know that I love you as a Christian brother."

Mr. White straightened his cravat. Glancing to the right and left, he mumbled uncomfortably, "Yes, yes, sir. I also, er, love you. As a Christian, of course."

The vicar slapped his hand on the table, threw back his head and laughed. "How you amuse—"

The minister could go no further. A large chunk of apple had lodged in his throat, and he began to choke, his face turning a brilliant red, his eyes straining outward in his desperation to breathe. Mrs. Suttner patted his back, her concern rapidly turning to alarm as her husband still struggled.

"Help him, somebody!" she cried. "He can't breathe!"

Eustace jumped to his feet and began pounding his father's back. "Cough it up, Papa!"

Alexander and Edward rushed to stand behind him helplessly. Several of the others half-rose from their chairs, and horror stamped itself onto the features of everyone.

"Don't hit his back!" Simon commanded, stirring from his shock to leap onto his chair and bound across the table, managing to send Fiona's glass crashing to the floor. He pushed Eustace aside and brushed away Mrs. Suttner's hands, much to the fury of Alexander and Edward, who tried to wrest him back. Simon, who was half a head taller than either gentleman and possessed muscles that only a daily session at the weight machine can bring about, swatted them both backward easily, and was not so busy that he didn't enjoy it immensely.

The minister's color had drained to a greyish pallor. His hands clawed his neck in frantic efforts for air, but feebly now. Simon jerked the man from his chair, positioned himself behind him, circled his arms around his waist, and allowed the minister to slump forward. Although Simon had never done it before, never even practiced it, he began the Heimlich, pumping the heel of one hand with the other beneath the vicar's rib cage.

"Work, work," he chanted to himself, trying to block out the sounds of questions and cries surrounding him. "Please work."

"What are you doing?" Alexander demanded. "Leave the poor fellow. Someone fetch the surgeon!"

Pump, pump, squeeze upward. He'd seen it done a million times on television. He could do it, he could.

The vicar slumped even lower.

"He is killing him!" screamed Mrs. Suttner. "Will someone not help me?"

"Dear God, deliver him," Mr. White prayed loudly, tears floating in his eyes. "Send your angels to guard over my brother."

"Come here, Claude, and put your lazy arms to work," Alexander spat. "The three of us will get rid of this madman."

There was a brief, disgusting sound as the apple segment shot from the vicar's mouth onto his wife's lap. Her scream cut off in mid-voice as her husband took a long, shuddering gasp of air. Immediately, she flung her arms around him and began to weep.

Simon returned the man to his chair—not without difficulty, because Mrs. Suttner would not let him loose—and undid the vicar's cravat while the minister drew in many noisy breaths, coughed excessively, and cleared his throat over and over again. When his color returned to almost normal, Simon backed away and began to circle the table to resume his seat. As he passed Alexander and Edward, he was delighted to see their looks of amazement.

"What did you do?" Alexander asked grudgingly. "How did you do that?"

"I'll show you sometime," said Simon, unable to keep all the smugness from his voice. When he sat down, however, his knees buckled at the last moment and almost shamed him as he half-fell into the chair.

"Thank you, young man," Mr. Suttner croaked over his wife's shoulder. "Saved my life."

Darby stood. "Mr. White prayed for the help of angels, and I do believe Mr. Garrett served very well in that capacity." Simon's heart leapt to see belief restored to her eyes. "Well done, sir."

To his great surprise and embarrassment, she lifted her glass in a salute. The others followed, even Alexander, though distrust was still evident on his face. Simon waved their accolades aside modestly, but in his most secret heart, he was very pleased. It had been the finest role of his life.

Chapter Four

"But who is he, really?" Evelyn whispered, when she was finally able to capture Darby by herself an hour or so after the choking episode in the dining room.

They were not truly alone, for the parlor was filled with the soft murmur of women's voices; women who, awaiting the arrival of the men from their enjoyment of cigars and claret, were pretending to revel in one another's company but were on the whole so ill-matched that many pauses and uncomfortable comments could be detected in their conversation, did one listen closely. The ministers' wives, for example, sat in chairs before one of the windows; and were it not for Aunt Gacia, who laughed often over nothing, and Mrs. Wallace, who commiserated tearfully with everyone, their discourse would have appeared as stiff as starched vellum.

The younger ladies fared little better. Seated on the sofa near the fireplace, Lenora, Evelyn, and Fiona had fired one question after another to Darby concerning her mysterious guest. Sitting across from them in her favorite winged chair, Miss Brightings gave them little satisfaction with her responses. In frustration the trio turned to other matters, hopping from local gossip to the recent arrest in London of a woman for stealing over a hundred of Queen Charlotte's keys. That none of them found the subjects interesting could be discerned from the frequency the young ladies' glances returned to Darby, whom they all believed hid much more intriguing news.

Finally Darby had escaped, declaring she meant to freshen everyone's tea with the service aligned on a table against the wall. Evelyn seized her chance and followed, saying she intended to help. And now, much to Darby's dismay, she stood closely to her friend and awaited her answer.

"He has told everything already, Evelyn."

Although she tried to sound convincing, Darby could not help feeling a weight in her chest as she spoke. She still had no inkling why her angel had found it necessary to lie. Could he not have appeared to her privately, thereby keeping his true identity hidden, a thing he seemed determined to do?

But perhaps it was as he said at table. She knew he had been trying to communicate with her, reassure her, with his story about the child. Perhaps there *were* special circumstances when lies were the lesser of two evils. Yet the idea continued to have a feeling of wrongness about it, and for an eternity of time her doubts had again surfaced, heated and relentless as molten lava. But he had cooled all that by saving Mr. Suttner's life, merely by touching him.

Did the others only realize it, they had witnessed a miracle this evening. It had been a better miracle than the heavenly music, if less pleasing aesthetically. There could be no denying Simon was what he said he was.

She wished she could tell Alex the truth before he made real trouble for himself.

She also detested lying to her best friend; such a thing

had never happened. Well, of course she had told temporary fibs necessary in the forwardment of the occasional
prank, but those were always made clear in the end. This
one, this very large one—could it ever be explained? *Evelyn, Simon Garrett is my guardian angel.*

It did not bear thinking about.

"Then you really did write him from an advertisement?"
Evelyn asked, her normally flat, quiet voice inflecting with
incredulity. "You hadn't seen him perform before? Was
that not a risk? He might have had a squint, or stunk like
a pig's foot."

The tongs in Darby's hand loosened and shook, splashing a lump of sugar into the pitcher of milk.

"Really, Evelyn, only see what you have made me do."
Darby scooped out the soggy lump and dropped it on the
edge of the tablecloth, to the side of the tray. She wiped
the milk from the tongs, then proceeded to transfer more
pieces of sugar from the large bowl in the table's cabinet
to the small one on the tray.

"Here, allow me to hold that, " Evelyn said, reaching
for the larger bowl and extending it in front of her. "You
might place a sideboard here instead of this little table;
then you could put an entire sack of sugar upon it. Who
would have thought a few women could consume so much
in their first cup of tea? By the by, this is too much work.
You should ring for the maid."

"Oh, it gives me something to do," Darby said.

"Keeps you from answering questions, you mean," Evelyn said.

"True. What a pity it hasn't kept everyone from asking
them."

Evelyn giggled, then grew solemn-faced again. "You
haven't once looked me in the eye this evening, Darby
Brightings, and I want to know the reason why."

"You are imagining things."

"Fie upon it. I cannot, *cannot* believe you would request a stranger to perform at your birthday ball."

"He wasn't so completely unknown to me as all that," Darby replied. When Evelyn quickened with interest, she added hurriedly, "I mean I knew what he looked like. He said his portrait was illustrated in the advertisement, remember?"

"Portrait? A pox on portraits. You know as well as I how they can deceive, though there was certainly no need for fabrication in Mr. Garrett's case. I must say you were fortunate there, for I've seen people with warts and hairy moles all over their faces look comely in portraits. So have you. You recall Lady Broomhilde's youthful memorial to herself in Strathley Hall? A painter's livelihood depends on his ability to overlook the brutal truth."

"I do know it," Darby said. "I've often thought how lucky it is Alex is not a portrait artist, for he would starve, since he is unwilling to hide the truth for anyone."

Her expression darkened suddenly. Biting her lower lip, she took the bowl from Evelyn and replaced it inside the cabinet, straightened the silver jug and bowl on the tray, then opened the lid of the tea pot to peer inside.

"There is not enough tea left," she said in dismal tones. "I shall have to ring for Maisy after all."

As Darby reached for the bell pull, Evelyn placed a restraining hand over her friend's. "Stay a moment," she said, all banter dropping from her voice. "The men will join us soon and we shan't have another opportunity to speak privately. There is something I wanted to ask you."

Fearing more uncomfortable questions regarding Simon, Darby looked over her shoulder at the other ladies. Conversation had ground to a standstill betwixt Lenora and Fiona; the young widow was paging through a magazine, and the minister's daughter attempted to capture a moth that had flown through the half-open window. Fiona was apparently unwilling to relinquish her seat, however,

and her occasional flailing, leaping efforts were limited by
the insect's pattern of flight. The older women by the
window were listening to Aunt Gacia's eloquence with varying degrees of interest on their faces, the one exception
being Mrs. White, who cast frequent, agonized looks
toward her energetic daughter.

"They will wonder why we're standing by the wall so
long," Darby said.

Evelyn's gaze followed Darby's. "No, they won't; only
look how they are enjoying themselves."

"Oh, very well," Darby said, a smile tugging at her
mouth. "What is this deep question that will not wait?"

Now that she had her companion's attention, Evelyn
fell exasperatingly silent and stared at her slippers. Darby
contemplated her with growing consternation. Evelyn was
shorter than herself, though not so petite as Lenora, and
slim as a waif. Dark brown hair fell in curls about her
head, and her small hazel eyes were often serious-looking,
effectively masking a wicked enjoyment of wit. With a delicate, upturned nose, olive skin, and small lips, she possessed the kind of prettiness often overlooked at first sight,
and only realized later as one came to know her better.
She seldom put herself forward, however, to those other
than her closest family and friends; which was just as well,
for she had a frank manner of speech that often sounded
bolder than intended.

"It's about Alex," Evelyn said finally, a blush staining
her cheeks. She waited, as if gathering the words she would
say next. "It will never happen, will it? Our old plans. The
dream you and I have shared since childhood."

Darby knew only a moment's confusion before she
understood. From the time the girls were old enough to
think of such matters, she and Evelyn had talked of their
future weddings. The pairs of siblings were so close in
age—Evelyn being only one year older than the twins and
Edward a year younger—and got on so well together, the

possibility of uniting themselves for all time could not
escape their imaginations. In earlier years, the girls had
coerced the boys into agreeing with this sensible plan, and,
though it was not often mentioned among them, it had
become a kind of standing jest that was not entirely meant
to be humorous. No formal declarations had been made,
but from time to time one of them would say something
that reminded them of their childish promise, such as,
"Shall Darby continue to direct the business after she and
Edward marry?"

It had become a strangely uncomfortable situation in
Darby's mind as she and Alex neared their majority. It was
almost as if their futures were decided, and then again,
they were not.

Now Darby looked down at the tea table and straightened a corner of the serving cloth needlessly.

"I understand you," she said. "What makes you suggest
it won't happen?"

"To say truth, I believe you and Edward will wed. He
would slay me for saying so, but he loves you madly, in the
event you haven't noticed that for yourself. He only waits
until he comes of age before making a formal offer."

"Oh, he does not love me madly," Darby said, appalled.
"*Surely* not. I mean, I love him, too, but . . . "

"Do not dare say you love him like a brother," Evelyn
said stiffly. "He had sooner have you plunge a dagger into
his heart, for he does not love you as a sister, I can attest
to that. You cannot have failed to notice how he bristles
every time Claude smiles at you, and the appearance of
this actor-friend of yours tonight has him fairly frothing
at the mouth."

"Oh, he has nothing to worry about there," Darby said,
instantly horrified. "Nothing at all, I assure you."

"I'm surprised. Mr. Garrett is most attractive."

"Yes, but what you are saying is—is *revolting!* Unthinkable!"

"Well, my goodness, Darby, I know he is only an actor, but it's not as if you were a titled lady who mustn't pollute her descendants with the blood of commoners."

Darby pictured again Simon's strong, sensitive face and luminous eyes and shuddered. "I'm not drawn to him at all," she said sharply. "Not in that way."

"Hm," Evelyn murmured. "Does that mean you've considered Claude?"

"Claude?" Darby exclaimed, then realizing the shrillness of her voice, glanced back to see Lenora staring at her above the pages of her magazine. Darby smiled apologetically, shrugged her shoulders, and explained, "We are only naming the men at dinner tonight."

It was partially true. Lenora accepted the explanation with a lifting of her eyebrows, then resumed her reading. Darby turned back to Evelyn.

"Claude is pleasant enough," she whispered. "But I could never shackle myself to a do-nothing."

"Then Edward has a clear field," Evelyn said, smiling a little. "Unless there is someone else I don't know about."

"No, there is no one else. Whom could I meet, never going beyond the potteries and Mirren? But as to Edward, I . . . well, I haven't sorted my feelings yet."

"Darby, you've had twenty years to sort your feelings."

"I know, but . . . " She looked more closely at her friend's stricken face, and a sudden realization came to her. "I'm a widgeon. This is not what you meant to ask me, is it, Evelyn?"

"Is it not?"

"No. You wished to speak about you and Alex."

Fresh blushes. "Lower your voice, please. I have the good sense to know there is nothing there. Not on his part, anyway."

"I'm certain you're wrong. He has a great fondness for you."

Despair came into Evelyn's eyes. "What you mean to say is, he loves me like a sister."

"No, I think . . . " Darby trailed away, torn between her fears and her affection for Evelyn.

"It is as I thought," Evelyn said, nodding slightly. "I've seen how he hangs on Lenora's every word. At dinner tonight he kept looking past me to watch her, and how he boiled as Mr. Garrett and she seemed to enjoy one another so much."

"Oh, *there* you are mistaken," Darby said, growing loud again. Forcing herself to employ quieter tones, she continued, "Mr. Garrett was only being kind, and Lenora flirts with everything capable of growing hair on its chest."

"You shock me," Evelyn said, laughing softly. "But you can't deny that the greater part of Alex's rudeness to your guest was because of jealousy. You did not know it, but before dinner I tried to maneuver myself beside your brother, hoping to achieve his escort. Yet when dinner was announced, he nearly knocked me aside in his effort to reach Lenora. Only when he saw she had taken Mr. Garrett's arm did he return to me."

"Well, Alex is a silly brute and will get over this infatuation soon enough," Darby said firmly. "Pay no attention; it will blow over like a summer storm, and he will come to his senses."

"Mayhaps," Evelyn said wistfully.

Darby determined to make her friend think of other things. "*Now* may I pull the bell?" she asked, feigning impatience. "I'm positive Fiona has grown thirsty in her efforts with that moth."

"Yes, do," Evelyn said nonchalantly, moving toward the sofa. "I myself am thirsty from all this talking."

Not long after the maid came to replenish their cups, the men entered, bringing a pleasing air of masculine jocularity that had something to do with boisterous voices and the aroma of tobacco, but not all; what it was precisely would ever remain a mystery to her. Darby always looked forward to the time after dinner when the gentlemen rejoined the ladies. One day, if she grew bold enough, she would refuse to retire after the meal and remain with the men, just to see if what she suspected was true—that they did indeed have a more congenial time together than the women. It would be worth smoking a pipe to find out.

No, she did not mean that. Could Simon hear her thoughts?

It did not seem he could, for once again Lenora pounced upon him like a cat on a mouse, pulling him aside for a tête-à-tête in the corner as soon as she saw him. If he knew what Darby was thinking, he would find some way to be alone with herself, to answer the thousand-and-one questions tickling her tongue.

Instead, he appeared content only to give her helpless glances from time to time across the room, as if he did not possess the ability to free himself from Lenora's wiles. Perhaps he failed to desire escape, for he gave every indication of enjoying her animated conversation. In fact, so much laughter and chatter began to sparkle from their corner that first Claude wandered over to join them, then Fiona, who, having knocked off her father's old-fashioned wig in her efforts, triumphantly brought the moth she had cupped between her hands for Simon's approval. In the way of things, the insect fled as soon as it was shown, and for several moments a lively game of bat-the-bug was played among the gentlemen, causing many shrieks from the ladies, until the hapless creature re-discovered the window and flew away.

Darby felt grateful her brother no longer spoke spitefully to Simon, but seemed willing to ignore him. She feared it was a temporary reprieve, for Alex could not disguise his feelings from her; and she sensed the tension growing in him everytime he looked at Lenora and her companion. Still, he was making an effort. Darby marked the especial attention he paid to Evelyn and hoped it would not raise her friend's hopes falsely.

She herself grew increasingly discomfitted as the night wore on. Edward never strayed far from her side. Ordinarily she would have thought nothing of it; but now that Evelyn had spoken, she feared the meaning behind his notice. Every glance now became a lover's look, every statement weighted with amorous significance. She could no longer view her childhood companion as a well-loved, comfortable old shoe; now she found herself thinking: *Can I spend my life with this man?*

Well, who better than a dear friend? She loved him, beyond a doubt. Still, her uneasiness made the hours crawl by at a slug's pace.

Simon never once came to speak with her. A sensible part of her brain argued that a private audience in such a crowd would be impossible. It was not as if they could take a stroll together in the garden; Alex would explode. But as the evening deepened, her curiosity and impatience twanged so badly she felt herself becoming cross. If Simon wanted to go unnoticed among them, why had he taken such a comely form? She counseled herself to put an immediate check on her emotions before she did the unimaginable, and became angry with her angel.

She continued to give herself the same advice as she dressed for bed that evening. She had no personal maid to assist, for such a luxury appeared burdensome to her, from what she'd observed of Aunt Gacia and Lenora's abigails. Slow-moving Persimone was forever getting her feelings hurt and running off to her room in tears—so often, in fact, that Darby had begun to view her outbursts with suspicion. And Lenora's Rena, though hard-working, possessed eyes like flint and a tongue to match. No, she had far rather dress herself.

The evening had gone well, considering that an angel had appeared in strange clothing and disrupted everyone; the vicar had almost expired; and two lamps had been broken in the pursuit of a moth. Almost everyone seemed to enjoy themselves at least once during the evening.

Excepting herself, of course. She had been on tenter-hooks since catching sight of Simon. And now, hours later, she was no more the wiser about his visit. It was maddening that they had found no opportunity to speak.

Darby jerked her nightgown over her head and fumbled at her buttons, ripping one off in her temper. She watched it roll across the carpet, then followed to kick it into the fireplace.

When she heard a soft knocking at her door, her frown deepened. It was doubtless Alex, come to scold her about inviting a stranger into their house without seeking his approval. Well, she would flap the thorny side of her tongue at him, wouldn't she?

Tossing her robe over her shoulders and looping its belt into a careless knot, she flung open the door. And bit her lip to stifle a scream when she saw Simon. Before he could speak, she seized his wrist, darted a frantic look up and down the corridor, then pulled him inside and closed the door.

"Are you trying to ruin me?" she heard herself say.

As his smile floundered, Darby cursed herself mentally. There, she'd made that sad look come into his eyes again. He began to apologize, and she shook her head and daringly pressed her fingers over his lips.

"No, no, it is I who am wrong," she said, pulling him toward a pair of blue chairs by the fire. "With your heavenly nature, you could not have thought how it would look, should anyone see you entering my bedroom at night. If I may make the suggestion, it would be best if you simply appear here, rather than walking to my chamber. The others think you are an actor, not an angel, I must remind you."

"I didn't think," he said, sitting down, regret lengthening his face. "Will they hear us talking?"

"Not if we keep our voices low. Father had thick walls built into this house for that very reason."

"You miss your father. I hear it in your voice."

Her eyes softened. "There is not a day that passes that I do not think of him. He practically raised us himself, since Mother died when Alex and I were seven. He was a special man. He treated us as if we were deserving of respect, and not children to be ordered about. It was his desire that we learn the business he began, and our days were ordered around it. Not that we didn't have ample time to play and learn other things, of course. But the pottery was the center of our lives, and never once did he treat me differently than Alex because I was a girl. That meant everything to me." She laughed suddenly. "But you know all this, of course."

He stared at her for a long while. Darby's pulse began to race when his eyes moved over her, then looked away. He gazed so intently at the window, in fact, that she was led to glance over her shoulder, wondering what might be looking in. When she saw nothing, she leaned toward him.

"Will you not tell me why you are here? The last time we spoke, you said I wouldn't see you again."

"I'll explain what I can," he said, his eyes still on the window. "But first"—he darted a lightning look at her, then away once more, his cheeks flaring with color—"could you, um, pull your robe a little closer together?"

Darby glanced down at herself, at the dressing gown that hung open to reveal her nightgown, which in turn exposed the upper half of her breasts. Flames of embarrassment heated her neck and ears as she whipped the robe about her, pulling it closed almost to her chin.

"I—I'm sorry I wasn't more careful," she mumbled

humbly. "I never thought—well, I imagined since you are invisible most of the time, you had probably seen me in my bath, and I didn't—that is—"

She stumbled to a stop, struggling with confusion. Shouldn't an angel be able to view her body without a second thought, even were she naked as a dog?

He met her gaze sadly. "You must think I'm a sorry excuse for an angel," he said.

"No, I—well, it is only . . . "

"I'm not what you expected, right?"

She paused. What was the correct thing to say? Would her guardian become angry with her? Was he capable of striking her dead? She breathed in shakily.

"Not precisely what I expected, no."

He straightened a little, his eyes becoming reflective. "You'll just have to think of me as a man." His words became more decisive as he spoke. "Yes, that's it. While I'm here, you have to think of me as a normal man, with all his limitations and—and temptations."

Recalling Simon's absorption in Lenora this evening, she felt cold. "But you are not a normal man. I mean, you possess your angelic powers and strength, do you not, even though you've taken mortal form?"

"What makes you say that?"

"Well, you saved Mr. Suttner's life."

When he laughed suddenly, she viewed him with surprise and some disappointment.

"I'm sorry, Darby," he said, recovering. "I'm not laughing at you, but myself. I seem to have a talent for tangling nets around me. Well, never mind. What I did for the vicar was something anyone can do, even a child. It's a simple procedure; I can show you how to do it if you want."

"Certainly," she said weakly. "Such a thing might prove useful more than once in a lifetime."

She could not look at him. Pushing herself from the chair, she walked to the window and gazed down at the moonlit garden. The cherubic statuaries placed among the roses glistened in a light spring rain. The cherubs appeared to revel in their various poses: faces raised heavenward, chubby arms gesturing outward toward the earth. So child-like they looked, so innocent.

Her heart throbbed in her ears.

"I have never heard of such an angel," she said, speaking distantly as if to the cherubim below. "The angels I've read about don't have human failings. They aren't concerned with how a woman dresses. They don't lie. And they certainly don't hold flirtatious conversations with coquettes."

Simon remained quiet for only an instant before asking, "Coquettes? Are you referring to Lenora?"

"Yes, of course I mean Lenora," she said, worrying at the lack of deference in her voice, but unable to do anything about it. Her head buzzed with questions, and this was all he wanted to talk about? "Everyone knows she is a shameless flirt, as should you." Not liking the alarm that inexplicably bloomed in his eyes, she turned back to the window, barely hearing his footsteps as he came to stand beside her.

"You don't like Lenora?" he asked stupidly, as if her answer really mattered. It was quite enough. Surely the flare of rage she felt was justified, and God would not kill her for it.

"You have placed me in a dilemma," she said, showing her teeth. "Now I must ask myself the question: Dare I speak truth to my angel, or should I lie expediently, as he has taught me to do?"

She felt an answering heat rising in him. He stood no more than a foot away from her, flames lighting the depths of his eyes. She retreated a pace and fingered her belt.

"I want . . . " His jaw worked. "I want to hear the truth."

"As do I," she declared, adding with cowardly haste, "But if you must know, I neither like nor trust Lenora."

He turned slowly and went to sit on the edge of the bed,

bowing his head and drooping his forearms across his knees. "Oh, man," he said despondently.

She felt an unpleasant mixture of bewilderment and alarm. A terrible apprehension seized her. What if her angel was unhinged, mentally? Could such a thing happen?

She started forward, intending to sit beside him on the mattress, then thought better of it. There was a wooden rocker beside the window, and she pulled it near the bed and sat, staring upward until he looked at her. Between the chair's lower height and Simon's tallness, she felt like a little child gazing up at its parent.

But such a strange parent he was. He had rid himself of his jacket before coming to her, and his white linen shirt with its cascades of lace looked romantic stretching across his chest and defining the muscles underneath, as similarly-dressed, sword-fighting heroes of the last century looked romantic in the illustrations she'd seen in books. And his hair; his silvery hair that he'd unbound from its ribbon to flow across his shoulders—that was romantic, too. She reined in her thoughts uneasily.

"Simon. What have my feelings toward Lenora to do with anything?"

At first it seemed he would not answer, for he rubbed his hands across his face and raked his fingers through his hair as if in the throes of great weariness, or indecision. When he finally spoke, the words burst from him like water overflowing a dam.

"Everything, Darby. What you think of Lenora means everything, since I've seen your brother values only one opinion above his own—yours. That's the reason I've come here again. I've got to make sure Alexander marries Lenora. He simply must."

Chapter Five

She stared at him with all the horror he feared she would, looking as if the power of speech had deserted her. Well, he'd been speechless, too, when he discovered the present owners of Brightings—Chesterton Place, they called it now—had descended from strangers instead of Alexander and Lenora Brightings, as they were supposed to do.

In the world he'd previously known—the world as it was before he warned Darby about the fire—she had died; and Alexander married Lenora, who bore him three sons, the oldest of whom became Elena's several-times-great grandfather.

Somehow by delaying Darby's death, Simon had changed all that. He'd caused a different world to exist.

Elena did not live in this new world and never had. And Tay with his sparkling green eyes, bubbling laughter, and plump little arms and legs always moving, had never drawn breath.

How could the sun dare shine in a world that knew no Tay?

And how much solace could Simon take in the fact that his wife—*ex-wife,* he reminded himself harshly—and child had not died brutally at the hands of one of his fans, a psycho who had declared her love for him in over five hundred letters? The guilt of not recognizing the woman's real threat, the guilt of being the unwitting cause of his family's murder, had been an impossible burden; but preventing them from tasting life at all was worse.

And all because his warning had delayed Darby's death—*had delayed it no more than a couple of months.*

He looked at her now with compassion. Why was this radiant, idealistic girl seemingly destined to die so young? Never mind the grey eyes flashing doubt, fear and repugnance at him; she was entitled. Hadn't he doubted himself during the past weeks; been almost paralyzed with it? He had begun to think he'd imagined Darby, Elena, Tay, and all the rest.

Darby began to speak, her lips and voice trembling. "What do you mean, Alex must marry Lenora? I don't understand."

"I know you don't. This is hard for you, especially since your feelings toward her aren't pleasant."

"You could not have told me a worse thing."

"Oh, come on, Darby, she's not so bad as all that. I spent some time getting to know her tonight—"

"So I observed."

"—um, okay, and she seemed quite nice, actually—"

"She *would* seem that way, since she centered all of her attention on you. Lenora ever enjoys fawning over men. Try being a woman around her and see how charming she is."

"But I saw her speak kindly to Miss White and others," he argued. "Aren't you being a little rough on her?"

"She's one step removed from a tart, and the distance grows closer daily."

"Whoa, Darby!" he said, laughing. "You're overreacting."

His mirth died when he saw she blinked back tears.

"I tell you, Simon, you cannot form an objective opinion about her because she was so taken with you. Another evening, it might be Alex or Claude or someone else. Had you visited us tonight in the guise of a humble old man, or a plain one—and I cannot understand why you did not—instead of this angelic beauty you have chosen to display, only then could you judge her dispassionately."

He couldn't help smiling. "Angelic beauty?"

"Surely you know how well you look," she said irritably. "You chose this form, did you not?"

"No, I'm afraid this is the way God made me," he answered meekly, a teasing look on his face.

"Oh." Her eyes lit briefly as if she wanted to join his amusement, but she did not succumb. "Well, in that case I must tell you this: Alex would be much happier with Evelyn, to whom he has been promised for most of his life. She is a lifelong friend and all that is amiable. Her reputation is above reproach. She—"

As Darby continued to extoll the virtues of Evelyn, her words ran together in his ears. Simon rose from the bed in agitation. This was what he had feared; Darby was the cause of the change in Alex's choice of wives. And she was still talking. He couldn't understand a word of it; he had to stop her.

"No, Darby," he interrupted. "Alexander can't marry Evelyn. No way."

Darby, too, rose and walked behind her rocker, holding onto the chair's back for support. "But *why*, Simon?" It was almost a wail.

"Because—because it has to do with destiny."

"Destiny," she repeated, as if the word was unknown to her.

"The family that Alex and Lenora will have . . . there's a descendant of theirs who'll be born many years from now. If they don't get married, that descendant won't exist."

She studied him with fierce concentration. "How can you know this? Is it given to angels to see the future?"

"Not all of it," he said uncomfortably. "I just know what'll happen if those two don't get married."

"Then are you saying that if Alex and Lenora don't give birth to this child, or cause this descendant to exist, something terrible will occur to mankind?"

"In a manner of speaking, yes." *Something terrible will happen to me.*

"What does this mean, *in a manner of speaking?* Devastation either occurs, or it does not; there cannot be degrees of it, surely."

"I never said it would devastate the world, Darby. But an earth without that child would be more . . . empty."

"But why cannot Alex and Evelyn become the ancestors of this person? Surely that could be arranged." She gave him a pleading look.

He brushed the hair back from his eyes. "No, it can't. If Alexander and Evelyn marry, they'll have a daughter. The Brightings line will die out; the estate will be sold to other owners." While disbelief grew on her face, he continued desperately, "You won't like this part. The potteries will go out of business, and the chinaware you and your brother produce will never become more than a local business."

She bowed her head, her long hair, loosened now for bed, hiding her face. He did not need to see her expression to know how she felt; her woe-filled voice said it all. "But if Alex and Lenora wed . . ."

"Everything will be for the best." A crafty thought made him add, "I probably shouldn't tell you this, but Brightings dinnerware will become known across the earth for centuries. You and Alexander will found a fortune."

A ghost of a smile curved her lips, then died. She shot a stabbing look at him, shook her head and began to pace before the window.

"I don't understand how you know all this. You speak as if the future is a road with many turnings, each one leading to a different destination. Is that how it is? Can a simple act like choosing one marriage partner over another be of such significance?"

"Sometimes it can," he said easily. But as her words struck him more deeply, he grew quiet. What was he doing, messing around with the past? He'd changed a thousand things when he was here for only a few hours. How many differences would he cause if he stayed a month? And what gave him the right?

The trees give me the right, he thought instantly, then dismissed it. His stumble into the past had been a freak of nature, like a tornado or an earthquake. There couldn't be any real purpose to it. He'd just do the best he could with the circumstances that had fallen his way. It was no different than he'd always lived his life. But how to make Darby understand?

"Do you remember when I warned you about the abandoned house?" he asked.

"Yes, and I haven't thanked you for that," she said, her voice warming. "You were right; after you told me about it, Alex asked me to accompany him to the Holley estate. He wanted to play a jest on our uncle; but your words came to mind, so I was able to stop us from getting burned. Thank you, Simon."

"It was my pleasure to be able to help you. But if I hadn't, you *would* have died that day. Call it another forking in the road if you want, but I think it's better you lived."

"Naturally I feel the same. But you aren't speaking of life and death over Alex's choice in wives, are you? Only that this descendant of Lenora's might not exist. You haven't claimed something devastating would occur in that event. So I must ask you: How can we know the future is not better without him?''

How did he know? By the aching in his heart. But what if she was right? What if leaving the future in its changed state was better for the greatest number of people?

No, he couldn't start thinking that way; he'd go crazy. He knew what he had to do. "It's just better, that's all," he said childishly.

"And yet, if what you desire comes to pass, Alex will be condemned to danger," she said softly. "How can you forget him in your plans?" She turned her back to him and stared into the night. "I did not wish to say this, but I see I must. You are consigning him to life with a murderess.''

"What?" he shouted, then flinched and looked toward the door. "What are you talking about?"

"You will say it is all conjecture and that I'm mad for speaking of it.''

He hurried to her side, then propped himself in the windowsill, forcing her to look at him. "Tell me," he said.

She swallowed. "Well, I have no proof; but when Lenora's husband died last Christmas, there was talk that she killed him. You see, we had all gone to Bath to spend the holiday with Reece and Lenora, taking rooms in the same hotel where they lived. One afternoon while Alex and I were attending an assembly, Reece fell from his bedroom window. I spoke with the hotel manager after it happened. According to him, Reece had been in his rooms all day, drinking heavily. When he sent his servant to fetch another bottle of wine, the manager, fearing the destructiveness of an inebriated guest, delivered it himself with a mind to judging Reece's temper. Just as he arrived at the door, Lenora flung it open, as if to leave, but Reece seized her and shouted, 'I shall tell all! They will learn the truth

about you from my lips!' or words to that effect. The hotel
manager was mortified at interrupting this domestic squab-
ble and, as Lenora did not appear to be in danger, he left
immediately. Moments later, Reece's body was found on
the pavement, four stories beneath their chamber.''

Simon breathed deeply. ''But if Reece was drunk, he
probably tripped and fell.''

''That's what Lenora claimed, and her story was believed,
at least officially.''

''But you think otherwise.''

''I cannot be positive, of course, but I suspect murder.
Their window opened to the floor, but outside the glass
was a tiny balcony made of iron; you know the sort of thing
I mean—curving bars that form part of the building's
ornamentation. This thing was waist-high and not meant
for guests to stand upon; I suppose it provided a convenient
place for the servants to wash the windows, though. To fall
from it, Reece would have had to squeeze onto this plat-
form and climb over the bars deliberately. It hardly seems
a thing he would do.''

''Sometimes, Darby, in a moment of despair, people do
crazy things.''

How bitterly well he knew it.

His family's killer, Sheila Wells, had been in despair.
And, in the weeks of crushing grief that followed her act,
he himself had dwelt in the shadowlands, thinking the
dark thoughts that could have led to an action similar to
Reece's. Ending his pain became an obsession.

How glad he was that he hadn't. Perhaps now he could
save Darby—again. Bring Elena and Tay back into being.
Make a difference in someone's life; an important difference. Something more vital than he'd done before—
existing only as a thirty-foot image in a darkened room,
birthing impossible dreams in the minds of strangers.

''You didn't know Reece,'' Darby disagreed. ''He treated
himself to every indulgence, be it whiskey, fine clothing,

or—or women, I'm sorry to say. He was not a man to end his life; he enjoyed it too much.''

Simon thought a minute. "You make me wonder why Lenora married him. A charming woman like her shouldn't have trouble attracting men."

After sending him a prolonged look of distaste, Darby said, "Reece Ellison seemed a fine match when they first wed. He had not gambled the greater part of his fortune away then, nor was he fat and indolent. As time passed, Lenora came to realize her error in judgment; this is why I believe she killed him."

"She's too small, Darby. How could she have pushed a pudgy guy over a rail?"

"Lenora is quite strong. And Reece was intoxicated, remember.''

Darby walked to her rocker and swung it around to face him, then sat. She gazed down at her lap and pulled the edges of her robe together across her knees, beginning to rock slowly.

Simon contemplated her, ice spreading through his body. Tattered thoughts were knitting together in his mind, and he didn't like the pattern they made.

"Do you have any idea what Ellison meant when he shouted he'd tell the truth about her? Do you think Lenora has secrets?"

"It wouldn't surprise me," Darby said, head still bowed. Suddenly she looked up, her eyes swimming with hope. "Do you believe that's the reason she killed him? That she was not merely tired of him, but did something awful— stole someone's jewelry, mayhaps; no, someone's husband, more likely—and when Reece threatened to tell, she killed him to protect herself from a vengeful woman, or the ruining of her reputation, or something like? *Do you mean to say you think I'm right about her?*"

Simon stared at Darby, transfixed. In spite of his chill, he began to sweat. Was the room growing smaller?

How could he say, *yes, you may be right about Lenora,* when he wanted Darby to like her, to encourage Alexander to marry the woman? How else to ensure Elena's birth?

But on the other hand, how dare he say, *Absolutely not; your imagination is running away with you; Lenora is a wonderful person,* when it could be she *was* a murderess—*that she might even try to cause Darby's death?*

Darby Brightings, twin sister to Alexander Brightings, drowned under mysterious circumstances on the evening of June 10, 1818, read the twenty-eighth page of the estate's crumbling historical record. He'd only had a moment to scan it before the sounds of sirens chased him from Chesterton Place. But the author's overwrought prose had branded into his brain:

Tragically, her death occurred during her gala twenty-first birthday ball. While family and friends danced to the strains of orchestral music, Darby drowned in darkness in the estate's secluded pond. Was it an accident as the magistrate claimed, or could it have been murder? If only an accident, why was she alone at the pond instead of enjoying her guests? And how to explain the horrible bruising on her face? Unfortunately, these are questions which can never be answered.

Well, he'd come here to answer them. And maybe he already had. He'd suspected murder as soon as he read the words. What else could he think, when Darby would have burned to death if not for himself? The two tragedies together formed a strong argument against accident.

But to simply warn Darby now was useless. Telling her to avoid the pond on her birthday would accomplish nothing if someone was determined to kill her. Not only would it cloud her days and nights with suspicions and fear, but she might alert the very person she should avoid. Since he had to remain until Alexander's love life was straightened out anyway—hopefully he could do it by their birthday—he intended to discover who meant to hurt her and why. If he couldn't, he'd stick to her like glue on the fateful day.

But *Lenora* as a suspect? It was hard to believe. Still, if she murdered once, she'd hardly balk at doing so again. But why would she? Was Darby going to discover her deep, dark secret?

His head felt like a chestnut about to burst in a fire.

Darby needs to trust Lenora so that Alexander will marry Lenora so that Elena and Tay will be born. But Lenora might be a murderess, might even try to kill Darby. So how could Darby trust Lenora? How could he? Around and around and around and around . . .

"Simon?"

Someone was calling his name, but he hardly heard the soft voice. Although his eyes were open, he saw nothing.

Surely Lenora was innocent. According to the record, Alexander hadn't been harmed; he'd lived a long, long life. Everything could still work, and he'd be able to prevent Darby's death as well. *Just keep your eyes and ears open.*

"Simon, can you hear me?"

She mustn't know his confused suspicions, at least not until something was proven. All could be lost before he began. He made himself focus on her face. "I hear you," he said in a hoarse voice.

"Please answer my question, then. Do you think I'm right about Lenora? For if I am, perhaps I, or you and I, could discover her secret."

"No," he said vehemently. "Don't even think about it. Absolutely not."

She knit her fingers together. "Are you disturbed because I may be correct about her, or do you already know the truth?"

"No . . ."

"No, you don't know; or *no,* you don't think I'm right?"

He cleared his throat. "No to both. I believe you're allowing your dislike of Lenora to colour your judgment."

The words ripped from his mouth painfully, as if his tongue were a scalpel.

She frowned. When she spoke, her voice sounded far away, as if she were thinking out loud. "Why is it that I feel you are lying to me?"

He breathed in sharply. There she went again, worrying about the flaws in her angel's character. She wanted him to be perfect, didn't she? Maybe it was a reasonable expectation, but it made him angry. He'd never be perfect, never, and the world's greatest director couldn't guide him to act that way.

She kept measuring him by her own standards; that was the problem. How could he, twentieth-century survivor that he was, dream to match the sheltered, moral character she'd formed in these innocent times? She was too pure. Probably a virgin as well. No, *undoubtedly* a virgin. This century could be paradise if he were not so—no. Stop. That sort of thinking had caused all his problems.

His anger flared irrationally. "You must think I'm sinless as God," he snapped, jumping from his perch on the window to walk back and forth beside her bed. He noticed she flinched as he passed. Yes, she'd do well to fear him, for though angel he was not, he held her life in his hands. And she had better trust him totally, or off she'd go sneaking into Lenora's private life like some foolhardy female detective in a novel and getting herself killed. He could read it on her face, see it in the defiant tilt of her chin.

"Well, I'm not," he continued, deliberately sounding harsh, though his anger floated away as he looked at her. "You're so concerned about my lies, as you call them, but let me ask you something. Do you ever read your Bible? If you do, you'll recall other instances where angels have misdirected people. You remember that passage about entertaining angels unawares? How could that happen if the angel didn't deceive his hosts in some way—claim to be someone other than what he is?"

He watched the rebellious light in her eyes fade. He'd never been so grateful at his mother's making him attend Sunday School. Bet Mom would be surprised at how he was putting his memories to use.

"Yes," Darby said, wonder in her voice. Gladness, too. "Is that what you're doing, then? This is why you've chosen to array yourself in those amusing clothes and claim to be an actor? You want my family to entertain you graciously without knowing you are an angel because it will improve them in some fashion?"

With a pang he saw her struggling to believe him. Every crumb of hope he offered, she grabbed and ran with it; but then he'd do something to destroy her confidence. Clearly he wasn't delivering an Oscar-winning performance but, God help him, the requirements of the role went far beyond his range.

"I've told you why I came," he said.

Her face fell. "Oh, yes. Alex must marry Lenora. Forgive me if I don't embrace that idea. I hope you won't think I'm being deliberately willful." Meekly, she added, "I shall pray that my attitude changes to what it should be."

"Um, there's an idea," he said uncomfortably. "And, Darby, here's something else. I don't know what you felt about the discussion over dinner tonight, or if it changed your mind in any way; but I'm pretty sure of what you think about angels in general; and I must tell you this: no matter what preconceived notions you have, you have to know that I'm not absolutely perfect in this form. Not in the way you expect. These clothes—they were a mistake. I should've been better prepared, but I wasn't. If I'd had more time . . . Well, I'm not one of your top-flight angels, see. If Gabriel is a general, I'm a private—understand? I'm the lowest of the low. I make mistakes and plenty of them. So you'll just have to expect that in dealing with me."

Satisfied, he nodded his head once, firmly, and folded

his arms. Through a strong force of will, he held her gaze without looking aside more than two or three times.

To his deep surprise, her expression lightened.

"Then . . . if you are not perfect, if you can make mistakes, perhaps you're wrong about Alex and Lenora!"

"No, Darby," he groaned, wondering why he hadn't seen this coming. "I mess up a lot, but not about that. No, no, and no." *Please God—if you're there—don't let me be wrong about this.*

"Perhaps time will prove differently," she said persuasively. "How long do you remain with us, if I may ask? Naturally, you are welcome forever. Do not let it be said the Brightings are not happy to entertain visitors, heavenly or otherwise!"

She was practically giddy with relief. He'd have to watch her every minute or she might end up drowning sooner than he thought.

"I'm staying until your birthday," he said sullenly.

"Well, that is a goodly, long visit! I will help you in every way I can. I wouldn't have presumed to offer such before, but now that I understand how it is with you, I believe you can use every aid at your disposal, even that of a poor human female."

Laughing lightly, she rocked to her feet and approached him. "Your clothing, for example. Uncle Richard's valet is a former tailor and sews all of his garments. I shall order him to stitch you up a few things, for no one else in this house is large enough to loan you his clothes. Beckett owes us a little labor, I should think, for his wages have been paid by the estate all these years."

She moved closer and touched his hair. When he stepped backward, surprised, she looked disconcerted for a second, then chuckled. "Your hair needs cutting, too, if you are to stay so long. Although it's beautiful—gracious, it feels like silk; do you wash it in rainwater? No, how silly of me; you probably don't have to wash it at all—anyway, the style is sadly outmoded and will cause comment, I fear. You won't mind having it clipped in one of the windblown styles, will you?"

"Cut my hair?" he replied in a hollow voice.

His long hair was his trademark; at least it had been in the world where Elena lived. "A Face for the Second Millineum," one of the scores of magazines he'd covered had headlined. "On Achieving Masculine Sensitivity: Simon Garrett," said another.

It hadn't been like that in the new world. His face no longer commanded the attention of the press; he was not adored by millions across the earth; he could not demand top figures at the box office.

He wasn't less talented in that world; he still acted in off-Broadway productions and had done a couple of small films, according to the biographical sketch he'd read about himself on the back of a program that he'd found crumpled inside a drawer in the Loma Linda bungalow he'd discovered was his after reading his address in an actor's directory.

Had it not been for all he'd lost in his family, he would've adjusted to that new lifestyle. It fit him more comfortably than the old one had; he wasn't penniless, and it was a relief to be able to buy a loaf of bread without being mobbed.

But he couldn't leave it at that, of course. He'd flown back to England to make things right, knowing it was worth any sacrifice.

But . . . *his hair!*

"Pray don't look so sad; it will grow back." She paused. "Won't it?"

"Hm? Oh, sure . . ."

She stared at him worriedly. "It won't—you won't be hurt if it's cut, will you? Lose your strength, I mean?"

"Lose my—" He began to laugh. "Darby, I told you I was an angel, not Samson."

She clasped her hands together. "Excellent; it's settled then. Simbar can cut it; he trims all the men's hair at Brightings."

"Simbar . . . he's the butler?"

"Yes, you saw him at dinner tonight."

"But he's bald as a bowling—bald as a—a turtle!"

Her laughter was throaty, abandoned, and deep, exactly the way he liked to hear a woman laugh—as if she were lost in her enjoyment.

"Don't worry. He only shaves his head because he spent a few years in India. Our butler believes his foreign sojourn distinguishes him from other mortals and is determined no one forgets it. He sometimes wears a turban, too, but pay no attention; we do not."

Her words did little to encourage him about Simbar's credentials, but he couldn't resist smiling when delight sent her spinning about the room.

"Oh, I shall help you in every way I can. Feel free to ask me anything, and if I know the answer, I'll tell you. Yes, we shall get on famously! And who knows what you and I might discover about Lenora."

He'd known she would get back to that. "You remember what I told you," he warned, easing toward the door.

"I will," she said. "I always heed your warnings. Are you leaving, then? Can you not—I don't suppose you're able to disappear to your bedroom in this form, are you?"

"No," he said, and coughed. "Not in this body, I can't."

"Then let me check the corridor first," she said, moving past him to open the door. "Oh, I have only just thought," she whispered. "May I listen to your heavenly music before you leave?"

"I'm sorry, I didn't bring it with me this time." He shrugged and patted the back of his satin breeches. "No pockets."

"I see," she said sadly. "Well, then." After looking in

both directions, she slipped her fingers around his wrist and guided him past. "Good night, my angel."

He stood outside her door as if turned to stone. Her fingers had sent a shock quivering through his body, hot as an electrical fire. He didn't want to think about what that meant.

"Good night, Darby," he whispered, and hurried away.

Chapter Six

Early the next morning, Darby saw something from her window that caused her to flee from the room, down the stairs and to the front door. In her panic, she could not make the lock turn and so began to pound the wood in frustration. Not only was she unable to open the door, but her hair, which she had not yet had time to put up, caught itself painfully in the buttons at the back of her dress. In despair, she ripped the long strands forward into two wild bunches across her shoulders, kicked the door resoundingly and began to cry.

"What's wrong?" exclaimed Alexander from the doorway of the dining room, a piece of toast in his hand.

She ran to him as though he were water on the desert. "Oh, Alex, thank God!"

When she seized him, the toast flew from his fingers and skittered across the floor. Alexander patted her back comfortingly while grimacing at the trail of orange marmalade behind her.

"What in blazes can be the matter to put you in such a fit?" he asked. "Did the king die?"

"No! It's my—it's Simon—Mr. Garrett! Someone is after him!"

"Good," said Alexander.

"No, you don't understand! Hurry and open the door for I cannot. Someone is chasing him through the park; I saw him racing behind the hedge from my window! Call Caesar and Augustus, do!"

"Very well, only calm yourself. Let me open the door first."

She released him and dashed the tears from her eyes while he opened the door. When he walked out, she followed closely, scanning in the direction where she had seen Simon last, then looking in the other two directions visible to them.

"It promises to be a beautiful Sunday," Alexander said, breathing deeply. "Look, the mist is already burning from the ground and lifting through the trees. Should be a smashing day for afternoon tea outdoors, do the Wallaces ask us after worship."

"Hush, Alex. You are being heartless and don't know anything." She pushed her way past him and rushed down the steps. Looking back and forth, she held her skirts high as she crossed the drive and the grass.

"Well, where is the fellow, then?" Alexander called, beginning to follow. "I wish you would stop; you look like a goose with its head on loose. There, I've made a rhyme; are you not proud of me?"

"No, I am not!" she shouted back. "And how can I know where he is? I told you to call the dogs! While you were dawdling, his pursuers may have caught him already!"

"I did not dawdle," he responded indignantly. "What did these fellows look like?"

A brief pause ensued. "I don't know; I didn't see them."

"You didn't see! Well, how did you know anyone was chasing him?"

"Because he was running, Alex," she said slowly, as to an idiot child. "Did you not listen when I spoke?"

He was within a few yards of her now, and a slow smile crossed his face. "Garrett was running, but you didn't see anyone chasing him?"

"Yes, that's what I've been trying to tell you," she said, pausing to catch her breath. "But from the way he ran, and the pain on his face, it was obvious something—I mean, some*one*—pursued him."

"Was it?" he said, joining her, his grin growing wider. "Well, I begin to think you're in the right of it, then. I *should* call the dogs." And so saying, he gave a piercing whistle, then shouted, "Caesar! Augustus! Cleopatra!"

Almost immediately, three setters bounded toward them from the direction of the stables, one of them barking loudly, the other two panting and appearing to smile as they loped along.

"There he is!" Darby cried, pointing toward Simon, whose head could now be seen in rhythmic, progressive intervals behind the hedge some distance away. "He appears to have run in a great circle for some reason. I still cannot see his assailants, but they may be hidden behind the greenery. Wait until we spot them before sending the dogs."

"What's that you say?" Alex asked. "Can't hear you. Caesar, fetch!"

While Darby loudened her protests, the animals looked up at him adoringly, questions in their eyes. Seeing their master point toward the hedge, they leapt off in that direction, baying and barking importantly.

The head behind the shrubbery bounced up one more time, perceived the dogs coming, and was seen no more.

"Alexander!" screamed Darby. "Call them off at once!"

She began to run forward again. "Come here, Caesar! Come back, Cleopatra!"

The female dog halted in her tracks, looked back at Darby sadly, and howled. With her tail tucked between her legs, the setter gazed longingly toward her fleeing companions. She began to follow.

"Don't you dare defy me, Cleopatra; you are my dog, not Alexander's!"

The setter immediately lowered herself to the ground and crawled on, whining.

"Bitch!" shrieked Darby.

"Such language, my sister," Alexander panted behind her. "And on Sunday, too. I thought you were reformed."

Still running, she whipped her head back and said viciously, "Call off the dogs or I'll show you how reformed I am."

"How you frighten me! But no one can stop them now, they are too excited."

"If Simon is harmed, I will never forgive you. Never!"

Alexander stopped running. "That's the second time this morning you've called him by his first name. What means this heavy concern for a stranger, Darby?"

"I am not speaking to you."

She stopped and pressed her hand to her side, breathing hard. They were almost to the hedge, but she would die if she ran any farther. How could Simon run so long without collapsing? Angels must have great stamina.

The dogs had long since disappeared behind the hedge and were ominously silent. She squeezed her eyes shut, visualizing Simon's torn, bleeding body.

A window slammed open in the house far behind them. "What goes on out there? Sounds like war!" called Uncle Richard from his second-floor bedroom.

Aunt Gacia, attired in dressing gown and frilled cap, crowded next to him and leaned forward. "You have awakened poor Mr. Lightner! For shame!" An instant later she added, "But we are not complaining, my dears! Of course you may do as you like in your own home! I have always said it and always shall!"

A few rooms down, Lenora also unlatched her window. Darby was not too exhausted to note that her step-cousin's hair flowed across her shoulders in golden waves, and her pink robe left little to be imagined in the early morning light.

The widow yawned fetchingly and leaned her arms across the embrasure. "What goes on? Am I missing an excitement?"

"You are missing nothing!" Alexander declared fervently, consuming her appearance like a starving dog, Darby saw with narrowing eyes. "Merely a little confusion over the actor. Forgive us for disturbing your slumber over such a trifle!"

"Trifle?" Lenora straightened, looking hungry as a wolf herself. "I would call that no trifle! Michelangelo's *David*, would be more apt!"

As one, Darby and Alexander turned to see Simon, a wide smile upon his face, emerge from behind the hedge. Jumping and fawning, Caesar and Augustus escorted him on one side, while Cleopatra nuzzled the arm on his other. When she caught sight of her mistress, Cleopatra lowered her head ashamedly but did not desert her post.

Darby's breath caught in her throat. Simon wore the breeches he'd worn the previous night, but his chest, calves, and feet were bare. Like tiny drops of rain, perspiration glittered on the pale hair that covered his chest. His breeches, also dampened with sweat, clung to his body and outlined the muscles of his thighs. She had not known a man's legs could curve so graciously yet look so strong.

All this she saw in the instant before Simon called cheerily, "Good morning. I see you set the dogs on me after all, Alexander. Guess it's lucky I have a way with animals."

He stooped to pat Cleopatra's head and scratch behind her ears.

Alexander, who had been too incensed to speak until this moment, stepped protectively in front of his sister. "What's the meaning of this exhibition? Why are you parading yourself indecently in front of innocent females? Darby, cover your eyes."

"Alex," Darby whispered warningly. She peered around her brother's shoulder long enough to see the surprise and indignation on Simon's face, then averted her gaze as she was bid. It was as she thought. Her angel had made another innocent mistake. Of course he would think nothing of appearing half-naked—probably would think nothing of appearing *entirely* naked for that matter. Like in the Garden of Eden, there would be no shame in heaven.

The thought made her grow uncomfortably hot. All of the blood in her body drained to her feet, and she felt faint.

But if there was no shame in heaven, why, then, had he become embarrassed about the gap in her robe last night? Was there one standard for men and another for women in heaven, too? If so, the golden city was not as enticing as she once thought.

"I wasn't parading myself in front of anyone," Simon disputed. "I was out here alone until the dogs woke everybody up and started people looking out their windows."

"That's my fault," Darby said from behind Alexander's back. "I caught a glimpse of you from my bedroom and thought something was chasing you."

She could sense the smile on Simon's face. "I appreciate your concern, Darby. I was just taking my morning jog."

"Morning jog?" Alexander repeated scornfully.

"Yes. If I'm going to eat eighty percent fat in my diet for the next month, I have to exercise or I'll be a blimp when I leave."

Alexander stared. "I suppose it's because you're an

American, but half the time I don't know what you're talking about. Not that it matters, for you never say anything worth hearing. In any wise, you have no excuse to make such a spectacle of yourself."

"Look, you, I wore this because it's all I have. I hope you didn't think I was going to sweat up my jacket and shirt, too. And I *did* try to run before anybody else got up. If I'm a spectacle, blame yourself."

Darby could feel Alexander stiffening. Why could these two not get along?

"Don't become angry," she whispered to her brother. "Please."

Uncle Richard's voice drifted toward them, unpleasant as a donkey braying. "What are you saying down there?"

"Yes, Alexander," Lenora joined. "Won't you move aside a bit? We can't see—I mean, we can't hear a thing!"

Alexander gave her an extended look of shock.

"Lenora, darling!" cried Aunt Gacia, trilling an alarmed laugh. "Do stop teasing Alexander, or he will think you mean it!" She turned to her nephew and pressed her hand across her heart. "She does not, you know. Lenora does not eavesdrop or want to see things she shouldn't." Pointedly she inquired, "Do you, my dear?"

A resigned expression crossed the young woman's face. "No," Lenora said pensively. "I had better dress for church like the good girl I am." She latched her window and turned away.

"Lenora sure has a great sense of humor," Simon remarked. "An excellent woman."

"Did I ask for an opinion?" Alexander retorted. "You go inside now. Any more nonsense and I will throw you out, birthday performer or not."

Darby exclaimed and walked in front of her brother. When he tried to push her back, she brushed his hands away. She was careful to keep her eyes away from Simon, however.

"I shall speak to Beckett immediately. He can begin tailoring your new clothes today. We'll also ask him to make some light apparel that will be suitable for your running exercise."

"Wait a moment," Alexander said. "Do you mean to provide clothing for this man as well as food and shelter? From the first I thought him a leech, and apparently I was right."

"Well, he cannot go about like that, can he?" she argued. "Think of it as your Christian duty, Alex."

"I'm thinking of it as your folly," he snapped, and walked away. After taking no more than a half-dozen steps, he turned back and seized her hand, pulling her after him.

"I fear you will have to miss church," Darby called over her shoulder, her gaze jumping over her angel's golden figure to the hedges and trees on either side of him. "I don't imagine your, er, clothing will dry in time. But this will be an excellent opportunity for Beckett to measure you for your clothes. Perhaps Simbar can be found to trim your hair as well."

"You're very kind," Simon replied.

"You have lost all good sense," said Alexander to his sister, and jerked her into the house.

Darby was so distracted during the morning service that when the time came to shake the Reverend Victor Suttner's hand afterward, she could not look him in the eye. She was certain that if the vicar had any notion of the scandalous direction of her thoughts during his message, he would harvest fodder for a month of sermons or more.

She could not stop thinking about her angel. When she sang the congregational hymns, she heard Simon's expressive voice speaking her name. Opening the book of Common Prayer, she read the words, but recalled Simon's:

I'm not absolutely perfect in this form. I make mistakes and plenty of them.

What, exactly, did that mean?

Could he, for example, make the mistake of taking her in his arms? Kissing her, perhaps?

How she had blushed and squirmed on the bench when *that* thought entered her brain. She was astonished lightning did not scorch her into ashes. Yet she could not stop her imaginings. Her gaze roamed from the vicar to the Old Testament stories depicted on the stained-glass windows to the dark, lustrous wood lining the ceiling and walls. She squeezed her eyes shut again and again. Nothing helped. Simon's image superimposed itself over all.

And not only this morning's bare-chested vision, either; she saw him in many guises. His laughable, costumed entry into their home last night. The earnestness with which he presented his horrible mission to her—a mission she was still determined to foil. His concern for her safety when she saw him before, and the odd clothes he wore then. And how he had appeared the very first time she spotted him in the wood—bearded, hair unwashed and uncombed, eyes tortured with sorrow—looking for all the world like a lost soul.

What terrible blow could bring an angel to such grief? Had he failed on one of his missions? It made her very curious of a sudden.

At least he no longer looked so abandoned, though a sad expression often stole across his face. She would like to see the sorrow gone entirely.

Her thoughts became so preoccupied that not only did she fail to listen to the sermon, but she had no inkling of its subject. Thus, when the service at last ended, she passed by the vicar as quickly as she decently could and hurried over to the Wallaces, who were standing on the grass a few feet from the road.

Alexander and the rest of the family followed. They

formed a companionable circle, one of many which dotted the churchyard, this being the most convenient time of the week for friends and acquaintances to greet one another and exchange gossip. The sun glared down, quickening everyone's Sunday-best into brilliant colors and warming the gentlemen's hats and the ladies' bonnets into hot coals. A few children, driven mad by the beauty of the day, dashed from group to group yelling, laughing, and making winsome nuisances of themselves.

As Alexander had forecast, Mrs. Wallace extended an invitation for afternoon tea.

"I want everyone to come," she said. "Bring Mr. Heathershaw and Mr. Garrett as well."

"Don't feel you must extend an invitation to them," Alexander said. "I'm sure they won't expect it."

"Even though they don't expect it, they'll be very glad of your graciousness," Darby smoothly added, giving her brother a forbidding look. "Both gentlemen enjoy company."

Mrs. Wallace scanned the faces surrounding her. "Did neither of them attend services this morning?"

"Heathershaw never comes, Mother," Edward said, condemnation strong in his voice.

"Mr. Garrett would have attended, but he had not the clothes," Darby added.

"The poor, unfortunate man," said Mrs. Wallace. "Tell him he does not need clothes to visit us." Her eyes widened. "Oh, dear. That did not come out quite right."

"We know what you meant, precious Hortense," said Aunt Gacia. "Unfortunately, Mr. Lightner and I cannot join you. We were awakened early this morning and need our naps."

"We do?" Uncle Richard barked.

"Yes, my darling," said Aunt Gacia firmly, drilling him a message with her eyes. "This way, they will all be able to fit into one carriage."

"Oh! Quite right," answered her husband, looking forlorn. "Hope you aren't having those sugared lemon things again, Hortense; hate to miss 'em."

Aunt Gacia continued as though uninterrupted. "It will be a tight squeeze even without us. Alexander, I shall depend upon you to sit beside our Lenora and keep her from being crushed!"

Alexander, eyeing Lenora and blushing like a girl, said he would be glad to do so. After Mrs. Wallace set a time for the gathering, the group dispersed to their carriages.

Over the cold luncheon that was served at Brightings on Sundays, Darby could hardly stop staring at Simon. He again wore his blue costume, but his hair had been cropped á la Titus and looked quite wonderfully different. To her way of thinking, the haphazard lengths suited him, bringing the lean beauty of his face to greater notice. She could not help missing the romantic aura of his longer tresses, however. To make amends for her vacillating feelings, she complimented the new style more than once.

There was little need for her to do so. Her aunt and uncle enthused over his fashionable crop, as did Lenora and Claude. Only Alexander remained quiet.

Simon took his shearing gracefully. He did not cast regretful looks at Darby for being the cause of it, though more than once his fingers reached to toss back hair that no longer existed.

After luncheon and an hour's rest, the young people set out for the Wallaces' in the family's best carriage. Alexander sat between his sister and Lenora while Simon and Claude sat opposite.

As they traveled, Darby tried to show Simon the coal fields that supplied fuel for the potteries. She often lifted her hand to the window, meaning to remark upon the wonders of nature that remained in spite of industrial growth—the river Trent, for one, or for another, the rolling countryside dotted with islands of trees. But every time she drew breath to speak, Lenora launched into her own observances. The chattering widow managed to command Simon's attention for the entire thirty-minute journey.

By the time the driver halted the carriage at the Wallaces' red-bricked, extended cottage, Darby's ears burned with irritation, and she knew her brother flamed beside her. He did not speak once as they walked to the front door.

When they were admitted, the housekeeper escorted them to the Wallaces, who were waiting in the withdrawing room. This chamber had long since ceased to surprise Darby, but now she wondered what Simon thought of Mrs. Wallace's decorating scheme, if an angel had time to think of such things. The older lady often voiced her opinion that couches and loveseats made unwilling companions, and her furniture reflected that sentiment. Solitary chairs, their styles ranging from Queen Anne to Sheraton with no perceived similarity in wood or upholstery, were set in a large half-circle around the fireplace. The floor was wooden with no rugs, other than an old hunting tapestry which Mrs. Wallace had caused to be placed in front of the fire. Upon it sat the room's one table, which was a low, round one. The walls were starkly white with no paintings upon them, Mrs. Wallace believing that decorations distracted one from the pleasures of conversation.

Darby often wondered why the overall effect of the chamber was not barren and institutional, but somehow it was not. Perhaps the pleasantness of the room's owners warmed it.

Upon their entrance, Alexander suddenly became animated. "You look like spring in that yellow dress," he told Evelyn loudly, taking the seat nearest hers. "Quite pretty."

"Why, thank you, Alex," Evelyn said, her eyes shining at this unaccustomed tribute. She smoothed a wrinkle from her skirt, then looked at him with shy hope.

Darby watched them glumly as she sat opposite in a satinwood Hepplewhite chair. She saw at once that her brother wished to make Lenora jealous, or to punish her for her attentions to Simon; and it dismayed her to think he would try in this manner. How could he be so insensitive of Evelyn's feelings? Did he think she had none?

But her friend's heart was not all that worried Darby. It seared her to know Alex's emotions were so deeply invested in Lenora. Surely his attachment did not mean Simon was right. She knew such a joining would spell everlasting hurt for her brother. And though she had rather be injured a million times herself than see Alex suffer pain, it was better he be wounded a little now than thrown beneath the axe later.

Perhaps Alex needed a sound thrashing to set his thinking straight. There was a time when she was the one to do it, but not anymore, not since their sixteenth year when he traitorously bloomed several inches taller than she.

"Have you lost your best friend?" asked Edward, leaving his mother to take the chair beside Darby. "You look like it."

"Do I? I'm sorry." She barely acknowledged him, having now become distracted by the spectacle of Simon trying to find a seat. He moved toward one, then, seeing Lenora behind him, stopped and gestured politely for her to sit. She smiled brightly and inclined her head for him to go first. Obviously he wanted to sit apart from her, and just as obviously she was determined he would not. He moved off again, Lenora trailing him like a baby chick, yet somehow managing to appear graceful rather than ridiculous. Had Darby tried a similar action, Alex would have laughed her to scorn.

Finally, Simon did the unbelievable and sat beside Alexander, there being no chair to his other side. Lenora selected the seat next to Mrs. Wallace as if she'd intended to do so all along. Claude eased into the ornate Adam chair beside Lenora and looked very pleased with himself.

Mrs. Wallace clapped her hands commandingly, though in truth there was scant conversation to be quieted. "I thought we might gather here awhile before going outside for our tea. It will be cooler a little later on, and you young people may wish to walk among the flowers."

She paused, waiting for the murmurs of agreement which immediately came, then continued, "I shan't mind being left alone when you do so, though I feel sad that Gacia and Richard did not come." Her voice began to thicken, and she brought her ever-present handkerchief to her eyes. "It does not matter, for I have grown accustomed to being by myself."

"Mother," Edward said consolingly, hurrying around the table to press her hand. "When do we ever leave you?" While his parent sniffled, he turned to face the others. "Forgive us. You all know"—his gaze flitted over Simon"—well, most of you know how tender-hearted my mother is, and that she is given to bouts of low spirits of late. The physician assures us it will soon pass, so pray do not mind a few tears."

Darby forgot about Alexander and Simon for the moment and gave Edward a consoling look. Except in the rare instance of his taking a dislike of someone, he possessed the sweetest of spirits and always had. Even in the midst of their most devilish pranks—of which he was often instigator—he would be the one to caution of possible devastating outcomes. Should a quarrel spring between two or more of them, Edward served as peacemaker. No one ever became angry with Edward himself. He cared too much, just as he cared now for his mother. He was intensely loyal to those he loved.

Darby guessed that Mr. Wallace's demise had something to do with the forming of Edward's character; her friend had to assume the role of family protector at the age of ten. She never doubted that he was the most worthy of the four of them.

Mrs. Wallace smiled bravely and brought Edward's hand to her cheek. "You are the best of all sons," she said. "And Evelyn the best of daughters."

"You are the best of mothers," Evelyn said with emotion, though she did not quit her seat beside Alexander.

"And we are the best of guests," Alexander commented, bringing a breath of levity to the gathering.

While they still smiled, Edward whispered to his mother, saw her nod, then returned to his seat. He scanned the circle with the air of one about to make an announcement, and Darby felt a moment's qualm as he gave her brother a knowing look. There was mischief brewing, she could feel it in her bones.

"My mother and Evelyn and I were talking over luncheon today about Mr. Garrett's visit," said Edward, turning his brilliant eyes on Simon. "Since he employs himself as an actor, we thought he might entertain us this afternoon with a recitation."

"What an excellent notion," Lenora said.

Alexander looked dubious and raised his brows.

Darby's heart sank. She should have known someone would try to embarrass her angel. But that it should be Edward, and just when she had been thinking nice thoughts about him! Well, he did it in an unfortunate attempt to please Alex, she supposed.

"Mr. Garrett mustn't be expected to recite on a moment's notice as if he were a performing bear," she said nervously. "I'm certain if he were given time to prepare—"

"What's wrong?" asked Alexander, immediately becoming animated. "Don't you think he can do it?"

Darby glared at her brother. "Surely if—"

"I'd be happy to recite," said Simon, standing and walking to the fireplace with an unperturbed air. "How do you feel about Mr. Shakespeare?"

"Ecstatic," Alexander said. "How do you feel about Mr. Gainsborough?"

Edward thought this very funny, and laughed loudly. His mirth died when he saw Darby's furious gaze upon him.

"Sorry," he said, his eyes wild as he attempted to restrain himself. "It's his clothes; I can't look at him seriously."

"But see how nice his hair is," Mrs. Wallace contributed. "I think Mr. Garrett looks very well. Please go ahead, sir."

"Thank you, ma'am." Simon looked at Darby and smiled. "I often memorize poetry as a mental exercise. It's been awhile since I've done the sonnets, though, so I hope I don't forget in the middle."

"We'll try not to be too surprised if that happens," commented Alexander.

Simon ignored him and lowered his gaze to the floor. Within instants, Darby felt a kind of power gathering about her angel, an energy building from some unknown source. Perhaps it came from heaven. Perhaps it flowed from themselves, for every person grew quiet, even Alexander. Simon began.

"Devouring Time, blunt thou the lion's paws,
And make the earth devour her own sweet brood;
Pluck the keen teeth from the fierce tiger's jaws,
And burn the long-liv'd phoenix in her blood;
Make glad and sorry seasons, as thou fleets,
And do whate'er thou wilt, swift-footed Time,
But I forbid thee one most heinous crime;
O carve not with thy hours my love's fair brow,
Nor draw no lines there with thine antique pen;
Him in thy course untainted do allow,
For beauty's pattern to succeeding men.
      Yet, do thy worst, old Time: despite thy wrong,
      My love shall in my verse ever live young."

A profound silence fell when he finished. Darby felt paralyzed by the lovely sound of his voice, the musical manner in which he pronounced the words, even if he did so with an American accent. He had recited almost without emotion, yet one sensed he felt the poetry deeply. His recitation stirred her as nothing ever had.

Mrs. Wallace burst into tears.

"What is it, dear lady?" Edward said, rushing to her side again. This time, Evelyn, her cheeks darkening with embarrassment, joined him to pat her mother's back.

"I—am—so—very—o-o-old!" Mrs. Wallace cried. "Time has—has carved its hours in my brow, and I—I— I shall never be beautiful again!"

"Now see what you've done," Alexander growled to Simon.

Simon paid him no mind, but squeezed between Evelyn and an irritated Edward to kneel on one knee before Mrs. Wallace. Seizing the hand that Edward did not hold, he kissed it and said,

> "To me, fair friend, you never can be old,
> For as you were when first your eye I eyed,
> Such seems your beauty still . . ."

Mrs. Wallace gazed at him for what seemed hours to Darby. Finally, the lady took a long, shaking breath. Relinquishing her son's fingers, she dried her tears with her handkerchief. After sniffing once more, she smiled timorously, then kissed Simon's cheek.

"I'm a silly woman sometimes," she said, patting his hand and releasing him. "But you are a darling boy. Thank you, dear. Do you have something else for us? You are most accomplished."

Edward and Evelyn, obviously relieved, returned to their seats. Darby began to breathe again, and the shifting postures of the others signaled the relaxation of tension.

Simon recited a few more sonnets, then was encouraged to read a passage from *Agamemnon*. Finally, he was permitted to sit down.

"I should like to recite something I wrote this morning," Claude said when the applause died. "It is not as good as Shakespeare, and I don't have Mr. Garrett's talent for performing. But it was composed from the heart."

"How marvelous!" exclaimed Mrs. Wallace. "We would be delighted."

"I'm not so certain," Lenora said. "Really, Claude."

"I beg your indulgence, fair Lenora," said Claude, pulling a sheet of paper from his waistcoat pocket and unfolding it. "This poem is not to you; or . . . mayhaps it is. You must listen and decide. It's entitled, 'Ode to My Mystery Love.'"

"Oh, famous! Shall we be able to guess who the lady is?" cried Mrs. Wallace, clapping her hands and laughing.

"I think you might, for she is present," Claude said as he positioned himself in front of the fireplace. There was little of Simon's grace in his posture; in fact, he looked so comically stiff that Darby wondered if he mocked her angel. As Alexander snorted and glanced at Simon, her suspicion was confirmed.

Claude shook his paper importantly, lowered it to his side, then frowned and peered at the floor as if looking for bugs. It was another blatant parody of Simon as he had been before speaking, and Darby's spine stiffened in outrage. As Claude's hesitation continued, snickers and chuckles could be heard, most of them sounding unwilling. Darby flashed Simon a distressed look, but he only stared at the table, a faint smile on his lips.

Just as the pause became agony for Darby, Claude raised the paper noisily and began to read in a voice laden with drama.

"Speak to me not of golden hair
And tresses dark as midnight;
Others may entangle there
And feast their soul's delight.
As for me, I must declare
A preference not renowned;
Give to me an earthen girl
And make her locklings brown—"

"Oh, it is Evelyn!" interrupted Mrs. Wallace, to the obvious dismay of her daughter. "Evelyn's locklings, er—locks, are brown!"

Claude stared at Mrs. Wallace and raised one eyebrow. "If I may continue, ma'am?"

"Yes, yes!" she said eagerly.

"This is ridiculous," Lenora muttered.

Claude gave the younger widow a look of exaggerated woe and cleared his throat.

"For brown are leaves that fall from trees
And brown the wren as well;
Brown the doe who laughing flees
To weave enchantment's spell.
And as for eyes, I don't despise
The gleam of brown or blue;
"But another shade!" my heart's soul cries—
And only grey will do—"

"Oh, dear," Mrs. Wallace said. "It cannot be Evelyn, then. Why, it must be Darby!"

"I've heard enough," Alexander said in a fury. "Can we not have tea now?"

"But I've not finished," lamented Claude, pressing the paper to his heart. "The best parts are yet to come. There are pretty descriptions about winter skies, bubbling storms, willowy tallness—"

Lenora's laugh rang like crystal. "How you amuse us, Claude."

"I believe I've had enough verse, too," Edward said. "Time to go outside, Mother."

"But, dearest—"

Edward walked to his mother's chair and tugged her upward. "Look at Alex, dear lady; he's white with hunger. You know what he is when his appetite is raging."

Mrs. Wallace could not refuse to provide relief for a guest, and family and friends ambled outdoors in various stages of puzzlement and relief.

The following hour on the stone-flagged terrace was the most awkward one Darby could remember spending at the Wallaces'. Along with leaf-thin sandwiches, assorted delicacies, and lukewarm tea, simmering looks and smoldering emotions were served in heavy quantities.

There was only one difference that could account for the change among them: Simon. Apparently his presence served to either exhume long-withheld feelings or to cause them. She found herself studying him, wondering if he purposed the undercurrents or spawned them by accident. Whatever the reason, she wished herself home and in bed. She had rather not be present to observe her brother lavishing attention on Evelyn while watching Lenora fawn upon Simon. And she particularly did not enjoy becoming the center of Edward and Claude's notice—especially Claude's, for his poem had embarrassed her mightily.

He had ever been gallant toward her, as gallant as he was to any lady; but there had never been evidence before today that his feelings toward her were so warm. She wished they were not. Now she struggled to divide her conversation equally between Claude and Edward, both of whom had

seized the chairs flanking hers. First it would be an offer
of a pastry from one, then the other would shift position
so the sun's glare would not fall into her *delicate eyes*. She
began to feel like a bird torn between two tomcats.

Thus, when only crumbs remained on the silver serving
tray, Darby was pleased to hear Mrs. Wallace suggest they
all walk in the garden. There was relief in the older lady's
voice as she spoke, as if she, too, had tired of the halting
conversations and odd silences.

Immediately did his mother finish speaking, Edward
jumped to his feet and offered Darby his arm. Claude
slapped his thigh, annoyed to be beaten in this game, then
presented his escort to her other side.

"No, no," Edward said, rushing Darby forward and away
from the gentleman's reach. "Don't mean to be rude,
Claude, but I must speak with Darby privately about—
about a suitable gift for Alex's birthday."

Claude swept his hat from his head and bowed. Edward
hurried Darby along until she was breathless.

The Wallaces allowed their garden to grow in a natural
manner, Mrs. Wallace detesting straight lines in her shrubbery as much as she hated couches in her drawing room.
Clusters of wildflowers grew in wide, curving sections, and
shrubs mixed with pinks and columbines scented the air,
achingly sweet. Darby had always loved this garden; in
effect it was a private and exotic maze with its grassy trails
winding on for acres. Many a childish war had been waged
here, and more than once she'd become lost among the
syringas, sweet williams, and peonies.

When they reached a branching of the path, he suggested they repair to the summerhouse and, before she
could draw breath to agree or protest, he pulled her down
a side trail.

They were very far from the others now. Darby had time
for only the quickest of looks over her shoulder to locate
Simon before the hedges hid him from view. As she

expected, Lenora clung to his arm, but her angel appeared
to be doing everything in his power to remain close to
Alexander and Evelyn. Claude, hands in pockets and whistling, trailed behind. By the look of things, Simon was
trying to maintain a conversation among all of them. Well,
good luck to him, for Alex's face was dark as a stormcloud.

Darby returned her attention to Edward, whose cheeks
were red with the exertion of pulling her forward at a trot.
Trickles of perspiration dampened his forehead and the
curly dark hair beneath his hat. After her conversation
with Evelyn last night, she had no wish to be alone with
him; only her strong desire to flee Claude could have made
her so thoughtless. Her popularity had unaccountably
soared within the last twenty-four hours, and she liked it
not at all.

"Why are we running, Edward?" she panted.

"I'm not running; this is merely fast walking."

"All right, then; why are we walking so fast?"

"Because I want to get away from everyone else."

Dread sounded in her spirit like a tolling bell. "Why?
Surely we are far enough now. I thought you wanted to
discuss Alex's gift."

He shook his head but did not speak again until they
reached the summerhouse. This tiny, frame building, con-
taining a single room that she had not entered in years, had
six exposures surrounded by a railed porch. Weathered
benches were spaced at regular intervals along the porch,
and he pulled her up the steps and led her to one.

"Whew. I'm hot enough to ignite a stack of wood," he
said, sitting beside her and leaning his back against the
house.

"And why should that be, I wonder? We haven't moved
so fast since we were children."

"Aw, I'm sorry, Darby." He loosened his cravat, peered
at her, then tucked a loose strand of her hair into her

bonnet. "Didn't mean to give you such a race, but I wanted you by myself for a few minutes."

"Why?" she repeated, then wished she hadn't when she saw a look of tenderness enter his eyes.

"When do you want to get married?" he blurted.

Darby stared at him speechlessly.

"I didn't say that very well," he continued. "Maybe I should get down on one knee. I will if you want."

"No! No. You don't have to do that." She turned her gaze to a distant stand of beech trees and swallowed before adding, "You surprise me, Edward."

"Surprise you? Haven't we planned this all our lives?"

"Yes, but I thought you were going to wait until you became twenty-one to ask me."

There was silence for the space of several heartbeats, then he said in resentful tones, "I wonder who told you that little nugget of information?"

"Oh, it does not matter," Darby said uneasily.

"It does to me, and I know who the culprit is: Miss Evelyn Tell-All Wallace, that's who."

"Oh, never mind that; the question remains: Why are you asking me now?"

He sighed and scratched his ear. "I'm afraid if I don't, someone else will jump ahead of me."

"Oh, Edward," she said, and laughed a little.

"Well, Heathershaw is penning you poems, isn't he?"

"Don't be ridiculous. I'm not interested in Claude."

"You say that now, but you might change your mind. Ladies like poetry and all that. I couldn't rhyme two words if my life depended on it. Heathershaw's not a bad-looking fellow, either, and he dresses well. You might be swept off your feet, since he has the advantage of living under your roof."

"Yes," she said, her voice dripping irony. "And the advantage of living off our hospitality, or rather, the hospitality of my aunt and uncle, funded by my brother and me. Don't think of it again; he is out of the question. How could I consider a man who has no prospects and seems determined not to form any?''

Edward remained quiet for a moment. ''You have great dreams for your potteries,'' he said faintly. ''I myself am not as driven as you are. You probably think I have no prospects either.''

''Don't be silly. You run your estate, and that is no mean occupation. Your farms are becoming well-known.''

''Yes, the dairy is growing, isn't it?'' he said eagerly. ''I think Father would not have been ashamed of me.''

''I'm certain he would be most proud,'' she said, viewing his boyish features with pleasure.

Her regard served to encourage him. ''When we're wed, I want to use the managing skills I've learned to help you run the potteries. I know Alex doesn't want to.''

She stirred uncomfortably and tried to swallow the taste of indignation in her mouth. Edward meant well, but she had not spent half her life directing the potteries to be replaced now.

''Well, you can't expect to go on as always once children come along,'' he argued, when her silence lengthened.

''Children! You are moving too quickly for me, Edward.''

''Yes, I suppose I am, since you haven't officially agreed to marry me yet.''

He gave her a look of such puppy-like anticipation that she laughed. ''I believe you should wait a year and ask me again.''

His mouth tightened. ''And leave you free to be caught by any male who wanders by? That Garrett fellow, for instance. I've noticed how you look at him. I think his story about being robbed is a tale suitable for a winter fire and hot chocolate. And, I don't mind telling you, I find your inviting him to your house the oddest thing of all. A stranger, Darby? He is a complete stranger to you?''

''Are you accusing me of lying?'' she asked in outraged

tones, forgetting for the moment that she *had* stretched the truth a little.

"No," he said, deflating. "No, I'm aware you never lie."

Drowning beneath waves of guilt, she said, "Let me reassure you that I'm not romantically inclined toward Simon." Shuddering suddenly, she saw again the depraved images that had plagued her during church. "You must stop worrying, Edward. Truly."

"Then you do intend to marry me?"

Of a sudden, her head became too weighty for her shoulders, and she looked down at her lap. "It's what we have always planned, isn't it?"

"Is that a *yes?*" he asked gladly. "Shall I tell the others?"

"No! You must give me time to think upon it, Edward."

"Oh, very well, I'll give you time, though you should know whether you want to or not by now. I want an answer by this week's end, do you hear? No locking my heart in your bower, Princess Rose."

Her lips quivered at her old title. "I'll try," she said in a small voice.

"Good girl. I'm going to kiss you now."

"You are?" she asked, drawing back a little.

"Yes, but try not to look so shocked, will you?"

"Oh, Edward, I'm not shocked; you have kissed me a hundred times before. It's only that I had not expected an announcement."

"This kiss is to be different," he said decisively. "I'm not holding a wooden sword this time, and Alex is not lying at your feet playing the slain dragon."

She laughed. "Very well, then, Prince Raleigh Don; only hurry before someone comes."

She closed her eyes and lifted her face expectantly toward his.

There was a moment's pause, then he kissed her quite abruptly. He did not pull her into an embrace or touch her in any way except for that brief meeting of lips.

"That should convince you that I'm serious," he said when he pulled back.

She pressed her fingers to her mouth, unable to think of anything to say. The kiss was sweet as Edward's always had been, just as Alexander's kisses were sweet. It was the kiss of a beloved brother.

"Remember, now," Edward said. "Next week you have to give me an answer."

"I'll remember," she whispered.

Chapter Seven

The coffee the maid left outside Simon's door was cold by the time he awoke on Tuesday morning. He brought the cup inside his room and tried to sip it anyway, but the dregs were thick as lily pads in a pond. He set the vile mess on his dresser and sighed.

He missed the twentieth century. Hot coffee. Hot showers. Television—he'd give his little finger to see a football game. Or a decent drama. One of his best buddies was in a soap now, and Simon loved to watch him every now and then so he could call him and offer critiques on his heavy acting. No, wait; that had been in the time before—Elena's world. God only knew where Larry was now.

Simon had only known a few people in the new world he caused. Even Dell didn't recognize him. After being thrown out of Chesterton Place, Simon had flown back to L.A. and burst into his agent's office. Dell claimed they'd never met, but if he'd leave a photo and resume at the front desk, the agency would get back to him.

There was nothing so paralyzing as finding he'd lived a

portion of his life without knowing it. In the new world, everything past the time he should have met Elena was blank; he could only remember his former past. How was that possible? Had he caused an alternate world to spring into existence? If so, shouldn't there be another one of him running around? But there hadn't been.

The nightshirt one of the servants had provided made him itch, and Simon scratched his chest while walking to the window. He stared down at the lawn without seeing it, old science-fiction stories leafing through his mind. Paradoxes, that's what those stories had called the seemingly irreconcilable contradictions caused by time travel. He would probably stimulate more paradoxes before he was done.

He'd be lucky to survive this experience with his mind intact. Never had he played such a desperate role before, not in all the movies in which he'd starred. What was an assassin or a cop to an inept time-traveler bumbling his way through the past, snuffing out lives every time he bumped his elbow?

Simon turned to the table beside his bed, where a pitcher of water and a porcelain basin were placed. He poured water into the bowl and slipped the nightshirt over his head.

In his former life, Elena's management of his career had often caused problems between them. (But it was the least of their problems; *he* was the greatest, and that guilt would never go away.) Countless times he'd accused her of being too aggressive, of using her wealth to open doors he didn't need opened. His talent—such as it was—would determine their future. That's what he'd told her, over and over.

Seemed she was right after all; contacts made all the difference. Elena had been the one to make him a star. And look how he'd repaid her.

Simon began splashing water and soap over himself. It

was a cold business. He'd like a bath, but after he saw the commotion it caused—maids boiling pots of water in the kitchens and hauling them upstairs—he couldn't ask. When he'd offered to bring the water up himself, one of the maids became angry, and the other cried, saying she'd be dismissed if she didn't do her work.

How did people live without bathrooms? If he were staying any longer than a month, he'd build something, though he was no plumber. And it wasn't only a bathtub he wanted. That disgusting chamberpot under his bed was worse than a litterbox. He wished he had money to tip the slop boy enormously, but all he could do was apologize when the kid came around. And he was going to have to stop doing that; the boy had begun to look at him like he was crazy.

He sighed, wishing there was something for him to do today. Yesterday he had explored the grounds and found the pond where Darby's murder, or accident, was to occur. Less than a mile from the house, it was hidden by a screen of widely-spaced trees topping a small hill. He was able to circle the entire lake within minutes. It was a romantic, pine-scented spot meant for lovers, not death.

He was bored without Darby. She left early every morning and didn't return until almost dinnertime. Alexander was gone most of the time, too; either in his studio or down at the potteries. Simon didn't miss Alexander, but he wished he were around to keep Lenora off him. She was as persistent as any Hollywood wannabee who thought the path to success ran through his bedroom.

Don't think about it.

Simon seized a towel from the table's cabinet and rubbed the water from his body. Long after he was dry, he continued to scrape the towel across his chest and arms and legs in rough strokes. He wanted to hurt, hoped to drive out his mental pain with physical discomfort.

Don't think about betrayal and what it did to your marriage. All that was finished. Nothing he could do about it now.

But there was something he *could* do; something decent for a change. He could stop thinking about Darby, about the way her eyes shined into his with innocent wonder, believing he was an angel. He could stop hearing her strong voice vibrating with morality and courage, something he'd thought had disappeared from the world.

But he couldn't stop. He saw her face everytime he closed his eyes. The old warning signals were squealing again, only this was not a simple physical attraction to be satisfied in a night. She had made him see her as a person, not just a body. And he was beginning to love being near that person. He hadn't felt this way since he met Elena.

But it was hopeless, utterly hopeless. He couldn't fall in love with her. It wasn't as if he could take her forward with him; they had tried that once already. And he had a life to get back to—unless he'd managed to wipe out his own ancestors on this little excursion.

Forget it. Let Darby continue to think he was an angel. It was the best thing for her. Surely he could do that one little thing.

He held his satin kneepants between forefinger and thumb. Absolutely disgusting to put them on again, but he had no choice. If only the costumery had carried more clothing from this period; well, maybe they had; he was the one who got the time wrong. And now he was trapped at Brightings, couldn't even go with Darby to the potteries until Beckett finished his clothes.

He pulled on his breeches and tried not to breathe. Every other night the maid would wash them for him, but this was the off-day. He had no desire to jog in them this morning; he might start drawing flies. Not that anyone would notice. No deodorants here, though all kinds of perfumes were used to mask the scent of underwashed bodies. At least most of the gentlefolk bathed enough to avoid being offensive—Richard and Gacia being notable exceptions—but the poor servants worked too hard to manage it.

Funny how accustomed a person could grow to odorless bodies. If someone from his era didn't wash, everybody knew it right away and ostracized him. Here, personal scent seemed as individual as hair color.

Darby smelled clean and sweet, like the rosebuds in her garden.

Before he put on his shirt, he shaved himself with the lethal straight-edge Simbar had given him and only sliced his chin once. If he'd had any sense, he would have brought a few disposable razors with him. But, wary of changing anything else in the past, he'd panicked at the last minute and left all remnants of the future behind.

It was hard to admit it to himself, but he still felt panicked. When he returned to his present, what changes would he find he'd caused this time?

He had to be smart, had to *think,* to step as carefully through this century as if land mines littered the ground. And the first thing he must do was direct Lenora's attention away from him. What a laugh on him it would be if *he,* not Darby, caused the break-up between Alexander and Lenora.

Most of all, he had to remain alert to guess who, if anyone, might try to hurt Darby.

When he finished dressing, he went downstairs and had breakfast alone. He had learned there were no early risers living here, other than Darby, Alexander, and Richard. He enjoyed the solitude of the early morning. There was a peacefulness in the dining room that he'd found in few places. The sun streamed through the windows, highlighting the sheen on the mahogany table and illuminating every nick and scratch. The breakfast dishes—always the same array of breads, meats, and eggs, but plenty of variety—steamed invitingly on the sideboard. From the kitchen came the sounds of pots banging and voices raised in argument, all cozily muffled by a green baize door.

While he was sipping his second cup of tea—now he knew why the English liked that drink; it was because their coffee was so bad—Lenora entered the room, and his feeling of peace dissolved.

She wore a burgundy velvet riding habit that outlined the graceful curves of her body. Her eyes sparkled when she saw him, though faint shadows beneath marred their brightness.

"I hoped to find you here," she said, moving to the sideboard and lifting covers off dishes. She picked up a plate, placed a muffin and a smear of butter on it, then sat across from him. "I wanted to find someone willing to accompany me on a ride this morning."

"I'm sure you'll have no trouble," said Simon.

She frowned impishly. "You are unkind, sir, to allow a lady to drop her line and hook no fish."

"I'm afraid you'd better fish somewhere else if you want me to ride with you. I don't know a lot about horses."

"That can be remedied in only one way," she said teasingly.

"Maybe so, but I don't want to remedy it." He made a great show of draining the last of his tea, then scraped back his chair, rising.

"A carriage ride, then?" she asked in a hopeful voice.

"Nope. Don't know how to drive one."

"Then you were not lying when you told Fiona White you couldn't drive. I can teach you. We might start with the gig."

"No, I don't think so. Thanks anyway." He circled the table and walked toward the door.

"You can't refuse. I don't know how it is you've lived this long without learning how to drive, but think what an advantage you'll have in mobility." When he continued to edge toward the door, she added enticingly, "You'll be able to visit the potteries at any time of the day without bothering the driver. And if you used the tilbury, you could carry a hot luncheon to Alexander and Darby."

He paused and considered. It would be good to be able to do that.

Sensing victory, Lenora smiled slowly. "Besides, you must admit you have nothing better to do with your time. I've seen you moping around the house like a lost bull."

"Since you put it that way, I guess I'll have to go," said Simon, unable to prevent himself from responding to her charm.

"Good." She took a bite of muffin and patted her lips with her napkin. "I shall tell Simbar to order the gig as soon as I finish my breakfast. Why don't you come back and sit down? I hate eating alone."

Less than a half-hour later, Simon took his seat beside Lenora in the Brightings's crisp black gig. The two-wheeler had green leather seats and polished brass fixtures. It was a fine-looking little sports coupe, Simon thought with a smile. The black horse attached to it looked fine, too.

Lenora took the reins in one hand, a whip in the other, and gave Simon a sly look beneath her lashes. "Watch me, now," she said. "In a moment you will be doing as I do. Only let me get the carriage onto the road where it is straight." And so saying, she cracked the whip, crying, "Go, Sasha!"

The mare tossed her mane and pranced forward. When they reached the road, Lenora pulled on the reins, then handed them to Simon. He immediately took one rein in each hand and shook his head when she offered the whip.

"You Americans," Lenora said. "Do you think you're driving a covered wagon? Here. Put both reins in one hand, holding them thus." She manipulated his fingers to her satisfaction, then moved his arm. "You must center your hand in front of yourself. No, bend your wrist; that's it. Keep your elbow close; that will prevent you from exerting too much pressure on Sasha's mouth. No, no; touch lightly; you don't want to make her a puller, do you? Now, take the whip in your other hand and crack it.''

"I don't like whips," he said, eyeing the horse with a sudden storm of love. He was going to drive a carriage!

"Sasha expects it," Lenora said dryly. "It is the sound, you know; you are not actually going to strike her. She is too fine a beast for that.''

"Um, okay." He raised the whip and flapped it feebly.

Lenora laughed. "You really do know nothing, do you? I thought you had a carriage that was robbed. How did you drive that?"

"Had a driver," he mumbled, raising the whip again.

"Be courageous, then, Simon—I hope I may call you by your first name?—now, crack it!''

He snapped the whip in the air, loud as a gunshot. Sasha jerked forward. Simon lost his balance momentarily, then braced his feet and concentrated on the position of his hands. After a moment, he risked a look at the countryside creeping by. The wind whispered through his hair. He could hear birds in the trees protesting the carriage's rumbling passage on the rough road.

He was exhilarated. He had never felt more accomplished, not even the first time he drove a Porsche.

"How am I doing?" he asked Lenora proudly.

"Well enough for a first-time driver," she said. "If you don't relax, though, Sasha will become nervous.''

Deflated, he lowered his shoulders and tried to relax. "How did you learn to drive? And don't tell me you've known how since you were three; I won't like it.''

She smiled briefly. "No, my parents didn't own a carriage. Reece taught me.''

Her expression grew thoughtful. Hoping to find out more about her relationship with her husband, he said,

"I understand Mr. Ellison died some months ago. I imagine you miss him very much."

She seemed to collect her thoughts before answering. "Reece and I had a rather ... tempestuous marriage, Simon. It is never good to speak ill of the dead, but my husband possessed a number of habits that made living with him difficult."

"You almost sound relieved he's gone."

Lenora glanced at him sharply. "Don't misunderstand. I loved Reece. His death devastated me."

She looked into the distance, her eyes sharpening. Simon followed the line of her gaze and saw a large carriage approaching from the opposite direction. Adrenalin began to spurt through his veins. He was relieved when she placed her hands over his and guided the horse to the side of the road. When the carriage passed by with yards to spare, Simon sighed deeply.

"You worry too much," she told him, a fetching glimmer entering her eyes. "Don't you know you are safe with me?" Her tone implied she was not speaking about driving.

"Am I?" he questioned warily. She was pulling him toward her with a power he knew only too well.

"Of course you are. I have always been discreet in whatever I do."

His mouth went dry. "Is that so?"

The horse slowed as Simon's grip on the reins loosened. He had never been able to resist a beautiful woman who desired him. It was the weakness that destroyed his marriage; Elena had endured his liasons for years before giving up on him.

The thought cooled him like icewater. He straightened virtuously, turned his attention to the dusty road, and flicked the reins. Sasha picked up her pace.

Lenora was undaunted by the change in his mood. "Yes, it is. I hope you don't think I accepted Reece's shortcomings without indulging a few of my own. A woman who remains docile while her husband does anything he likes is spineless, in my opinion. Now in my case, I have a particular fondness for the company of handsome gentlemen. Yet never have I betrayed a trust. There are no expectations on my part when I form ... attachments. It is the joy of companionship that I seek, nothing more. Do you not find that a refreshing attribute in a woman?"

"Um. Have you had a great many of these attachments?" He awaited her answer with trepidation. Was he wishing a nymphomaniac on Alexander?

"Not so very many. Enough to know what it is I look for, which is simply pleasure." She gave him a deep, meaningful look. "I'm not at all like other women, am I? Not like Darby, for example, who would require a marriage license before allowing a gentleman to kiss her hand."

Dear God, she was a feminine version of himself. Ignoring the reference to Darby, he said, "You must have many admirers. Claude Heathershaw, for one; I've noticed he pays you a lot of attention."

He cared little what she thought about Heathershaw, but he didn't want to seem too pointed in his interest in her feelings for Alexander, which *did* concern him greatly.

"Claude." Her lips twisted scornfully. "Of late, he appears more drawn to Darby than myself."

Simon's heart jumped and began to race. Was she jealous? Would she try to kill Darby in a jealous rage? But that made little sense; she seldom displayed interest in Claude, who was no prize, anyway; and Lenora seemed like a practical woman. If she married again, surely it would be to advance herself.

"What about Alexander?" He could scarcely keep the pleading note from his voice.

Although her features remained pleasant, he sensed doors closing within. "Alexander? He is a dear boy. I have a great fondness for him."

"He seems to like you."

She kept her gaze on the road for several instants. When she turned back, the look she gave him was nakedly sensual. "I don't want to talk about Alexander. I had rather talk about you."

"No, you don't; I'm not very interesting. Your father and step-mother seem to like Alexander, I've noticed. They wouldn't mind if the two of you became closer, would they?"

The heat faded from her eyes. "I'm no longer a little girl to be led by my father's wishes."

"Yes, but you can't help agreeing it would be a nice solution all around. It would keep the family together, wouldn't it?"

"What I do with my life is my affair."

He couldn't blame her for feeling that way. "Okay. So what *are* you going to do after Alexander inherits? Do you and your parents have plans?"

"I have just remembered that I promised to help Gacia hem Papa's new handkerchiefs," she said, her lips pursing together. "You had best turn back. Here, I'll show you how."

Stifling a grin, Simon allowed her to help him. If he hadn't learned a great deal about Lenora, at least he'd managed to make her angry. Maybe now she'd focus her attention on Alexander.

That afternoon, Beckett delivered boots, a pair of tan pantaloons, a white shirt, gold brocade vest, cravat, and fawn-coloured jacket to Simon's room. Simon eagerly threw down the copy of *Childe Harold's Pilgrimage* he'd been trying to read and surveyed his new clothes.

"Soon's I can, I'm to make you another waistcoat and *frac*, then a suit for evening," said Beckett, who was a small man with features that reminded Simon of pictures he'd seen of Napoleon. To strengthen the illusion, the valet held himself excruciatingly straight, and nothing marred the crisp lines and clean perfection of his own clothes. "By tomorrow I'll be finished with the running garment you wanted, though I've never stitched anything so dashed loose."

"Your work is beautifully done," said Simon, examining the tiny, even stitches in his jacket.

"It is, ain't it?" Beckett agreed, the whining tone in his voice warming. "I take pride in what I do, though there's some what don't appreciate it."

"Where did you get the boots? Don't tell me you're a cobbler, too."

"No, there's a bloke in Mirren. Don't look too close; the boots ain't so fine as what you'd get in London, though a sight better than that odd pair you're wearing."

"It's amazing you did all this so fast."

Air puffed from Beckett's cheeks. "Mr. Lightner says to say I'm working to please Miss Brightings. Anytime she has need of me, she must call; even if it means my employer must suffer for the lack of my services." His face darkened, and he added confidentially, "Between you and me, sir, he ain't sacrificing much. I still have to do everything he wants, only I do the extra work while others lie abed."

"I'm sorry."

Beckett gave him a long-suffering look. "If it wasn't this, it would be some other thing. Truth to tell, I like sewing garments for young gentlemen, though I guess you ain't no gentleman since you're an actor. Still, it's pleasing to dress a body that makes my work look good, unlike some I could name but won't. Try on the clothes now and show me if I measured right."

After satisfying Beckett's curiosity regarding the fit and receiving hurried instructions in how to tie a cravat, Simon thanked the valet, escorted him to the door and closed it. Stripping off the new clothes, Simon gave himself his second chilling bath of the day and dressed again. He even washed his hair, since there was time enough for it to dry before dinner. It was too short to feel right, though.

When the hour arrived to go down, he couldn't help admiring himself before the cheval mirror. For the first time since he arrived, he looked like he belonged here. He had not felt so stylish since he'd been a presenter at the MTV Awards.

"You're succumbing to peer pressure," he told his image in the mirror. He grinned at his foolishness while thinking, *Wonder if Darby will approve?*

The smile died. Thoughts like that were pointless. His purpose in coming here had nothing to do with pleasing Darby. He came to rescue her and restore life to Elena and Tay. Nothing more.

Thus it was a grave but striking stranger who entered the parlor a short while later. He found it hard to remain solemn, though, when receiving the attention his new clothes brought. He couldn't help feeling especially gratified when Darby looked at him with surprise and—did he imagine it?—admiration. She glanced away quickly, however, and he couldn't be sure.

He was not as pleased to note that Lenora viewed him with comparable pleasure. She seemed to have forgotten her morning's irritation with him. Although Gacia demanded Alexander escort her step-daughter into the dining room, thereby deciding upon Lenora's dining partner, the widow nevertheless managed to direct many of her remarks in Simon's direction.

There was not enough of them to allow of private conversations anyway. Simon quickly claimed Darby's arm before Claude could, but it did him little good to sit beside her. She looked charming in a white gown shot through with gold threads, but he could only stare at her so long before Alexander's steely glare knifed the corner of his eye and cut his attention away.

As dinner progressed, Simon came to believe Darby

wanted to say something in particular to him; but everytime
she turned to him confidingly, someone demanded her
notice. His hunch was confirmed when the maid slipped
on a patch of spilled soup and, after brilliantly juggling
the dish of peas she carried, suffered only the loss of the
lid. As the glass fell loudly to the floor and shattered,
drawing everyone's startled notice, Darby seized her opportunity and whispered in his ear that she needed to speak
with him alone.

After dinner, Simon returned with the gentlemen to the
parlor, chatted awhile, then wandered slowly toward the
doors leading to the garden. Hopefully Darby would follow
and speak her mind. He meant to be accommodating only;
as soon as he heard what she had to say, he would return
inside and not linger beneath a spring moon. Even if it
was only a crescent, it looked dangerous to him.

He walked across the bricked terrace, down the steps,
then ambled past groupings of roses with cherubs centered
within them. Towering over the flowers, a few solitary oak
trees were allowed to spread their branches; a circular,
wrought-iron bench was wrapped around each.

Without conscious choice, he headed toward one of the
benches and sat. Hopefully Darby could find him here;
from this angle, he couldn't see into the parlour windows.
He'd have to watch for her.

The new leaves above him fluttered sweetly. He leaned
his back against the tree and stared at the sky. Wisps of
clouds floated beneath the stars, hiding, then revealing
the glimmering suns in un-smogged splendor. It was very
quiet; no traffic, not even the horse-and-buggy kind, passed
on the road; and the murmur of voices from the house
could not reach him here. The wind brought a not-unpleas-
ant whiff of stable to his nose. A dog barked somewhere
faraway.

Simon closed his eyes, and within moments, he slept.
Absurd dream fragments drifted through his mind. He

jogged around an asphalt track while Darby juggled glass jars filled with peas. One jar after another shattered on the pavement. Just as she launched the last one at his head, Simon heard a voice calling his name. He jerked to bewildered wakefulness, opening his eyes to see not Darby, but Lenora. He sprang to his feet.

"Lenora! I was just going inside."

"You were sleeping," she disputed, her lips curving upward. "Do I make you uneasy, Simon? You seem so whenever I'm near."

"What? No, of course you don't make me uneasy. I do have to go inside now, though." He placed a hand on his chest. "The night air chokes me up."

"Does it now?" She sat, straightened her skirt prettily, then patted the seat beside her. "Sit down for just a moment. I have something I wish to say to you."

He hesitated. Every instinct advised flight, but he might learn something important. Keeping a safe distance between them, he sat.

"I think I may have been rude to you this morning," she began. "You asked me questions which seemed impertinent. I resented your inferences about Alexander and myself, but as I thought more upon it today, I had to ask: Why does Simon want to know this? And I could only conceive of one answer. You don't wish to trespass on another's interest."

"Um, no, that's not—"

She leaned toward him and placed her finger across his lips. "Hush now, let me finish. You intrigue me, Simon. I have never met a man like you, and I would like to know you better. What I said about myself this morning was true. You need not trouble yourself with my plans concerning Alexander. You and I . . . we may enjoy one another without any bonds."

Slowly she drifted closer, her lips parting slightly.

Simon dreamily pushed aside the finger which rested

on his mouth. In a dry voice he asked, "Then you *are*
serious about Alexander?"

"No more about him," she breathed, and smoothed her
hands across Simon's vest and circled his waist. He crushed
his back against the tree, his arms raised helplessly. As if
hypnotized, he watched her face draw nearer. And then
she pressed her lips to his.

He could have escaped. Later, when he reviewed the
moment in his mind, he knew he should have resisted.
But at that moment he endured, intending to break away
gently and spare her feelings. At least he did not enjoy the
kiss, or if he did, it was only the smallest amount. Certainly
he never lowered his arms and responded as once he would
have. Surely that proved his intentions were good.

But none of that meant anything when he finally did
release himself and look up. Darby, her eyes blazing grey
fire, her hair flying from its pins, was running toward them
as fast as her narrow dress would allow.

His heart stopped.

Seeing his expression, Lenora whirled around. She had
time only to relax slightly—Simon wondered briefly who
it was *she* feared was coming—before Darby grasped her
shoulders and wrenched her from the seat to the ground.

"You—you—hussy!" Darby shouted. "How dare you?"

From her half-sprawled position on the grass, Lenora,
her mouth and eyes rounded in perfect circles, gawked at
Darby. The widow's skirt had slipped above her ankles,
and her elbows were planted in great clods of dirt. She
looked so comically shocked that, had Simon not been
afraid of Darby himself, he would have laughed.

As it was, he tried to stand, intending to begin explana-
tions if he could think of any; but Darby stood so close
that he managed only to lean against the tree, the bench
cutting into the back of his knees like a blade.

"Darby," he began, "don't—"

She whipped around to face him, slapped her hand

squarely on his chest, and pushed. Having no other choice, he sat and stared directly up at her, an appeal in his eyes that had nothing to do with acting.

"And you!" she cried. "You—horrible, horrible—*thing!*"

Words appeared to desert her then, and rage-filled tears flowed down her cheeks. Clenching her fists, she turned and walked a few paces away, looking at neither of them.

"Have you lost your senses?" exclaimed Lenora, stretching her hand toward Simon for assistance, since her skirt was narrow and allowed little maneuvering.

Simon braced Lenora's struggle from the ground, but he kept his eyes on Darby. When the widow safely achieved her stance, he released her hand immediately; the very touch of her skin was now repulsive.

Darby's shoulders were shaking with suppressed sobs, as if her heart was tearing. He had broken her with that little kiss, just as he'd shattered Elena with worse. But with Darby, he'd not stopped with hurting her feelings; he had shaken her faith. What could she be thinking now, believing an angel of God would act like a cheap lothario?

Darby's spirituality was one of the things he admired most about her, since her strong character seemed to spring from it. He almost envied that faith, almost regretted that he couldn't believe those old tales himself; it might be a comfort. What had he done to her?

He'd have to tell her he was not an angel. But if he did, would she allow him to remain at Brightings? He knew there would be no chance, not with this righteous anger burning inside her.

Darkness descended over his shoulders like a familiar old coat. He'd forgotten how bad he could feel. Until now, he hadn't realized he had become happy here, spinning his life around Darby's rescue, Darby's words, Darby's smile. He noticed the difference now, though, now that the lightness had bled from him.

He stepped softly to Darby and touched her shoulder. "Don't cry," he said hopelessly. If only he could find words to excuse his actions, but he could think of none.

Darby shrugged off his hand and stepped away. She crossed her arms and dug her slippered toe into the soil banking one of the rosebushes.

"It was merely a kiss," Lenora said in a vexed voice as she dusted dirt from her sleeves and the back of her gown. "We haven't sullied your maiden eyes with something more scandalous. I don't know why you are acting so missish unless . . ." Lenora's tidying efforts ceased momentarily, and a look of comprehension spread across her features. "Oh," she said with a faint smile, "so it's like that, is it?"

Darby swung around angrily. "I don't know what you mean. It's not like anything, except I don't expect those staying in my house to behave like animals."

"Animals?" Lenora squeaked. "A simple kiss between two unmarried adults is behaving like animals?" She turned to Simon. "You *are* unmarried, aren't you?"

"Yes," he answered, and so distracted was he by Darby's scornful eyes that he almost confessed he was a widower. "Please forgive me, Darby."

"Forgive you?" Lenora stepped in front of Simon, forcing him to look at her. "Why should she forgive you for such a small thing? There *is* something between the two of you, isn't there? I thought it strange that Darby would invite someone she didn't know to stay in the house like an honored guest. So what is it? Are you betrothed, or is it something else altogether?"

Simon frowned down into Lenora's speculative eyes. At least he hadn't hurt *her*. She seemed as delighted to discover what she imagined to be intrigue as she would have been to create her own. In the right century, she would have made a fine gossip columnist.

"Betrothed!" snapped Darby, dashing the tears from her eyes. "You are an idiot if you think that."

"I told you I'm not perfect," Simon observed humbly.

"Ah," Lenora said knowingly. "He has told you he's not perfect. What else has he said?"

"Nothing but words," Darby declared. "Lying, deceitful, untrustworthy words."

Lenora's laughter rang across the garden. "Oh, yes, I understand perfectly now. And you've been secretive because you mean to keep this scandalous liason from Alexander's ears, and I don't blame you. Well, Simon, now that I know why you resisted me, my faith in myself is restored."

Darby became very still. "He . . . resisted you?"

"I did," Simon agreed eagerly. "I resisted her."

Darby ignored him, her eyes piercing Lenora across the bricked walkway.

The widow appeared to be enjoying herself immensely. "Yes, he did. Somewhat. Darby, I'm delighted. I thought you were a stiff stick, but I was wrong."

Simon held his breath while several emotions passed through Darby's eyes.

"Rubbish," she said after a moment. "You're insinuating things that are untrue."

He began to breathe again. Darby's face looked less forbidding than before, he was sure of it.

Still smiling, Lenora tilted back her head. "You'll have to forgive me for treading on your territory. I didn't know, I promise you."

"Oh, be quiet, will you?" Darby looked from her to Simon, then glanced toward the house. The door to the parlour had just slammed, and Alexander now walked into sight. "Oh, this is all that was needed," she murmured, and immediately straightened her shoulders while rubbing her eyes.

Simon muttered something under his breath, and both women looked at him in surprise.

"Darby?" called Alexander, walking toward them. "What are you doing out here?"

In a strangled voice, Lenora whispered, "I won't tell him about you and Simon if you promise to do the same for me."

Darby's gaze flew to Simon. Although hostility still gleamed in her eyes, she was asking him for guidance. He nodded his head in quick, desperate jerks.

Alexander's boots crunched against the bricks as he came to stand beside his sister. With condemnation in his eyes, he viewed each one of them in turn, staring longest at Darby.

"What goes on here? Have you been crying?"

"Something flew into my eye," Darby answered.

"What was it, a bird? You look terrible; your nose is red as a strawberry."

"It hurt," she said in a sad little voice, making the weight on Simon's chest grow heavier.

"Well, is it out now?" Alexander viewed her skeptically as she nodded. Giving Simon a suspicious glance, he offered his arm to Darby. "Come inside before something else happens, then."

"I believe I'd like to go inside as well," Lenora said, seizing his other arm, to Alexander's obvious satisfaction.

"I guess I'll turn in, too," said Simon, but no one so much as glanced at him. He shrugged and followed the others into the parlor.

Chapter Eight

Later that evening when the house grew quiet, Darby splashed water on her face and lit an extra candle. Even though her emotions ached like raw wounds, she was having trouble staying awake; and she would need to remain alert for at least another hour before daring to visit Simon's room.

She had not been able to steal a moment alone with him all night, and she wanted to ask his advice. Why she bothered, she was not certain. He was such a weak, paltry angel. Truly, she would do better to trust her own counsel than that of a creature who could not defend himself against such as Lenora.

He had said he resisted the merry widow. Well, she'd seen that kiss, and it did not look like he fought very hard.

Darby's lips turned downward. She sat in her rocker and covered herself with a shawl. Although her ivory dress had long sleeves, she always grew cold at night. Reaching for the book of sermons on her table, she opened it and began to read.

After ten minutes, her eyes grew so heavy that she put the volume aside and occupied herself by chewing her fingernails and thinking. By the time her self-inflicted hour passed by, she had stirred herself into a boiling stew.

She was able to maintain composure enough to close her door quietly and slip through the corridor on soundless feet. Arriving at Simon's door, she knocked softly. After waiting several endless seconds and hearing no answer, she knocked again. When he still did not answer, she took a deep breath and turned the knob. It was unlocked. She edged inside and closed the door behind her.

He had left the candle burning by his bed; a dangerous practice, since he slept so soundly. She would have to warn him about that as she had warned him of so many things. Perhaps fire held no fears for him, since he was not mortal; but it did for her.

Knowing she should not, she tiptoed to his bed and watched him sleep. The candlelight flickered over the fair hair tumbling across his forehead, the remarkable dark brows, his long curling lashes. Looking at him now, she could not doubt he was an angel. If only he acted more like one.

He had pushed aside his covers while he slept. His nightshirt reached only to his knees, and its top buttons gaped open. She felt a sudden, mad desire to press her lips to his cheek.

Her face began to flame. She should not be here. Never had she been in a man's room, other than Alexander's, but he did not signify. She'd thought visiting an angel's chamber would be of similar innocence, but now she realized her error.

With her gaze pinned to his face, she began to back away. She could not see that the handle of the water pitcher on his bedside table was sticking out; thus it was his fault, not hers, when her elbow struck it a glancing blow. The pitcher clattered toward the edge, the bowl it nested within sliding, too. In a heroic effort, Darby lunged desperately and caught both before they broke upon the floor, though water spewed in all directions, mostly upon her dress.

In the catching, she had stumbled to her knees, and now her head bumped the table noisily, causing it to rock. Clenching her teeth to hold back the hot words which threatened to burst from her mouth, and with both hands still clutching the pitcher and bowl, she watched Simon's razor tilting toward the floor. The table returned to its former position, but the blade plummeted. It struck the carpet with a soft thud.

With a crazed expression, Darby looked at her angel. He had continued to sleep peacefully through all—until the razor landed. And now his lids were slowly opening over eyes that glimmered like diamonds, and with as much comprehension. When recognition, then confusion, entered those eyes, she felt a wave of heat pass from her head to her toes in spite of the dampness of her gown.

"Darby?" he asked in a sleep-thickened voice. "What are you doing?"

"Nothing," she snapped, setting the pitcher and bowl on the floor and struggling to rise. Her hand squished into a particularly wet spot of carpet, and she winced but managed to attain her feet. "I had a little accident, that's all. If you turned the handle of your pitcher toward the wall as is proper, none of this would have happened."

She bent to retrieve the ceramic pieces and demonstrated her meaning by showily restoring them to the back of the table. With an angry glance at him to see if he paid attention, she stooped a second time and retrieved the razor.

"You're all wet," he said, still sounding bewildered as he looked from her to the table to the floor and back again. For a moment she suspected laughter threatened in his eyes, but he lowered his glance so quickly she was not certain. In a hoarse voice he added, "Let me get something to wrap around your shoulders."

When he rose from the bed, she was pleased to see a look of alarm cross his features as he realized he wore only a nightshirt. Now she was not alone in her embarrassment.

"Where is that robe?" he muttered, throwing his blankets back and forth. Finally, he found the garment—a moth-eaten, old red thing, Darby saw, making a mental note to find him a better one—pulled it on, and tied the sash. Snatching a blanket from the bed, he walked toward her.

"I don't need it," she said, raising her chin. "I was just leaving."

He stopped, though he still extended the blanket toward her. "Why? Did you sneak into this bedroom just to throw my water on the floor?"

She glared at him haughtily. When he offered the blanket to her again, demandingly, while chewing his lower lip in a futile effort to hide his amusement, she shuddered to feel her mouth responding in traitorous twitches.

"Oh, very well," she said crossly, seizing the blanket and tossing it around herself. "I did have a reason for coming, so I may as well stay a moment."

"Please do." He gestured with exaggerated politeness to the straight-backed chair beside the fireplace. There was only the one chair, and while she sat in it, he slouched on the rail at the foot of his bed.

She stared at him disapprovingly, the silence lengthening. Merriment continued to shine from his eyes, and she did not like it.

"I hope nobody saw you enter my room," he said. "I wouldn't want you ruining my reputation."

She immediately caught the allusion but failed to see the humor. "Your angelic reputation is safe with me, though I fear the same cannot be said of all your acquaintances."

That killed the laughter in his eyes, she was pleased to note.

"I'm sorry about Lenora. I mean, nothing really happened, but I know to you it might have looked as if something did."

"Yes," she said acidly, "I'm certain it was my error, but I could have sworn you were kissing her. Even she admitted it. Cannot you?"

"She was kissing *me."*

"And you could not stop her—big, strong angel that you are."

"I *was* trying . . ." His voice faded, as if he suddenly realized the futility of protesting.

His inability to form better excuses fueled her anger. "It seems if you were going to kiss anyone, it would be *me,* since I'm the only one you entrusted with the secret of your identity."

Darby's eyes widened in shock. From what wild spring had those words burst? Horrified, she covered her face with her hands. She could hardly see Simon in the spaces between her fingers, but he was regarding her with an ominous silence. She squeezed her eyes shut and began to pray for forgiveness.

His voice came as if from a great distance.

"Do you want me to kiss you, Darby?"

"No!" she said firmly. "No, I didn't mean it. I'm sorry."

When he remained silent, she opened her eyes to a squint. That terrible look of sadness had come into his face again, and she had put it there. He was disappointed in her. And why shouldn't he be? Imagine anyone so depraved as desiring to kiss an angel! Even Lenora wouldn't have done such a thing, did she realize what he was. Or most likely not.

Tears sprang to Darby's eyes. She should be shot.

"Don't you dare cry," he said, and moved as if meaning to go to her. But as soon as he stood, he sank back to the bed, proving she disgusted him so thoroughly that he could not comfort her. Tears began to spill down her lashes.

"You haven't done anything wrong," he added earnestly. "Not a thing. It's me, Darby. I'm the problem."

"No, you aren't," she sobbed. "I'm too—too possessive. I think of you as m-my angel, and I don't want to share you with anyone else."

This time he did leave the bed and come to stand over her. With a tender, sorrowing look in his eyes, he touched the top of her head, and with his fingers traced the path of her tears, erasing them gently.

"I am yours," he said.

Darby stared up at him, hoping for something she could not name. The pain in her heart lessened, and her mouth trembled into a little smile.

Although his eyes remained clouded, he smiled faintly in response and moved his thumb across her lips as if sketching them, making her shiver. When he lowered his hand and returned to his perch on the bed, she felt consoled and disappointed all at once.

"You have more character than anyone I've ever met," he said, his voice sounding hollow. "Don't put yourself down, do you hear me? Never do that. You are so . . . so pure, so good. I don't know who would be worthy of—well, enough. Maybe you'd better tell me why you wanted to see me."

"Hm?" Her head was spinning with his praise, and for a moment she could not think. "Oh. Well, before I speak of that, there is something else I've been thinking about since—since we were all in the garden." Indignation flared within her again, but she pushed it aside. "When Alex came toward us, remember how quickly Lenora pledged us to secrecy? She said she would not tell him of *our* liason"— Darby wrinkled her nose scornfully—"if we did not speak of *her* involvement, or whatever it was, with you."

Simon nodded, a curious look on his face, as if to say he did recall it but did not understand its importance.

"Well, there it is, don't you see?" Darby exclaimed, growing excited enough to bounce from the chair and pace in front of him waving her hands in extravagant gestures. "Why should she be worried about what Alex thinks of her if she does not plan to trick him into marriage?" She studied Simon's face eagerly. "You still do not understand, do you? Oh, I know that you desire they wed so your important person will be born. But I think Lenora has schemed to marry Alex all along and may have killed her husband in order to do so. Don't you find it suspicious that she didn't want my brother to know you kissed her?"

"I *didn't* kiss her," Simon replied distractedly, trying to follow Darby's line of reasoning.

"As you say, then. But can you not admit the possibility that I'm right? Alex will not be absurdly rich, but his fortune is considerable. Certainly he is in better straits than poor Reece was."

She was dismayed to see a furrow appear in his brow. Obviously he wanted no one to dash cold water on his plans. Well, he could not hide from the truth; he was an angel.

"I don't know, Darby. You're stretching things a little, I think."

"Am I?" she challenged.

He shifted on the bed as if he were uncomfortable. "It's worth thought," he admitted, "but I don't know if Lenora is really after him. I mean, it's plain your aunt and uncle are trying to throw them together, but Lenora's actions don't fall in line with that. Flirting with other men is a dangerous way to reach her goal. Had I been responsive, Alexander would likely have found out."

Darby shook her head stubbornly. "Lenora thrives on this sort of adventure. If you'd seen her behavior among gentlemen when she was wed to Reece, you would never guess she was married."

"A lot of people enjoy playing games like that," he said slowly, an odd expression on his face. "Even if she does have a wandering eye, you can't simply conclude she murdered her husband. We don't have enough information."

"If we knew more, though . . . if it transpires that Lenora *is* guilty, you won't insist upon completing your mission, will you? Surely you won't expect Alex to marry a murderess!"

He held her gaze for a long time before lowering his eyes. She felt a moment's trepidation at the glimmer of fear she saw there. Or had she imagined it?

"I . . . can't answer that right now," he said. "And don't go snooping around where you're not wanted. Are you listening to me? No trying to find out anything. I—I command it, as your angel. Understand?"

A taut moment passed between them as she struggled with her own willfulness. But she could not argue with heaven, not when its wishes were so plainly presented. Defeated, she nodded slowly.

Simon watched her closely, then sighed, sounding relieved. "Now, did you say there was something else you wanted to talk about?"

Subdued and disappointed, she returned to the chair.

"Edward has asked me to marry him," she said.

Had she thrown her skirts over her head and howled, Simon could not have looked more surprised. "Edward?" he asked stupidly, as if he had never heard the name before.

"Yes, Edward Wallace. You have met him."

"Um. I remember."

"Well, I wanted to ask your advice. Do you think I should say *yes*?"

He ran a hand across his mouth, his gaze wandering

back and forth along the carpet beneath her feet. "Why ask me?"

"I thought if anyone would know, you would."

Still avoiding her eyes, Simon cleared his throat. "How do you feel about Edward?"

Her eyebrows lifted when he pronounced Edward's name as if he did not like him. "I love Edward," she said devoutly.

"Do you really?" The curtness in his voice both surprised and pained her. "Then marry him, by all means."

"Well, you see, this is the way of it," she said consideringly. "I love him because I have known him all my life. There is not a feeling of . . . oh, I don't know how to say it." She almost told him then of her sisterly feelings when Edward kissed her, but stopped herself in time. Since she had made such a furor over Simon's kiss, he would probably condemn hers in turn. Instead, she finished, "He does not make me feel . . . in the way I believe I should, to be married."

"Oh, I see."

"Well, you need not look so amused. I don't find it a laughing matter."

"You're right; it's not." The brief look of humor faded, and he crossed the room to stand before the window and gaze outward. "What does Edward do? Does he have a job?"

"You don't know this? He runs his family's farm. They have a dairy that is becoming well-known."

"So he's not trying to latch onto the Brightings fortune."

Darby stiffened until the top of her head was as tall as the chair's back. "Do you think he wouldn't consider marrying me without being paid for it?"

Simon turned wrathfully, startling her. "A man would have to be a fool not to want to marry you!"

"Oh." Shocked with pleasure, she squirmed a little and relaxed her shoulders. "Thank you."

As the quiet lengthened, Darby lifted her gaze from her lap and looked at Simon. Something silent and serious passed between them; something beyond words but as tangible as the blanket beneath her hands.

In that moment, she realized she had fallen in love with her angel. And as certain as she knew her name, he loved her, too.

The stunning awareness of this horror rushed the blood to her cheeks. With stinging eyes, she stood, the blanket falling to the floor.

"I—I have to leave," she said. And felt agony when she saw his eyes fill and redden with this new, unspeakable knowledge they shared.

"Yes, I guess you'd better."

But he did not move; apparently he was rooted in place beside the window, one hand clutching at the draperies as if to a lifeline. She walked to the door alone, but before she touched the knob, he spoke her name softly. She turned and waited.

"Marry Edward," he said. "He seems to be a good man. He's kind to his mother and sister, and I'm sure he'll be the same with you."

Darby gazed at him. *In this moment,* she thought with a sense of fate, *I have grown up. And I will never truly be happy again.* She opened the door, not caring if every member of the household lined the corridor to shame her.

"Thank you for the advice," she told him in a breaking voice. "I—I will consider it."

Chapter Nine

Simon had not slept when the maid tapped on his door before daybreak the next morning. He'd instructed the servant to awaken him in time to have breakfast with Darby so he could accompany her to the pottery. Now, staring at the ceiling with salty eyes, he wondered if he could go through with it.

"I'm awake, thanks," he told the maid through the door. He had to get up, even if the thought of seeing Darby filled him with dread. Last night at dinner, he had asked if he could visit her workplace, and she was expecting him. But he continued to lie in bed while the darkness beyond his window warmed to pink.

What he wanted to do was run outside, flee into the woods and dash beneath the ash trees like a coward. Whatever awaited him in the future had to be easier than pretending he didn't love Darby.

But he couldn't run. For the next few weeks he was anchored to the past, tied by obligations that must be met, even if his heart cracked into dust fulfilling them.

He deserved any pain he suffered. Months—and a whole world—ago, he buried his child and the only woman he'd ever thought to love. That they were no longer husband and wife at the time of her death was his fault. Afterwards, they'd remained friends. Neither one of them had bothered to change their wills, which was how he came to inherit Brightings.

Now even that bond seemed shallow in comparison with his passion for the enchanting girl he had come to save. She was different from any woman he'd ever known. Elena had been bright, sophisticated, and assertive. Darby was strong, too, but there was an innocence, a vulnerability, about her that made him feel protective. And he was drawn to her idealism, her unapologetic morality, like a guilt-blackened moth to the flame.

Elena never really needed him. Within weeks of the final decree, she had begun seeing other men. It was, in fact, her engagement to a dentist that caused her murder and Tay's. Simon's deranged worshiper had incinerated them both to punish Elena for causing him pain.

Again, his fault.

And now he'd involved Darby, charmed her into his orbit like a python entrancing a nightingale. He could have remained remote and detached, but by allowing his own feelings for her to show, he'd caused her natural awe of a heavenly visitant to grow into something more. And Darby would not recover easily. She might never be the same after he left. He certainly wouldn't be.

Some angel he was. He seemed not only determined to save her from death, but to ruin her for life.

Even though he didn't like the sound of it, marriage to Edward Wallace was probably the best thing for her. He didn't want Darby mourning her angel like a nun for the rest of her days.

But what if Darby didn't *want* to marry Edward? She hadn't sounded very enthusiastic last night.

Simon jerked upward, propping himself on his elbows. Outside the window, the rising sun mirrored the fiery sense of doom he felt.

In spite of his outward appearance as a nice guy—Simon knew better than to believe outward appearances—Edward might be unstable. What if she refused him, and he became so disappointed he'd want to kill her?

Don't trust anyone, Simon told himself. Not Lenora, not Edward, not anyone.

The thought stirred him from bed. He bathed, dressed in his new clothes, then went downstairs to the dining room.

"Well, well, you made it just in time," said Uncle Richard from the head of the table. "Darby said you might be going with us this morning."

Alexander threw his napkin onto his empty plate and pushed back his chair. "I don't know why you want to come. The workers won't like your spouting sonnets at them."

"Alex, please," Darby said. She gave Simon a troubled, lingering look and rose. "We usually leave at this time. Perhaps you could bring a muffin or piece of fruit to eat in the carriage?"

"I'm not hungry, thanks."

"Then we should depart."

Darby circled the table as her uncle and brother joined Simon at the doorway. Simbar, his naked head shining beneath the chandelier, awaited them in the hall distributing hats and gloves. Simon was surprised to receive a black top hat that made him think of old vaudeville routines with taps and canes. Darby explained it had been her father's. He suppressed his smile and put it on as the other men did theirs while Darby tied the ribbon of her straw bonnet beneath her chin. The velvet ribbon matched the violets on her dress, he saw with a feeling of tenderness. Then, since it was expected of him, he reluctantly drew

on a pair of the late Mr. Brightings's gloves, which were
far too tight. When they were all properly swaddled from
head to fingers to toes—Simon wondered why they did
not cover their faces, too—the foursome left the house
and entered the carriage that awaited them.

Alexander claimed the seat beside his sister, forcing
Simon to share the bench opposite with Uncle Richard,
whose girth did not leave a great deal of room.

"You haven't seen the pottery, I believe," Darby said to
Simon as the coach began to move. "When we traveled to
the Wallaces' home on Sunday, we journeyed in the opposite direction."

Simon did not disagree, though he had viewed the twentieth-century version of the factory on his ride to Brightings
from the airport. As he recalled, the pottery was located
about five miles from the house.

Uncle Richard folded his hands on top of his belly and
stared worriedly at Darby. "Hope Old Sam is well today,"
he said. "Mr. Triagart's growing impatient for his urn.
Don't blame 'im; he loved that old terrier of his. While he
waits, he's having to store Muddykin's ashes in a cookpot."

"That's no fault of ours," Alexander said. "You're the
one who keeps making the individual orders. The money
is in moulded quantities, not single pieces. Darby has told
you so a hundred times."

"Ah, but local patronage and good will—"

"—is all very well," Darby interrupted. "But it does not
support our ninety-three workers."

"Are you abandoning hand-crafted items entirely to go
into mass production?" Simon asked, not liking the idea
of progress as well as Darby apparently did; but then, she
had not seen the skies blackened with it.

"Some work is done by hand," Darby explained. "Alex,
for one, spends a portion of his day painting our more
expensive porcelain. But it's not economical to craft odd
pieces that require the services of a thrower like Old Sam

when pressers can stamp out many more items in the same amount of time. And the quality is uniform.''

Spoken like a true industrialist, thought Simon. One side of his mouth lifted in an ironical smile. Darby was more progressive than he, man of the future that he was.

Uncle Richard's jowls quivered as he cleared his throat. "Don't mind us, Mr. Garrett. My niece and nephew have their way of looking at things, and I have mine. And who's to say which way is right?"

"The profit-sheets are most objective," Darby answered.

"Hah! That's my business partner talking!" burst Uncle Richard with an overdone twinkle.

"Not for much longer," sang Alexander under his breath.

"And you, young sir," declared the older man to his nephew with no apparent lessening of spirits, "I was glad to see you and m'daughter walking arm-and-arm last night. Mended your argument, have you?"

Alexander scowled. "What argument?"

"Ho, you try to deny it, do you? You think no one noted how you've been cutting Lenora these past few days?"

"Your meaning escapes me, Uncle."

"Now, now, don't try to pull that innocent act with me; I wasn't born in a blarney field. Lenora dropped tears telling us how you ignored her on Sunday, spending all your time with that Wallace chit."

"Evelyn is not a chit," Darby said coldly.

"I didn't ignore Lenora; she ignored *me*,"declared Alexander at almost the same instant. "For *him*," he added bitterly, glancing at Simon, who would not meet his eyes but shifted his weight closer to the door.

Uncle Richard laughed heartily. "That's what I thought you'd been thinking. I told Lenora there was nothing to it, but she was certain you were angry with her. You know what m'daughter's like, children. She's a warm-hearted girl and likes to make everyone feel at home. That's all her attention to Mr. Garrett here meant. Nothing else. Sorry to disappoint you, Mr. Garrett, if you were hoping different. She is *dashed* fond of you, Alexander. *Dashed.*"

Alexander folded his arms. "I see whom I want, *when* I want."

"Of course you do, m'boy! Who ever thought or said differently?"

Silence reigned in the coach for the remainder of the journey. Simon was deeply relieved when the kilns of the pottery came into view.

Less than half the buildings he'd known in the twentieth century factory were here, but the pottery was impressive nonetheless. And strangely archaic-looking. The bottle kilns, looking for all the world like old-fashioned milk jugs, loomed taller than their accompanying, three-storied warehouses and the flint mill banking the Trent. And he was wrong about the pollution, he saw; the sky was thick with it.

Darby noticed his frowning observation of the smoke and said, "If coal were not so cheap, we could not exist competitively. The kilns are unfortunately not very efficient; it requires at least two pounds of coal to fire one pound of clay."

"Um," he grunted noncommittally. The factory he'd known was powered with electricity, but that was far in the future.

Nodding to the occasional worker who hurried by, he followed Darby and the men across a dirt-packed yard littered with coal-carts, broken crockery, lumber, piles of bricks and rusted fragments of equipment, the original uses of which he could only guess. When they entered the nearest warehouse, Simon paused inside the door, his senses so thoroughly assaulted with noise, heat, and activity that he could not think for a moment.

The enormous chamber was open to the rafters, except for a balcony of rooms reached by an open, wooden staircase—offices, he decided. Although he noted a number of decent-sized windows, the bricked walls and floor, the mass of people and equipment, gave the impression of darkness broken by flashes of fire from the ovens.

He had never been inside a factory before. It reminded him more than a little of an artist's rendering of hell.

While he stood mute, a pale-faced woman hurried toward them. Before she arrived, Alexander turned to Darby, shouting, "I'm going to see the new engravings!"

Darby nodded, then waved aside Uncle Richard as he voiced his intention of finding Old Sam. By this time the woman had joined them, and Darby looked at her inquiringly, saying, "Yes, Mary?"

"It's my Millie, miss," the worker said, rubbing her hands in her apron. "She's sick today."

"Again?" Darby said impatiently. "This is the second or third time this month."

"Second, Miss Brightings. She ain't pretending, I promise ye. Her hands has broke out in turrible spots and hurt her something awful."

Darby touched the woman's arm sympathetically. "We're going to have to think seriously about this, Mary. It seems that removing the transfers is not the right work for her, and—"

"Oh, no, miss! She just has to get used to it, that's all. She likes taking the papers off 'cause 'tis easy, but keeping her hands in water all day ain't. She'll toughen up in awhile."

Darby lowered her voice, and Simon moved closer to hear. "Mary, I know you need the funds. I'm not thinking of letting her go. We'll find another position she can do better."

"But there ain't nothing," said Mary, her face twisting. "You know Millie ain't very smart for her years. You give Clemmy her old job, and I jes' don't know what else she can do."

"We'll find something, don't worry. Just take care of your little girl."

With a distressed expression, Mary nodded and walked away.

Darby turned to Simon. "I'll give you a brief tour, then you can walk around on your own. I have a meeting with the miller and his men in an hour; after that I spend the rest of my time wherever I'm needed. Today we're running a new design of Alex's, and I'm anxious to see how it turns out."

Simon thought she looked excited, not anxious. The noise and the incessant movement quickened her like a stimulant. "How old is that woman's daughter?" he asked.

"Hm? Oh, she's seven or eight; I'm not certain."

Darby moved onward, looking back at him in surprise when he didn't immediately follow. He walked forward on feet that suddenly felt heavy as cement.

There followed a mind-numbing lesson in the pottery business, all introduced by Darby in brisk, precise sentences. He saw the moulds that had been discussed in the carriage; these, she told him, were made from either plaster of Paris or lightly baked clay; both facilitated the drying of the final product as well as shaping it. Two men were engaged in making them, there being a steady need for different styles and replacements. A design would first be made in alabaster, then a stoneware duplicate from which the plaster moulds were cast. For dishes, flat hollow-ware was used; the men stamping them out were called pressers.

He saw biscuit, or once-fired ware, being dipped in liquid glaze in large, wooden tubs. The more expensive china was fired twice and dipped in a glaze almost completely made of flint glass.

"The lead glazes are not as healthy for the workers," Darby explained. "As to the composition of the plates themselves, we have followed Mr. Wedgwood's lead in using the whitest Devon clay we can find. Our dishes are as economical and elegant as his Queen's ware, though we supply our own decoration—all of it Alex's. The time is soon coming when even the humblest cottager will be able to afford beautiful dinnerware.'' She added lightly, ''Father often said it was our beholden duty to banish delft, pewter and wood from every table.''

When Simon responded with only the most perfunctory of smiles, she looked a little puzzled, then urged him to the next division of work. As they moved from one area to another, the workers under observation would eye them with brief interest, then return to their tasks with scarcely a pause. Darby spoke loudly to be heard over the clatter and shouted instructions of one laborer to another.

''A soft-paste hybrid is employed for our finer porcelain. Hardpaste is of course preferred on the Continent, as it is more similar to the oriental. But like Mr. Spode, we've found adding felspar to the bone-ash makes a cross between the two, and it is easy to work and produce in great quantities.'' Plates were stacked on a nearby shelf, and she held up a cream-coloured dish with a gold band circling the outer edge. ''This is an example of our fired gold; we mix gold-leaf and honey together before we fire it; it does not rub off easily as the old gilding did.''

She showed him the ovens, large enough to enter and lined with shelves. As he watched, men and boys walked into the sweltering kilns, round cases stacked on their heads.

''Those stone carriers are called saggars,'' she said, misreading his absorption. ''The objects to be fired are inside them. The saggar protects them from the smoke.''

''It's unbelievably hot in there,'' he said. Although they stood well away, smothering heat radiated outward from the bricked kilns; he felt his shirt growing damp.

Darby smiled. ''The ovens reach almost 1400 degrees centigrade when in operation.''

They moved past men operating mechanical lathes,

saggar-makers, and clay-beaters. "When my uncle is no longer an impediment, one of the first things we intend is to experiment with the design of our kilns. Alex thinks circular ones might be more efficient."

She paused longest to explain the operation of print-transference. "Here is where Alex's art comes to life," she said. "The engravers cut designs into copper plates, then heat and ink them with metallic oxide and oil. When the excess is removed, an impression is made from them onto moistened paper."

She strolled to another table, where women, Mary among them, pressed the inked paper to dishes, then rubbed rollers across them. "Once the design is trans-ferred, the girls rinse off the paper in cold water. Then the plate is heated to remove the oil. After that, it's glazed."

Three little girls stood with their hands plunged into vats of water, peeling off the papers. Darby walked toward them and whispered something. Three pairs of hands lifted. She inspected them approvingly, then darted a look at Mary, who observed her with an anxious expression. Darby nodded at the children and squeezed Mary's shoul-der without comment.

They wandered on. Darby led him outside to view the flint mill.

"The flint is needed to strengthen the clay for higher temperatures," Darby said. "Now that we have a steam engine, the crushing process is easier and safer. When my father was a child, the flint was reduced to particles by means of iron mortars operated by brute force, then sieved through lawn. But the workers sickened and died because they breathed the dust into their lungs. Now it is ground to a powder beneath the water, then mixed into slip."

"How practical," commented Simon.

"Yes, it is," she said, looking at him curiously. "Well, I must meet with the miller now. Do you wish to accompany me, or would you rather wander about on your own?"

"I'll look around myself, thanks," he mumbled.

"Very well. If you tire, my office is the second one at the top of the stair."

He nodded but did not move. She hesitated, scanned his face with a hint of a smile in her eyes, then walked toward the framed building that housed the mill. He watched her disappear inside, then turned to a warehouse he'd not viewed yet and entered.

More of the same here. People working hard, looking irritable, looking pale and thin and worn for their years. Little children toiling beside their parents. Adolescents taking on greater responsibilities, receiving no understanding for the clumsiness that their quickly-growing limbs gave them. One boy received a harsh scolding for dumping a stack of saggars that Simon knew was far too heavy. The child, red-faced with shame, was forced to sweep the broken pieces from the scalding floor of the kiln.

Simon wandered into another building which contained mostly supplies, then returned to the first warehouse. He walked among the laborers asking questions, offering praise, expressing interest in their work; and all the time his eyes were moving restlessly, his ears listening woodenly, his heart sinking like a stone in the river Trent.

He was heading toward the stairs when a small boy rushed toward him carrying a bucket and dipper. With one foot on the bottom tread, Simon waited.

"You tirsty, sir?" asked the child. "I got water."

Simon glanced at the communal ladle, thought of a million diseases, then looked into the boy's hopeful eyes. "Sure," he said, and accepted a couple of sips.

When the child reached upward to reclaim the dipper from Simon's hands, his sleeve fell back, exposing a stretch of dark, shriveled skin reaching from his wrist to his elbow. Simon instantly felt horror and struggled not to show it.

"What's your name, son?" he asked.

The boy smiled shyly. "Clemmy."

His hair was as fair as Tay's had been, though Clemmy's eyes were a rich brown against a too-white face. He was not much bigger than Tay either, though Simon knew this boy must be older. Steeling himself, he asked.

"I jes' turned six, sir." 'ow old is you?"

Simon forced himself to chuckle. "I guess that's fair. I'm thirty-one."

"Gor, *dat* old? Granny's thirty-four *I tink*, but 'er 'as lines on 'er face."

"Really? That's too bad."

Simon tried not to stare, tried not to think how much Clemmy resembled Tay. The boy didn't, not really. Tay was only three when he died, and his eyes were green as a budding leaf, his skin tanned and glowing with health.

"What happened to your arm?" Simon asked gently.

Clemmy looked blank, then saw the direction of Simon's gaze. "What, dis?" He set the pail on the floor and pulled back his sleeve cheerfully. "I got too close to Joe when 'ee was dipping plates in de 'ot bath. Won't niver do *dat* again!"

Transfixed, Simon stared at the scar while the child continued to extend it proudly. He could think of nothing to say. When a woman in a coarsely-woven brown dress scurried toward them, Simon lifted his eyes with almost sleepy reluctance.

"Clemmy!" the female whispered harshly. "Don' bother the gennulman. Go back to work now."

The boy heaved a large sigh and walked away.

Simon stirred to awareness. "Thank you, Clemmy," he called. The child must not have heard him, for he did not turn again.

"Please don' mind 'im, sir. My boy's still learning."

Simon sent the coldness in his heart to his eyes. "He's doing very well," he said, his lips moving hardly at all. "For a baby."

"Oh, he ain't no baby, sir. Miss Brightings don' let 'em come in 'til they's six year old."

Simon could not look at her any longer. He placed a shaking hand on the rail and began to climb the stairs.

Chapter Ten

Pride beamed in Alexander's eyes. "Well, here it is. What do you think?"

Darby edged beside her brother, who displayed a plate at arm's length. She took the dish in her own hands, holding it by its outer edge, and walked closer to a window to study it. After a quick glance, she looked up. The clatter of activity surrounding her was as comforting and familiar as her own heartbeat. The only distraction was the steady gaze of Alexander and the two men behind him. At her stare, the three of them busied themselves by shuffling their feet, clearing their throats, and looking unconcerned.

Lowering her eyes a second time, she viewed the plate with deeper concentration. Drawn in blue ink on a cream-coloured background, a boy and girl walked up a hill. A bucket dangled from their clasped hands. At the top of the hill stood a picturesque well.

"It's utterly charming, Alex," she pronounced. "Much better than before. We all know Jack and Jill will eventually fall, but what child wants to eat upon their terrorized faces?"

"I don't know, Darby," he said. "*I* would have."

"Yes, but that is *you*. Most children are not so blood-thirsty."

"Har," one of the men, Bull Thornton, laughed. "You don't know chillrun much, does you, Miss Brightings?"

"My boys wud druther 'ave 'em drippin' blood from their cracked noggins," added the other, Joe Rasher.

"That may be true, but mothers will be buying these sets for their little ones," Darby said. "Or so I hope." More to Alexander than the others, she appealed, "Tell me again that I've not made a mistake. The middle class *is* growing, and a separate set of dinnerware for their nurseries will become necessary. True?"

Alexander lifted one brow. "I have to reassure *you?* You're the one who told me no one could resist my Mother Goose sketches."

"And no one will," she said with conviction. "I cannot wait to see Little Jack Horner with the plum on his thumb." A lofty look entered her eyes. "Have you shown this to Uncle?"

An answering expression crossed Alexander's face. "Not yet. He should be deep in his morning nap by now." He began to smile. "But not for long."

"Alex, what have you done?"

"Oh, nothing much." His eyes began to twinkle. "You know how Uncle always props his feet on his desk when he sleeps? Naturally, he puts a great deal of weight on the back legs of his chair when he does so. A *very* great deal. Well, no chair can endure that kind of abuse forever." Alex lowered his voice conspiratorially. "Especially not after its legs have been sawed halfway through."

"Oh, Alex." In spite of minding her dignity in front of the men, she began to laugh. Behind her brother, Bull scratched his nose and grinned while Joe pretended not to hear. "I hope I'm in the building when he awakens," she added, then began to look around in a searching manner. "Has anyone seen Simon?"

"No, I'm pleased to say," said Alexander, the humor dying from his face.

Joe stepped forward. "You mean that gennulmen wot was with you, miss? Last time I saw 'im, 'ee was 'eaded for yer office."

She began to move toward the stairs. "Thanks, Joe. I want to show this to him."

"Must you?" Alexander called after her. "You're spoiling my moment of triumph."

Darby paid him no mind but strode eagerly across the large room to the stairs. She was anxious not only for Simon to see the first of their new line of nursery ware, but to receive his impressions of the pottery. This work was her life's blood, bred into her bones and tied to her heart. Hopefully he would understand that and approve.

During their tour, he had reacted with less pleasure than she expected, but perhaps that was because of the awful revelation of the night before. He was undoubtedly ashamed of his feelings, just as she was. Surely it was this which caused his aloofness and not some heavenly disapproval for her working in a man's world. It would be hard to bear if her brother and her dear, departed father were more forward-thinking than her angel. In truth, it would be alarming.

Darby reached the top stair, crossed the wooden balcony to the second room, and placed her hand on the doorknob. After taking a swift breath, she twisted it and entered.

Simon was standing before the window looking out, his tall frame a dark shadow against the bright daylight. At the sound of her entrance, he looked around briefly, then returned to his former stance.

This was an ominous beginning. What could be holding his attention so long outside that window? Nothing. There

was only scrubby countryside and a smithy down the road.
She stared at the taut form of her angel and knew fear.

"Hello," she said tentatively.

"Hello, Darby," he responded in a voice so low it
sounded miles away. He did not turn this time.

She walked behind her desk, placed Alex's dish upon a
stack of papers, and sat in the large oak chair that had
once been her father's. There was comfort to be gleaned
in the familiar clutter of her office—the desk scattered
with orders to be filled, bills to be sent; the cabinets of
files next to the door; the black leather chair on the other
side of the desk; the portrait of Alexander and herself,
painted last year by one of her brother's friends, on the
far wall—and just now, she needed comfort.

"Won't you sit down?" She cleared her throat to remove
the wobble from her voice. "Would you care for something
to eat? M. Donelle always packs us a cold collation for our
luncheon."

"I'm not hungry."

"Oh. Since you did not have breakfast, I thought perhaps you might be." Darby's fear began to sharpen into
vexation. "Please sit, Simon. I want to show you Alex's
latest work."

He turned slowly. Moving like a stiff old man, he walked
to the leather chair opposite her desk, contemplated it as if
it might bite him, then sat. He was behaving most strangely,
would not even lift his eyes to look at her. Well, she was
bound if she'd ask him what was the matter. He could tell
her if he wished.

"This is the plate," she said, and was pleased to hear
strength returning to her speech. Her hand trembled only
slightly when she pushed the dish toward him.

Although he looked, Simon did not move to take it. She
fought against growing annoyance. Now that he was away
from the window, she noted an unusual pallor to his skin.

Perhaps he was ill. But that was silly; angels did not become sick.

"Well?" she asked impatiently. "What do you think?"

He regarded the plate a while longer. When he spoke, his lips scarcely moved.

"It's lovely. Someday collectors will pay a fortune for a complete set."

Her ire vanished instantly. "Do you think so? Dishware for children is a risk, I know; Uncle Richard nearly gave himself an attack of apoplexy when I suggested it. Well, I cannot take credit for the idea entirely; had Alex not sketched a woman inside a pumpkin for one of our younger workers, I would never have thought—"

"How many children would you guess burned themselves for that plate?"

"—of it . . . myself . . . I beg pardon?"

"How many babies were sacrificed in the making of that plate?"

"What?"

For the first time he looked at her directly. With a flash of shock, she saw his eyes were bloodshot and desolate. Never, *never* had she seen him appear so sad, not even at their first meeting. What could be wrong? Why was he talking about sacrificing children? Had last night caused his mind to slip away entirely?

"Oh, yes, look innocent, Darby, like you don't know what you've been doing." He clenched his fists on the arms of the chair, then pushed himself upward. Whirling around, he paced the few feet between the chair and the wall. For an instant he stared at the portrait of Alexander and herself; it seemed to ignite him further, and he twisted back to face her. "You may look innocent, but it is the innocent you prey upon. How can you sleep at night? And stop pretending you don't know what I'm talking about."

"I *don't* know, Simon," she said, agonized. "Have you come to believe I'm some sort of pagan devil-worshiper?

Let me assure you that is not the case; I have never sacrificed a child, nor an animal for that matter. Should I— would you like me to order the carriage so you may go home and rest for awhile?''

"I'm not talking about literal sacrifice and you know it. I'm talking about those little children you have down there working in dangerous conditions when they should be playing, or in school. That tiny boy with the burned arm— he's no bigger than—than a mite! A breeze could blow him away, Darby!''

"Oh," she said, comprehension dawning. "I have heard these notions before. You hold the view of the reformers, don't you?''

"And you don't, obviously." He began to pace back and forth in front of her desk. "How could I have been such a fool?''

"Children work in every factory in this country." Her voice sounded weak again.

"Even I know enough history to realize *that*. But *you*, Darby?''

He was trying to make her feel ashamed. She burned with the injustice of it. Standing, she propped her hands on the desk and leaned forward. "I'm not certain what history has to do with anything, but these children work because their families need the income.''

"Oh, do they? And what does little Clemmy earn for his day-long labours, may I ask?''

She hesitated before answering. "The smallest children are paid a penny a day.''

"A penny! Dear God, Darby, what can you be thinking?''

She was growing hot. "A penny often makes the difference between bread and want at supper. Perhaps you don't realize it, Simon, but children are not efficient workers. It takes several of them to do the job of one adult. I employ them as a kindness to their families. If I did not, many of them would be left alone at home unattended. Here at least they are supervised, and here they receive valuable training for their future vocations."

"Future vocations," he derided. "More of the same drudgery for the rest of their lives, when school could train them for a better existence."

"Could it?" Reminding herself she spoke to an angel, she breathed deeply and tried to make her voice sound more placating. "Saying Clemmy's mother would allow him to attend school, which I doubt, and saying such a school existed for worker's children; what would he gain there? Would he learn to read about homes he can never own, foods he will never be able to eat, clothes he cannot afford? What you are suggesting will breed only dissatisfaction."

At this, tears filled Simon's eyes, and he turned his gaze ceilingward as if to prevent their falling. Darby's stomach tightened like a fist; her eyes began to fill, too. His anger, his disappointment, were incomprehensible to her.

When Simon collected himself enough to speak, he no longer shouted, but his voice throbbed with emotion. "And what *you* are suggesting is that he remain in blind ignorance, without hope." He briefly pressed the heel of his hands to his eyes, then walked closer to the desk. Lowering his fists to its surface, he said, "You, Darby, are a *fake.*"

She straightened and stepped backward as if he had slapped her. Her lips moved, but no words came out. She had been struck dumb.

He had not quite finished. "A self-righteous, sanctimonious *fake.*"

Words began returning to her now; she felt a cauldron of them boiling inside her throat. "How—how dare you? I know you are an angel, but surely that doesn't give you the right to insult me. Or to be my judge."

He nodded shortly, lifted his chin and viewed her through his lashes. "You can forget about the angel thing right now. Let's just talk, you and me, one being to another.

All this time, you've been judging *me*, haven't you, Miss Sunday School? Oh, yes, you worried about me, didn't you? Plagued me over my little sins. I spin a story to explain my presence at Brightings, I sit with a beautiful woman and let her kiss me, and *you* fall all over yourself rubbing my nose in it and acting like Saint Virgin of—of our Church of the Hypocrites. And I, of course—bumbling fool that I am—*I* fall for this line of phony palaver and slobber all over myself in guilt. When all the time you, *you* have been fostering this monstrous exploitation of children and smiling about it!''

His eyes were firebrands blazing into hers. She reacted in kind, pulses of heat radiating from her body. Simon's form began to waver before her eyes. Perhaps he was going to disappear now; or perhaps it was only her tears that made him shimmer.

"You have said to speak with you as one being to another, and I shall," she said between clenched teeth, her voice sounding more grief-clogged than she liked. "You have accused me of horrendous crimes and forced me to defend myself. If I have been doing wrong, and I still am not convinced I have, it was not intentional. Work has always been the lot of poor children, even in Biblical times. At least the ones downstairs are not slaves as they would have been in olden days."

"They're hardly better off; maybe less so."

"Simon, I would never willingly harm anyone. If you believe such about me, you have been an even less observant guardian than I thought. I ask you now in all fairness: If I have been guilty of cruelty by following the practices of every businessman in England, how was I to know?"

"You should have known." He spoke almost in a whisper, clutching his fists to his chest. "In here."

"But I didn't," she responded in correspondingly quiet tones. "I thought I served these families well by employing their offspring."

"If you paid the adults a decent wage, they wouldn't need their children's pitiful offerings. A penny a day, Darby. You're buying their youth and health disgracefully cheap."

"What do you want me to do, Simon? Walk from my office and announce that henceforth no children will work in this pottery? What do you think would happen to them then? Even if I added their wages to their parents', nine out of ten children would be forced to seek employment in another factory or be apprenticed into service."

"They could go to school."

"School? Where? Shall I fetch our carriages and send them off to Eton?"

He scowled at her sarcasm. "If there aren't any schools nearby, you could start one."

She paused, torn between incredulity and distaste. "I? Start a school?"

"Why not?" The fury faded from his face as excitement grew. "To make things easier for the parents, it could be here on the premises. There's space enough for a couple of classrooms in that warehouse next door, the one you store things in."

"A school at my pottery? In my warehouse?" She heard herself parroting him but could not help it; the idea was too nonsensical to assimilate. In a faint voice she added, "Someday I had hopes of filling that building with surplus wares."

"Fine. When that happens, you can build a little school-house out back."

Her eyes narrowed at this. "And who will pay for this little schoolhouse? Do you think the Brightings' funds limitless? I fear you mean to put the pottery in danger."

"The expense would be very little. If you can't sacrifice next year's carriage or a few dresses for the well-being of others, then it's your soul that's in danger, not your pottery!"

His words fanned her wrath into an inferno. "You speak to me as if I am frivolous. We don't buy a new carriage every year, and if the truth be known, I have very few gowns. Alex and I are not luxury-mongers; rather, we channel our profits into the business to expand it."

"Then you're saying this factory is more important than the people in it. Now I understand everything. You should've told me, Darby. I'd never have come, if I'd known this pottery was your god!"

She pressed her hands to the sides of her head, clenching handfuls of hair between her fingers. "It—is—*not*—my—*god!*" she shrieked.

At that instant, the door to her office was flung wide, and Alexander charged into the room. "What goes on here?" he demanded, looking from one to the other with a combative expression. "Has he troubled you, Darby?"

There was an extended silence as Darby and Simon, cheeks flushed and chests heaving, continued to glare at one another. Finally, Darby lowered her gaze. Simon had said a great deal of hurtful things to her in the past few minutes. She might never be able to forgive him, but he was her angel and she loved him in spite of everything, God help her.

"It's all right, Alex. We were just . . . discussing matters of business."

Alexander looked at her in disbelief. "Matters of business with *him?* Next you will tell me you've been consulting Clemmy as to his preference for Chinese or French rococo on porcelain."

Not liking to hear Clemmy's name just now, she pressed her lips into a tight line. With a furtive, still smoldering glance at her angel, she said, "Simon has given me something to think about."

"I daresay," retorted Alexander. "He has given *me* a great deal to think about, too."

Simon directed a tired look at Alexander and might

have responded further; but at that moment, a horrific
sound of cracking wood and startled screams reached their
ears, followed by a heavy, rattling thump against the wall
behind Darby's desk.

"Uncle Richard!" exclaimed Alexander. "He has awakened!"

Darby felt a kernel of amusement, but her heart was too
heavy to appreciate the prank as she normally would—
especially when she saw Simon's eyes remained dismal.
Alexander, grinning hugely, made an unnecessary motion
demanding silence. Within seconds, further noises began
filtering through the wall.

"Cover your ears, sister," he mouthed. "It might be best
if you didn't hear our uncle's words just now. I'm sure he
will come to regret them."

More sounds ensued. Wood scraping against wood.
Another thump, then something heavy clattering to the
floor. Silence for an instant, followed by weighty footsteps
and a door opening. Footsteps resuming, approaching.

Gleefully, Alexander leaped to perch on the corner of
Darby's desk. "And you believe we should go on with the
children's dinnerware," he declared as the doorknob
began to turn. "I think you're right. We need not press
too many at one time, and—oh, hello, Uncle. And how
are you? Are you ready for luncheon?"

Uncle Richard, his hair rumpled into a peak at the crown
of his head, his face pale except for two circles of red on
his cheeks, fingered the torn seam of his jacket while looking back and forth between the twins. "I suppose you know
nothing of this," he said.

"Know nothing of what?" Alexander asked innocently.
"Is something wrong? Did you have a bad dream?"

"M'chair broke," Uncle Richard said in a flat voice.
"Don't guess you heard anything about it."

"Who, me? Why should I know anything about your
chair? Though I've told you often enough that we should

purchase new office equipment. *You're* the one tightening the purse strings, you know.''

"The chair was fine until this morning."

"Well, you know how some things are, Uncle. When furniture grows old, it very often looks all right for years and years, but then one day it suddenly snaps." Tightly holding his grin at bay, Alexander clicked his fingers to illustrate.

"Yes, no doubt," said the older man sourly.

An indignant look passed over Alexander's features. "Say now, you're not accusing *us* of anything, are you?"

Darby was surprised at the vehemence that flamed in Uncle Richard's eyes, but it quickly flared and died. "No, no," he said. "Far be it from me to suggest it. Even if you did such a thing, it would be a good jest, since I did not die as I might've."

A feeling of scorn welled in her heart. Did the man have no sense of dignity? The closer came her birthday and Alex's, the more her aunt and uncle groveled. They hoped to ingratiate themselves into their hearts and house, she knew. But did they realize it, such behavior only served to make Alexander and herself more contemptuous of them.

Still, she could not help feeling a little sorry for the man. "Shall we call the carriage, Uncle Richard? Would you care to go home and rest?"

"I would," he said fervently.

"I'll go with you," Simon said, and crossed the room. Taking Uncle Richard's elbow, he opened the door and guided him from the office without acknowledging Darby in any fashion. She watched him leave with a feeling of rage and loss that made her ache.

For the remainder of the day, she was of little use at the pottery. She could not stop thinking about Simon's words. It was unfair of him to believe she harmed children by employing them. Neither she nor Alex nor their father before them had ever been brutal or uncaring to the little ones; rather, they had been kind. Children were patiently taught their jobs and never beaten, even if the child failed to learn properly. The same compassion could not be found in many employers.

She'd always thought of herself as enlightened. But Simon was terribly disappointed in her, had accused her of making the pottery her god. What an absolutely horrid thing to say, and so untrue. Wasn't it?

Shortly before time to leave for the evening, Darby walked from her office to the balcony and watched the activity below, feeling the old stirrings of pride and dreams that the view always gave her. But now for the first time, she looked, really *looked*, into the faces of her workers. Some of them appeared happy, snapping quips back and forth; others seemed bored, disgruntled, even sad. The children in particular wore expressions of resigned endurance.

Did they, like her, have dreams? She had never considered it before, or if she had, she never dwelled upon it. Dreams would be a curse for people such as these, for how could they fulfill them? Had anyone asked her prior to this day what her employees wanted from life, she would have responded, "Food on the table, ale to drink, a shelter over their heads." Now she wondered, and the wondering made her uneasy.

Simon had ruined everything.

She descended the stairs and found Clemmy sitting on the floor beside his mother, Jane Goodehouse, who was hand-painting a transferred outline onto a platter. When Darby asked to speak with Clemmy privately, Jane became agitated.

" 'Ee's only taking a little rest, miss," she whined. "Get up, son. Go fill your bucket."

"No, do not," Darby said. "It's almost closing time. I

only want to ask him something." Conscious of Jane watching anxiously, Darby extended her hand and pulled the boy a few paces away. Crouching to his eye-level, she smiled and asked, "What would you like to do when you grow up, Clemmy?"

Looking surprised, he shrugged. "I dunno, miss."

"Oh, come now. There must be *something.*"

He glanced over her shoulder to his mother. Darby turned and saw Jane hurriedly resume her painting. "You may say anything you like; there is no right or wrong answer."

Looking thoughtful, he narrowed his eyes and explored his ear with a finger. "Dipping plates. I'd like dat."

"Is that all? There is nothing else you want, not in the whole wide world?"

"Can't tink of it. Oh, in de whole world?"

"Yes. Anything."

"A bucket of cherry pudding," he said solemnly. "And a rocking chair for Mamma."

Darby slowly stood upright. She didn't know whether to feel elated or disappointed. She felt vindicated that the child expressed no great ambition, but now she wondered, *Does he dream no dreams because he has no hope?*

That question and similar ones occupied her thoughts throughout the journey home and during dinner. She spoke only when spoken to, and then in the most dutiful manner. Neither Claude's flirtatious chatter nor Alex's worried looks (on the few occasions he tore his attention from Lenora) stirred her mood.

Simon was even worse than she. Over dinner, he ate sparingly and looked only at his plate. Except to answer a question of Aunt Gacia's about his plans for his upcoming performance at the birthday gathering, he spoke not at all. Afterwards, when the men joined the ladies in the parlor, Simon was not among them.

Without a thought for what the others might say, Darby

excused herself and went in search of him. She found him slumped in her father's leather chair in the library, a poker dangling from his fingers. The room was chilly, and a new fire crackled in the grate. When she entered and closed the door, he looked up, then leaned forward and stabbed the coals.

"I was just going to bed," he said, speaking to the flames.

"Were you? Is that why you started the fire?" Watching him closely, she slid into the chair opposite him. When he showed no signs of flight, she added in a soft voice, "This was always my father's favorite room."

"Mine, too."

"Truly?" She looked dubious, then a little amused. "I didn't realize you'd been in here before, but I keep forgetting you are an angel and can go anywhere. I haven't sat in this room more than twice since my father died. It makes me sad to do so."

"Don't let me keep you," he said, speaking so quietly she could scarcely hear.

Choosing to ignore his rudeness, she said, "I spoke with Clemmy this afternoon."

"Oh? Why? Did he fall behind in his work?"

"No, and I would not scold him if he did. You're not making this easy, Simon." She drew in several deep breaths to steady her voice. "I asked Clemmy what he wanted to be when he grew up."

"Did you?" Simon could not have sounded more disinterested.

"He wishes to dip plates and buy a chair for his mother."

Simon gave her a direct look. "And I suppose that means you were right. Clemmy is of a separate species from yourself. He was bred to do menial work and is happy with his lot."

Her lips tightened. "That could be. But again, it's possible his way of life prevents him from envisioning a better existence."

"I would say that's more than possible."

"But if that is so, Simon . . . if all children attend school as you suggest, and that schooling provides them with new skills and knowledge . . . what happens if no one wants to work in the pottery anymore?"

"Well, what if it does?" he asked, his voice rising. "That won't occur because there are varying levels of intelligence and ambition in every person; but if by some strange stroke of fate it *did* happen, do you think children should be kept in ignorance merely to maintain a labor force?"

"No, of course I don't! It's only that—oh, for all the—" She rubbed her temples in vexation, then dropped her hands to her lap. "What I'm trying to say is that I've thought about what you said. If I have been wrong, I want to know. I can change, Simon. I don't wish to cross heaven in this."

A distant gleam lit his eyes. "Don't change anything unless *you* wish to, Darby. Don't do it because you think I want you to, or because you're afraid you'll be punished if you don't."

"To be totally truthful, what I wish is that you had not brought this problem to my notice. But now that you have, I cannot rest until discovering if you're right. I don't wish to wrong anyone, but neither do I want to squander our funds. I've been thinking about it all afternoon. Do you believe it would be worthwhile to start a school for a short period of time, just to see if the children take to it?"

She was gratified to see the look of relief on his face. "I was hoping you'd reconsider." His elation dimmed slightly. "How short? It takes awhile for children to learn."

"I've thought about that, too. How long was it you said you planned to stay with us, Simon? Until my birthday?"

"Probably. It depends on my mission. Why?"

"It seems to me your mission is being accomplished without much interference from you," she said with a degree of bitterness. "Since Lenora discovered, or thinks she discovered, that you and I"—Darby flushed and

averted her eyes—"I mean, since she began to believe that
we—"

"Since she thought we were a couple," supplied Simon.

"Yes. Since then, she has directed her attention toward
Alex again, and he has responded like a schoolboy." Under
her breath she added, "Lenora's motives are transparent
as glass, yet my twin is blinded by dazzling eyes and golden
hair."

"Let's not argue about that again. Yes, I've noticed
things are going well in that direction." With some reluctance he added, "If it looks like they're going to make it,
I'd better leave the day after your birthday, as I planned."

"Only three weeks, then," she mused, then grew silent.
"Can you not stay longer?"

"It's best if I don't."

She studied him a moment more; then, forcing brightness into her voice, said, "The trial term will be three
weeks."

"Why so short? It'll be hard to see improvement in
that amount of time. Wait a minute. Darby, you can't be
thinking—"

"And why not? Alex and Lenora are fulfilling your
desires. You have nothing else to do."

"But I'm no teacher."

"Well, surely you don't expect *me* to do it. Children are
all very well in short doses, but all day long . . . I would go
mad."

"No," he said worriedly, "I didn't think you would play
teacher; you're too talented and suited for the work you're
doing. But me? Surely there's someone else who'd do a
better job."

She almost laughed in pleasure. *Talented and suited for
her work,* was she? And she'd wasted energy worrying that
he would condemn her for it. Life was full of surprises.

Seeing the insecure expression in his eyes, she could
not stop a teasing note from entering her speech. "What's

the matter, Simon? Are you ready to show others where they need improvement, but unwilling to undertake something improving yourself? For surely ministering to these children will be of an *edifying* nature." She lifted her eyebrows. "Well?"

He coughed a very long time, sounding almost consumptive. "Um," he hummed eloquently. "Three weeks? Sure. Why not?"

Darby's lips curved as she extended her hand. "We are in agreement, then. And you are not angry with me anymore? You no longer think I'm a hypocrite or a fake?" Very deliberately, she avoided that other embarrassing term he'd used. She wanted him to continue thinking she was a virgin, since she was; but she did not like being called a *saint* in such a derogatory way. He'd made chastity sound prudish, and that was not right.

Looking ashamed, he shifted forward and clasped her fingers between his hands. "I was never angry with you, only disappointed for awhile. Even then, I was too harsh."

"You said I was *self-righteous*, too," she added in an aggrieved voice, almost growing vexed again as she re-lived those awful moments in her office.

"I know. Sometimes you are, a little. No, don't fly off the handle again. I'm sorry I said those things. I have no right to expect perfection from you. Not when I'm far from perfect myself."

"So now I'm this very imperfect creature," she said coolly.

"Is that what I said, Darby? Did you hear me say that?"

"Not precisely, no. But it seems you are still casting judgments."

He chuckled. "No. For a few hours I forgot just how much a person can be influenced by his—her civilization. You're a product of your society, just as I am."

She could not maintain her irritation, not with his skin touching hers so warmly that even her toes felt hot. "Yes," she said softly, staring at his strong hands. "And how good it is that your society is a heavenly one."

It took him several seconds to respond. "Yes, isn't it?" he said. Giving her a melancholy smile, he released her fingers.

Chapter Eleven

During the journey to the pottery on the following morning, the tension inside the Brightings' carriage was running high. Since making the announcement over breakfast about starting the school, Darby had endured non-stop criticism from her brother and uncle. Simon felt her distress more than he did his own. He considered backing down for her sake but could not; Clemmy's peaked face and button eyes would haunt him for the rest of his life.

"This is ludicrous," pronounced Alexander for the tenth time. "Darby, I'm tempted to go against you in this."

"For once we are in agreement," said Uncle Richard while fingering his mustache. "Young lady, I beg you to reconsider. You'll make us the laughingstock of the village. Don't want to use my authority, but I will if I must."

Darby paled. "That is your legal right as our guardian, but it's a power that ends shortly. I've told you I want to try the school for only a few weeks. If you force me to delay, I'll insist upon a longer trial when it becomes my right to do so."

Uncle Richard gave a bark of laughter. "We're a bit high in the instep about our rights, hey? Considering it's your brother who inherits the whole, and you know what *he* thinks about your school."

"Hold a moment," said Alexander contentiously. "Whatever *I* inherit, *Darby* inherits, no matter what the rules of primogeniture. That is how Father intended it, and that is how it shall be. And if she wants to start a school or a—a trapeze academy, then we will."

Darby's eyes glowed with approval. "Thank you, brother."

Alexander nodded and stared grimly at his uncle. Simon exhaled slowly. He'd hoped the young man's loyalty to his sister would win out in the end, and it had. Or perhaps it was the sudden realization he and his uncle were espousing the same opinion. Whatever the reason, Simon was pleased to see Darby relax.

Uncle Richard waved his hands resignedly. "Oh, very well. If you're both determined to do this, I'll not stand in the way."

The gentlemen's capitulation seemed easy in comparison to the workers'. When Alexander made the announcement from the stairs in the main workroom, the outcry ranged from restive grumblings to shouts.

"I done all right and I niver 'ad schooling!" declared one.

"If our chillrun learn to read, they'll git uppity! Might even think they're better'n their folks!" yelled another.

But not all objected.

"Did you say we'd still git their wages?" asked Jane Goodehouse.

"They'll be paid the same as if they worked," Alexander replied.

"But only when they attend the school," Simon added.

"No getting them work elsewhere." Gloomy looks testified that some had already thought of this.

After the laborers were sent back to work, Simon spent the remainder of the day enrolling students and preparing the classroom. He learned that by their teens, most young-sters were able to earn an adult's wage and resented the idea of being thrown into a classroom; so he enrolled no pupils over twelve unless an older child requested it. As it turned out, none did; and few of the younger ones wanted it. In spite of their protests, he gathered fifteen students between the ages of six and eleven and put them to work sweeping floors and moving boxes and equipment from the room he'd chosen in the storage warehouse.

There was little time to contemplate his newest role. He'd spent half the previous night thinking about it, and he could not fool himself that he was going to flame into an educational firebrand. He had always liked children, but only one or two at a time. Even worse, he had an inbuilt abhorrence of rules and routine, and every school he'd ever attended had plenty of those. All he hoped was that he could provide a start for these children. Something had to be better than nothing.

Most important of all, the school provided him with an excuse to be near Darby. Maybe here he'd learn who her enemy was. At least he would be on hand to protect her. Her opponent might be a disgruntled employee, not a member of the family as he originally thought.

He shuddered to think about what he was doing to the future now. He'd read nothing about the Brightings pottery educating children, not in either timeline. But what was he supposed to do, nothing? Looking into the pinched faces of the youngsters working around him, he could not stop his heart or his hands from moving to help.

The selected room was large with adequate ventilation from two good-sized windows. After searching through the building, he found three rectangular tables and enough wooden chairs to provide seating. By the end of the day, the classroom was as ready as he knew how to make it. He called the solemn-faced children together, instructed them to come bright and early on the following morning, then dismissed them. It was then he realized that Clemmy was nowhere in sight.

"Try 'is mam," said a freckled girl named Sally Castle to Simon when he asked. " 'Ee likes to hide under 'er table."

But Clemmy wasn't there, nor was he in any of the rooms Simon searched after returning to the building that housed the school. It was not a good start, losing a child his first day as a teacher. Dreading a confrontation with a distraught mother, he returned to the main warehouse. It was then he spotted Clemmy at the far end near one of the kilns. He was little more than a shadow in the distance, but Simon could not mistake the silhouette of a small boy holding a bucket.

When Clemmy caught sight of Simon approaching him, he started as if intending to flee; then a look of bravado entered his eyes, and he held his ground.

"What happened to you, Clemmy?" Simon asked. "We missed you at school."

The little boy tossed a lock of hair from his eyes. "I don' like school. I like work."

"Aren't you being too hasty? We haven't really started yet. You might change your mind when you find what it's like." *Then again, you might not, seeing who your teacher is.*

"I make money for my mamma."

"You'll still make the same amount of money, Clemmy."

The child's lower lip began to tremble. "I like work."

Simon knelt on one knee and tilted his head. "What's really wrong, son? Are you afraid of school?"

"I ain't! Nobody can say I'm 'fraid!"

Jane Goodehouse, who had been watching them from her worktable across the room, put down the plate she was painting and rushed to her child. "What trouble are ye causing now, Clemmy Goodehouse?"

Tears filled the boy's eyes and spilled down his cheeks. "Georgy said Mr. Garret wud drash us if we din' know our lessons."

Simon's heart turned over with compassion. "I've never thrashed anyone in my life, Clemmy."

"Georgy says all teachers hate chillrun and dat's why dey teach, so's dey can hit 'em."

"Well, that's not true in my case. Now stop worrying, and put down that pail. I'll see you tomorrow morning." He nodded to Jane, then went upstairs to Darby's office to await closing time.

There were few secrets in the pottery, and the story of Clemmy came to Alexander's ears. Over dinner that evening, he shared it with the others at table, concluding merrily, "The children object to the school even more than I! Perhaps they will revolt and put an early end to it."

"I hope so," Uncle Richard said. "Don't know how we can keep up production without their hands, and you two are always wanting that above everything."

Darby forked a morsel of veal and suspended it before her mouth. "I'm interviewing for temporary workers tomorrow."

"What?" Alex exclaimed. "If we're already paying the children their normal wage, how can we afford to hire other workers?"

"It will not break us," she said, and began chewing her meat, her eyes on Simon.

"We must be doing famously then, Mr. Lightner," Aunt Gacia said with enthusiasm. "Your guidance has brought the platery to a new level of success, hasn't it? Note that, children; note it well. Perhaps now, Mr. Lightner, you will permit me to purchase the Indian silk for the twins' birthday? It will be more elegant than damask for a mature woman like myself."

"You would look elegant in homespun," Claude contributed, throwing Gacia into giggling protests.

"Do as you like, m'dear," responded Uncle Richard, waving his hand dismissively. "Extravagance appears to be the order of the day."

Lenora, who had remained unusually quiet since the subject of school had been mentioned, said in a serious voice, "I think it's a marvelous plan."

"Oh, thank you, dear," said Aunt Gacia eagerly. "You will weep when you see how brilliant are its colors—"

"No, I meant the school. I think it's a good idea to educate the children."

A startled silence met this remark. Simon stared, expecting to see scorn or cynicism on Lenora's face. He saw only sincerity.

Claude's fork clattered to his plate. Lowering his lids over bright, quizzical eyes, he commented, "Do you truly? One must wonder why."

"I think everyone deserves a chance to improve themselves. Besides, won't a worker who can read and figure be more valuable?"

"You surprise me," Alex said.

Aunt Gacia looked alarmed. "You are surprising him, Lenora. Speak truth now; you're feeling ill, aren't you, dear? Only tell us, and we'll excuse you until you are better."

"I'm not ill," she said. "I'd like to help with the school, if you need me."

Simon's pulse quickened. Was she trying to start with him again? The look she gave him across the table was not flirtatious, but maybe she was masking her feelings. Why would a woman like her want to become involved with a band of children? She *must* be after him.

Claude began to laugh. "What an excellent jest. Well scored, Lenora."

"Oh, thank heaven," sighed Aunt Gacia. "For a moment I thought—"

"I'm not jesting. I have always enjoyed children and would like to help teach them, if Simon will allow. I don't mean to interfere."

Simon felt Darby's eyes impaling him. But he couldn't deny a little help would be welcome. If anyone other than Lenora had asked, he would have jumped at the offer. As it stood, though . . .

"Are you certain it's the children you wish to aid, Lenora?" asked Claude slyly, directing a pointed look at Simon. "Or are you only searching for novelty again?"

Uncle Richard's voice rumbled worriedly. "Yes, Daughter. Can't allow some misguided impulse of—of generosity to take you from your duties at home."

"I have no duties at home. I'm bored all the time."

Alexander's hostile gaze had been flitting back and forth between Lenora and Simon for several moments. "Perhaps boredom is not the best reason to teach."

"Oh, it's not, it's not. Dear Lenora, listen to him," begged Aunt Gacia. "Sweet Alexander is right. You *must* hear him."

"All right," Lenora responded in a heavily resigned voice. "You are all correct, of course. It is not only that I hoped to teach to relieve my ennui; I confess I desired to be near the pottery. I have always wondered what it is Alexander and Darby do there. The school seemed to offer a perfect opportunity to observe and converse with them at odd moments of the day. But I realize now that I have been foolish, so think nothing more of it."

While the dining room crackled with conflicting emotions, Lenora began to eat her veal with an unconcerned air. After a moment, Alexander cleared his throat.

"I see no reason why you should not teach if you want to," he said in defensive tones.

"Indeed not," Aunt Gacia agreed. "Lenora is nothing if not kind-hearted. And intelligent, too, with an inquisitive mind. But not *overly* so, of course."

"Since the classroom is Simon's, perhaps he should speak his mind," Darby said challengingly.

Simon felt himself shrinking as all eyes turned to him. Maybe Lenora was being truthful in her insinuations; maybe she *did* hope to spend more time with Alexander. Elena had accused Simon many times of having an inflated ego. He had to stop thinking everything revolved around himself.

Moreover, he was trembling in his boots thinking about tomorrow.

"I *could* use the help," he heard himself say.

While Claude laughed uncontrollably, Darby tightened her lips. After glancing resentfully at Simon, she did not speak again the entire evening through.

By mid-morning on the following day, Simon had resigned himself to a secondary position in the classroom. After several increasingly impatient attempts to explain the nature of the alphabet, he had been swept aside by a laughing Lenora, who proceeded to make a game of the sounds each letter made. It was she who remembered to bring paper and quills, and the children bent to their practice with more eagerness than Simon thought possible. After awhile he began to suspect their compliance was due more to adoration of Lenora than any incipient desire for learning. Even Clemmy was captivated. When he tried to bolt from the classroom early that morning during Simon's attempt at teaching, Lenora drew the child aside and whispered to him for several moments. After that, he began to respond more than anyone.

Simon fell into his element at story time, though, when he delighted the children with hair-raising tales of fantastic adventures he recalled from Tay's books and cartoon videos. That the stories had yet to be written troubled him not at all. He was becoming increasingly bold in his time infractions, but what did the children care?

That afternoon, he also insisted on leading exercises and games. They had no equipment, though, and after one little girl received a bloody nose from a game of dodge-rock, he spoke to Lenora of his determination to procure ropes and balls at least.

"We should bring something for them to eat, too," Lenora said. "Have you seen what these children bring for their lunch? Some have no more than a piece of stale bread. It's disgraceful. No wonder they are so thin."

"I know. It wouldn't have to be expensive—freshly-baked bread and lots of it, with butter. And cheese and milk, maybe."

"And fruit, to put color in their cheeks," she added.

Simon agreed, then marvelled again at this very different woman whose face came alive, not at his presence, but at the proximity of children. He could not help remarking upon it as they sat outside watching the older students play while the younger ones slept in the shade of the warehouse on old packing blankets.

"My love for children surprises you?" she asked. "That's because you know very little about me. Confess now, Simon. You believed I used teaching as a ruse to seduce you. Last night at dinner, your face was alive with your fear of it."

He smiled ruefully. "Was it? I'm sorry."

She laughed. "Never mind, you are safe with me now. I would not have Darby's wrath fall upon me for the world. The truth is, I've enjoyed children since I was a youngster myself. My mother was ill much of the time, and the supervision of my younger brother often fell to me."

"You have a brother? I didn't know."

She looked into the distance. "Had. He died of the fever that claimed my mother's life."

"Oh, my God, how terrible for you. I had no idea."

"It happened a long time ago." She smiled faintly, her expression growing more thoughtful. "And then, when I lost my own baby, I thought never to be around children again. Especially after Reece died."

"You . . . lost a baby?"

"She was stillborn after I fell down a flight of stairs." In a testy voice she added, "It was an accident."

Simon could think of nothing to say. He suspected something dark lay unspoken behind her statement, but he could hardly question her; the wound seemed too raw.

The following day was Saturday, and school did not meet since the factory was open only until noon. A two-day downpour dampened plans to have the Wallaces to dinner on Saturday night, and on Sunday, no one, not even Darby, wanted to attend church in mud-caked shoes.

During the next week, Simon and Lenora fell into a routine at the school. Lenora directed the reading, writing, and arithmetic lessons in the morning. After a nourishing luncheon funded by the ever-loosening Brightings' purse, Simon conducted exercises, stories and singing.

He found himself forgetting for long periods that Darby remained in danger. No threatening villains appeared to lurk in the shadows, and the school came to occupy his thoughts to a degree that surprised him. The children were a kind of substitute for Tay, he supposed; especially Clemmy. But that was not all of it. He found a purpose and a nobility in the work that no role had ever given him. And most shocking of all, he felt a guarded friendship blossoming between Lenora and himself.

There were few problems with the children themselves. Most had learned self-discipline from their jobs, and other than a personality conflict or two among the youngsters, they presented none of the discipline problems Simon thought they would. Perhaps it was because the class was so small.

In a moment of inspiration, he decided to have the children perform for the birthday ball. "It'll be more meaningful than anything *I* can do," he told Lenora. "And it might make Darby and Alexander view the school more sympathetically. I have to find a guitar, though."

"I think Alexander is already convinced," said Lenora. "He comes to watch the children often enough."

Simon snorted. "He comes to see you."

"That may be, but he appears to be enjoying their progress in reading especially. Clemmy amazed him this morning by printing his name and sounding out the letters. Darby now . . . if she'd only visit us, perhaps we could convince her, too."

Simon shook his head hopelessly. Darby was avoiding the school and himself with a pointed determination. Every night he tried to interest her in Lenora and his—and increasingly Alexander's—excited chatter about the school. And every night she buried her nose in her book of sermons and contributed nothing.

Chapter Twelve

Very early on Thursday morning, not long after the grandfather clock tolled midnight, Darby heard the sounds of pebbles hitting her chamber window. Plagued with thoughts of Simon, Lenora and Alex, she had not yet slept, and now she alertly pushed her feet into her bedroom slippers, pulled on her robe, and padded to the window. Just as she peeked outward from the side of the drapes, a fresh assault of pebbles clattered on the glass. She cried out in alarm; then, realizing whose face peered up at hers, she tugged the draperies aside and opened the casement.

"Edward!" she whispered vehemently. "You have nearly killed me with fright."

"Sorry; couldn't help it," he whispered back. "I have to see you." His bright eyes entreated her in the moonlight. "You promised to give me an answer, remember?"

Darby groaned to herself as she recalled Edward's proposal of marriage. In truth, she'd forgotten to think about it these past days, so distracted was she by Simon's disloyalty to herself with Lenora and her mixed feelings about the school. "There will surely be a better time than the middle of the night," she complained.

"You said you'd tell me at the end of the week, and I've waited almost two."

"That's because I haven't seen you. Won't you wait until Saturday, when you come for dinner?"

"I can't bear another minute. If you don't join me now, I'll bay at the moon like a wolf and wake everyone!"

Darby sighed. "Oh, very well, I'm coming." She walked as softly as she could from the room, down the stairs, and out the parlor door, it being quieter and easier to unlatch than the front.

Edward awaited her on the terrace. With one hand hidden behind his back, he stood between a pair of iron-worked chairs. When they both were seated, Darby said, "Truly, Edward, I don't know why we must discuss this now. Should anyone see me sitting with you in my nightgown, it would cause a scandal."

"Not if you're going to be my bride." He withdrew his hidden hand and offered her a battered rose. "Well, are you?"

Darby reluctantly took the flower. Unable to look into his earnest face, she stared at the rose and felt moisture gathering in her eyes. "Oh, Edward."

"I picked it off one of your own bushes. Not very romantic, I suppose."

"No, it is not," she said, giggling tearfully. "But it's so like you. You're a dear, Edward . . . the best friend anyone could ever have."

"Hopefully I'm such a good friend that you never want to part from me."

"Oh, I never do. I trust our friendship will always remain; but . . ."

"But you don't wish to marry me," he finished, then jumped up and stalked to the railing. "Have I agonized for two weeks only to hear you won't have me?"

For one crazed moment, Darby imagined throwing herself into his arms and crying, "No, no, you have misunderstood; I will marry you." It was what Simon had advised. But Edward deserved a wife who truly loved him, and she did not. Her heart was already lost—irredeemably lost, without hope of return or reciprocation.

"I'm sorry," she said so softly that he was forced to read her lips.

"You're sorry," he huffed. "And so you should be. Is it Heathershaw or that actor who's stolen your heart? Neither one is worth a farthing."

Darby wiped her eyes on her sleeve, then went to lean against the rail. "I won't lie to you, Edward; I do love someone, even though I know that love is hopeless. But, having experienced this—this painful, excruciating . . . *joy,* I believe that what you feel for me is the fondness of long friendship, not the deep love necessary for marriage. I cannot deny you the pleasures of such a union someday. You are the finest man and deserve—"

"Oh, stop it, will you? Don't speak to me of love and friendship or tell me how I love you. *I* know my own emotions, not *you;* and I'd like to chop my rival's head off his shoulders. Why won't you tell me who it is?"

She shook her head mutely and looked at her hands.

Balling his fists, he swept past her and ran down the few stairs to the grass. "Don't expect us here for dinner Saturday night or your birthday. I can't watch you throw our future away for—for nothing! A foolish dream!"

She watched him stride away and disappear around the corner of the house. There came the sound of a horse's snort, then hoofbeats. She sank into the chair, a storm of tears rising. Nothing grieved her more than hurting Edward. But it was the right decision, the only decision, she could have made. How sad it was she could not order her heart as she did her workers.

And what to do with herself now? Simon was killing her.

His growing friendship with Lenora hurt her more than his supposed romance had, strangely enough.

Darby no longer feared he would succomb to the widow's machinations, not after the conversation they had when she became convinced he loved her. To be truthful, Lenora did not appear to exert herself in that manner to him either; her flirtations seemed confined to Alex now, which was bad enough in its own way. But it galled to see the three of them talking night after night of the school and the children as if it were all a great game instead of an experiment, when it was *she* who had fought to give Simon the right to start the entire venture.

And had they forgotten the experiment was supposed to end when her angel left? For days, Alex had not mentioned putting the children back to work. Perhaps he had changed his mind and wanted the school to continue. If so, who would run it? Lenora? Alex? If she did not feel so badly, so *left out of things*, she would have laughed at the idea of either one of them heading it.

Were it not for Claude Heathershaw's fawning attentions to herself, she would feel no one loved her anymore.

Sitting in the hard chair beneath an uncaring moon, her eyes and mind cleansed by a bath of tears, Darby heard her thoughts with clarity for the first time in a week. And then she did laugh. She was reacting like a spoiled child. She had allowed her mind to become ensnared in pettiness when all the time it was a deeper cut that threatened her well-being. The school had diverted her from thinking about it for awhile, that was all; but she could push it aside no longer.

Simon was leaving soon. Her amusement crumbled.

What would she do when he left? How could she live without her angel's physical presence? It did little good to imagine him watching over her invisibly; she wanted to see his expressive eyes when they spoke together; to feel his hand touch her lips, soft as an angel's feather.

Before a fresh squall of tears consumed her, she returned inside and locked the door. Half-blinded by watery eyes, she picked her way up the stairs. As she started to enter her room, a sudden noise made her pause. Another door was opening down the hall—Lenora's. When Claude exited in his nightshirt and robe, followed by a gesticulating Lenora in a nightgown that little disguised the ripe body beneath it, Darby felt her eyes bulging from her head.

Hearing her gasp of shock, both of them stood motionless, returning stare for stare with Darby. She was the first to move. Feeling oddly unreal, she shook her head angrily and rushed inside her room.

Seconds after closing the door, she heard light footsteps racing down the hall, then a scratching on the wood. With her back pressed against the door, she whispered furiously, "Go away! I don't want to speak with either one of you!"

The scratching persisted. Afraid above all things that they would awaken her brother, she jerked the door open a crack. Instantly, Lenora positioned her face within inches of Darby's, and Claude's loomed above.

"Please let me in," Lenora begged. "I can explain."

"No, you can't," Claude whispered sternly. "Allow me a moment, Darby, and *I* will explain."

While Lenora glared over her shoulder at Claude, Darby said bitterly, "There is nothing either one of you can say. Go away and leave me alone."

"You won't tell Alexander, will you?" Lenora beseeched desperately. "At least not until you let me talk with you."

Darby moved to close the door. "I make no such promises. Now do you leave, Lenora; surely you must be cold. You don't want to catch something."

Claude, a look of humorous appeal crossing his face, clutched the door and prevented Darby's shutting it. "Lenora and I were just talking over old times. She was showing me a miniature she had made of Reece. Weren't you, Lenora?"

Darby leaned all her weight against the wood. "You—must—think—I—am—a—gudgeon."

"No, we don't," Claude said breathlessly, pushing against Darby's resistance. "It's you I love, Darby. Truly. Don't you remember the poem I wrote?"

"If you don't release this door," Darby gasped, "I—will—scream."

A grim, hopeless look came into Lenora's eyes. "Come, Claude," she said. "Let her be."

Claude exchanged an unreadable glance with Lenora, then shifted his gaze to Darby. After studying her face, he gave a defeated shrug and whipped his hands from the wood. The door slammed. Darby locked it, then leaned against it panting, fearing someone would investigate the noise. All she heard were the sounds of footsteps retreating.

She lifted her chin and stared at the ceiling. She cared not a whit about Claude's perfidies; she had never taken his overtures seriously anyway. But she had been breaths away from accepting what she believed was a new Lenora. Now her heart ached for what she must reveal to her brother. Were all of them—Alex, Edward, Evelyn and herself—doomed to hopeless loves?

What should she do? Even though she halfway regarded him now as a traitor, she thought, *Simon will know.* With only a passing notion of how it would look if *she* were seen by anyone, Darby opened her door, saw the hall was unpopulated, and slipped around the corner to Simon's room.

She had learned he was a sound sleeper on her last visit to his chamber; therefore, she was not surprised when he failed to answer her knock. After waiting only the smallest amount of time, she opened the door and was jolted to see him not in bed as she expected, but seated in a chair facing the window.

At her entry he whirled around, his bedside candle dancing light and shadow across his features. Seeing her, he stepped backward, shrouding himself in the fainter illumination of the window. But it was too late; she had already noted the savaged eyes and the lost expression on his face. Oh, he might murmur her name, then busy himself tying the sash of his robe and raking his fingers through hair already growing shaggy, but he could not mask his sorrow. What troubled him so deeply? Could it be the same grief that pierced her heart? But that would be hoping for more than an angel could give.

"Simon?" she ventured, hating the yearning tone she heard in her voice, but it could not be helped; for the moment she did not even recall why she came. "What is wrong?"

He made no reply, only looked away from her.

She circled the bed and walked closely enough to feel his breaths upon her skin. Lifting trembling fingers toward him, she stroked the wetness from beneath his left eye. As she reached toward his other cheek, he clasped her wrist.

"Don't," he whispered.

She lowered her hand, her gaze fastened to his. "Why do you weep, Simon?"

He did not answer for a long time.

"Do you believe in God?" he queried finally.

She was astonished. "You ask me that with yourself standing there?"

"No, no. Pretend you never met me. Did you always believe in God?"

"Of course." Her reply sounded impatient, but she felt impatient at such a foolish question. Seeing the haunted look in his eyes, though, she searched for a more meaningful answer. "How else to explain the wonders of this world? Surely such a beautiful Creation could not happen by accident."

"But what about the ugly things? The disasters, the murders, the endless suffering of the innocent?"

"I have heard it said that man brings evil upon himself,"

she replied, bewildered. "Why do you ask these questions? Are you testing me, Simon?"

"Maybe I'm testing myself. If man *does* cause evil, why does God permit it?"

She thought carefully. "Mr. Gravitt says that no earthly Father would lock his offspring in a cell simply to keep him from harm, no matter how concerned he is for his safety, for the child would never grow up and learn to make his own decisions or experience life. Therefore, God allows mankind freedom with both its pleasures and its consequences."

Simon looked down. "Consequences. Better to call it torture. And do you know what torture is, Darby? It's being able to see or imagine how your life *could* be, had you made the right choices. I want so much, but there are things I can't have. I reach my hand out to grab what I need"—he gestured in the air, pantomiming—"and when I open my fingers, nothing's there."

She stared at his hand as if mesmerized. "What is it that you need, Simon?"

His gaze drifted back to hers, looking so sad and full of longing that she felt tears spring to her own eyes. Then, with a deliberation that made her ache, he leaned toward her.

She now had no doubt what it was Simon thought he needed. Blood pounded in her ears. Her angel was going to kiss her, and she was not going to stop him. Was there no end to her wickedness? *Was there no end to* his?

But when his lips were within inches of hers, he froze, straightened, and stepped sideways, clearing his throat. "Why did you come here?" he asked politely, eyes averted.

The mood was broken. She did not know whether to applaud or scream. It had been a narrow escape. Why, then, did her heart pound with regret?

Suddenly recalling the events prior to her entering this

room, she said, "Oh. I have just seen Claude leaving Lenora's bedchamber."

His attention sharpened. "Did you?"

"Yes, and they were both dressed in their night raiment."

He hesitated. "Well, Darby, the same could be said for you and me, and nothing indiscreet is happening between *us*. Don't go accusing people of things when you don't have all the facts."

Her disappointment grew warm. "You say that only because you don't want anything interfering with your plans." She tightened her lips. "And I'm not so certain nothing indiscreet happened between us."

"I never laid a hand on you!"

"Oh, I know *that;* I know it very well. But something almost did happen here, and you cannot deny it." She blushed at the sound of her own admission.

"*Almost* is not the same as *did*, Darby, and you have to grant Lenora the benefit of doubt. Don't be so holier-than-thou. It drives me crazy when you do that."

"Alas, does it? Would you care to know what drives *me* crazy, or mad, or whatever? Your noble understanding of everything pertaining to Lenora, no matter *what* she does!" She began to pace, gesticulating extravagantly. "But of course I know why you do it. Above everything else, Lenora must marry Alex! It doesn't matter to you if she possesses the desires of a Cyprian—only let Simon's mission be accomplished! And now, I suppose, the school is added to your list of reasons to canonize Lenora. Well, it will never do. My brother is more important to me than that, and I will *never* allow him to be misled into lifelong unhappiness."

"I don't expect you to," he said, suddenly placating. "If I find she is—is like you say, then I won't . . ."

"Yes?" She folded her arms. "You won't . . .?"

"I—" A light knocking could be heard at the door.

Looking vastly relieved, he moved toward it. "Someone's knocking."

"So it seems," she said scornfully.

His steps halted. "Don't you think you should hide?"

Darby's eyes rounded. "Oh!" Wild-eyed, she glanced around the chamber for a suitable place, then dashed into his dressing room and pulled the door closed to a sliver.

When Simon opened his chamber door, Darby was dismayed to see Lenora edge into the room and look past him inquiringly. "Where's Darby?" she asked. "I know she must be here."

To Darby's intense irritation, Simon said nothing. Why did he not push the merry widow back into the corridor? Darby would have done as much for him. But he simply stood there like a great lump, and now Lenora was staring at the closet door and beginning to smile. And then, with the relentlessness of a figure from a nightmare, she drew near.

"Thank God I found you. I tried your room again, and when I couldn't get an answer I decided to look downstairs. On the way I heard voices and guessed you might be with Simon."

"I don't know why you'd think that," said Darby, frowning at how ridiculous her defense sounded since she was indeed here. Grumpily she emerged from the dressing room and leaned against the rail at the foot of the bed.

"Well, I certainly didn't believe you'd be guilty of what you thought Claude and I were doing, even if you were hiding in Simon's dressing room. I know you too well for that, Darby."

"I don't understand what you mean by that, either," returned Darby, who could not be pleased by anything Lenora said.

Simon pulled his chair near the bed and gestured toward it. As Lenora sat, he commented, "Darby told me you had a visitor tonight."

"I thought she would. That's why I'm glad I found the two of you together. I realize what you saw looked compromising, Darby, but I assure you nothing happened between Claude and me."

"See?" Simon said, childlike in his eagerness. "I told you nothing happened."

Darby grunted her disbelief.

"Well, the two of you are in exactly the same circumstances, and I haven't accused *you* of anything," Lenora reminded her.

"Yes, but as you said, that is because you know me," Darby replied. "The reason I believe something happened in *your* bedroom is because I know *you.*"

"Well, thank you very much," Lenora said coldly.

"Ladies ..." Both of them looked at Simon, who stretched his hands entreatingly and smiled. When he seemed unable to think of anything further to say, the women returned their hostile gazes to one another.

"You will understand better when I explain," Lenora began. "Claude was a good friend to both my husband and me, as you know—"

"I'm certain Reece rests happy knowing your friendship continues," interjected Darby, her words sizzling like drops of acid.

"I will admit Claude and I had a liaison," Lenora went on, obviously struggling to keep her temper. "But not since my husband died."

Darby rose, towering over her adversary. "You are a terrible woman, Lenora. Do you expect us to believe that you acted dishonorably during your marriage, but now—now that you're unfettered, you've developed a conscience?"

Lenora eased out of the chair and straightened to her full height. "Reece had his liasons, and I had mine. As long as we were discreet about it, neither of us minded what the other did. It was unconventional, I realize, but our relationship was strained."

"Unconventional is not the word I'd choose," Darby said.

"You'd be surprised at the marriages that are unconventional in that way," Simon said unexpectedly. "I'm not casting blame, Lenora, but . . . how many?"

"That's a most impertinent question," she said. "Were I not here to throw myself on your mercy, I would refuse to answer it." She fingered the fringe that hung from the sash of her robe. "Besides Claude, there were one or two others, briefly. Claude lasted longer because of proximity—he traveled with us much of the time—and because I imagined he was . . . amusing."

"But you don't find him amusing anymore?" Simon persisted.

"No." Her face darkened. "He pressures me to resume our former status, but I will not."

"And if you believe that," Darby said, "you will believe anything."

"It is the truth!" Lenora cried.

Simon moved excitedly. "Did Reece know about your affair with Heathershaw?"

"He learned of it," Lenora said in a small voice, "a few days before he died. He was angry because I'd chosen Claude, his friend. He . . . felt it was a betrayal of sorts."

Darby exchanged a speculative look with Simon. "Was this the cause of your argument on the day Reece fell from the window?" she asked, deliberately moving her gaze from Simon's when he showed alarm at her question.

Lenora regarded her in a strained silence. "How did you hear about that?"

"If you recall, we were visiting you at the time."

"Yes, but I thought you and Alexander attended an assembly that day."

"And so we did, but what does that matter? Your common, liquored display gave exercise to more than one tongue at the hotel.''

Lenora lowered her eyes. "I see. How elegantly you put it. Yes, the affair was the major portion of our disagreement." She laughed humourlessly. "Reece even threatened to tell everyone I was—a" She darted a look at Darby—"I was immoral. As if there was anyone who cared. I suppose you think I received what I deserved, but I was half-mad with grief the last few months of my marriage and hardly knew what I was doing."

"Grief? Oh, yes, the baby." There was little sympathy in Darby's voice. "We were all sorry you lost your child, but you're not the first mother to be so unfortunate; yet to my knowledge, no others have taken lovers to console themselves."

"What do you know of it?" Lenora blazed. "How easy for you to pass judgment on people, you with your beautiful brother who loves you more than his own life, you with your factory to run and handsome suitors falling at your feet! What do you know of failed dreams, of genteel poverty, of disappointment! How dare you cast aspersions on the way I live my life, when you have never known brutality or want!"

Lenora was trembling with anger. In the sudden quiet of the room, Darby's ears began to ring. Simon went to the widow and clasped Lenora's arms in a soothing gesture.

"Brutality, Lenora?" he asked gently. "Did Reece . . . hurt you?"

Without looking at him, she said, "Yes. Not often, but moreso near the end. When he lost at the gaming tables he fell into rages, and that was happening more and more."

Simon's fingers tightened on her arms. "You told me you lost your baby through an accident. That wasn't true, was it?"

Lenora's gaze dropped to the floor. Almost imperceptibly, she shook her head. "Reece pushed me down the stairs. He said—he said he would not be responsible for another man's child. And that—that was before I ever . . .''

She was unable to continue. Simon, gazing at Darby with expressionless eyes, enfolded Lenora within his arms while she wept.

Darby watched them, horrified. If Lenora lied, she was the best actress on earth. Although Darby did not condone Lenora's behavior, she had gone a long way toward understanding it. She could not even feel jealous that the widow was experiencing something she never would—the feel of Simon's arms around her, the sound of his heartbeat beneath her cheek. Moving stiffly, Darby placed a hand on Lenora's back. It was as much a gesture of apology as comfort.

"I'm sorry," she said.

Lenora mumbled something, wept awhile longer, then broke away from Simon. He handed her his handkerchief, and she dried her eyes and blew her nose.

"You must forgive me," she said, composure returning. "I've spoken more than I should. It was not my intention to re-live old troubles. I only hoped to beg you both to remain silent about what Darby saw this night." Her hopeful eyes flickered between them.

Darby took a deep breath and prayed she was not about to disappoint her angel again. "I'm very saddened by what you have revealed, but you're asking me to hide something from my brother whom *I* love more than my own life."

Lenora laughed thickly. "I see you're throwing my own words back to me. But be honest with yourself. Have you never hidden anything from Alexander?"

Lenora's expression took on a crafty look as she glanced from Simon to Darby, causing the younger lady to think, *This is the merry widow I know and detest.*

"I have never hidden anything that might hurt him later," she responded. And so that Simon would not scold her for piousness, she added swiftly, "But I'm willing to remain quiet so long as *you* tell him."

"I . . . tell him?" Lenora pressed shaking fingers over her mouth.

Darby rejoiced to see approval shine in Simon's eyes. "It will be easier coming from you," he said.

Lenora's gaze wandered blankly around the room. "Very well, I shall. But give me a little time, will you?"

"I see no purpose in delaying," Darby said.

"A *little* time," Simon said decisively. "Not a lot. Soon."

"I will," Lenora said gladly, then glided to the door. "I want you to know, Darby, that I truly love your brother. At first he seemed like a child to me; but now I've come to appreciate his many good qualities; especially since he's shown interest in the school. I've learned he's a gentle man and capable of deep affection and loyalty. Those traits are remarkably important to me. And though he *is* short-tempered, it's in a way entirely different from Reece."

"You need not describe his character to me," Darby said in irritation.

"I know. I only wanted to convey to you how highly I esteem him, and that if he returns my regard in the way I think he might, I will make the most loyal of wives. You need not fear I would ever betray my marriage vows. That is behind me."

Darby swelled with vexation. "And I wish to convey to *you* that Evelyn Wallace has been promised—in a manner of speaking—to Alex since we were babes. Evelyn would make a loyal wife, too, as well as a chaste one with an unblemished character."

Lenora winced. "Your aim is true, Darby, and you know precisely where to strike. But let me ask you this, would you consign your brother to a loveless marriage simply because it appears more socially acceptable? For I'll tell you this, if you do not already realize it: Alexander does not love Evelyn; he loves me."

"You think so now," Darby said, her voice quivering. "But speak to me later, after you have talked with him about your past. You may discover another trait that I well know. Alex is not very forgiving."

"And neither are you," Lenora whispered, opening the door and entering the hall. "Good night, Simon."

"Good night, Lenora," he said.

Darby waited a moment, then ran to the door and peered out. Seeing no sign of the widow other than smelling the scent of lavendar, she closed the door and returned to Simon. "Do you think she killed Reece for revenge?"

Simon did not answer immediately. He looked so forbidding that by the time he did, her excitement had drained away. "You are some piece of work, do you know that?" He sounded disgusted, as if he wanted her out of his sight.

She knew instantly the source of his anger, and this time she vowed he would not make speeches about how much higher his opinions were than her own, even if he *was* from heaven. "I only want the best for my brother. No, do not tell me I'm a Sunday girl, or whatever it was you called me that time. If Lenora is best for Alex, then so be it. If he is willing to accept her after she tells him the truth, *I* will; I'll not so much as present an argument against her. But he must have all the facts first."

Simon's face relaxed. "Really? That's how you feel?"

"She would not be *my* choice, mind, but if Alex chooses her . . . yes. That's how I feel." Even if it killed her. Her angel had changed her that much.

"Well." He sat on the bed and crossed a leg over his knee. "I'm impressed. There's hope for you yet."

She felt absurdly pleased. "I'm glad to hear you think so. Now . . . do you think she murdered Reece in revenge for killing her baby?"

"Do I think she killed Reece? No, no, and no. Once again I ask you to look at her and tell me how such a tiny woman could throw a man off a balcony."

"I grow weary of hearing how petite she is!"

Simon laughed. She was gratified to see his good humour returning, but hers had flown out the window. "Also," he said, "in spite of what you think, I don't believe Lenora is the type to murder anyone. Heathershaw, now, is another story—was he there when it happened?"

"Yes," she said, her voice full of doubt. "But he was taking a walk when Reece died."

"Did anyone see him?"

"Well, no . . . but Claude is not the murdering type, as you call it, either."

"You think that because he flatters you constantly."

The annoyance with which he said this brought a smile to her lips. "Oh, does he?"

"Don't pretend you haven't noticed."

Her heart leaped in delight. He was *jealous!* She bit her lower lip to refrain from laughing out loud. "Even if I had, do you think I'm incapable of objectivity?"

"Yes, I do," he said, still irritated.

She pondered that for a moment, then decided to let it pass. "But why would Claude murder Reece?"

"Maybe he desired Lenora for himself."

"If that was what he wished, he wasn't very successful. And now he gives every appearance of wanting me."

Simon's eyes darkened. After a moment, he said, "Who wouldn't?"

Darby stared at her slippers. "Well, Edward for one." She said it reluctantly, though in truth she had waited all this time for a chance to confess it to him. "Not after I refused him this evening."

"You saw—" His voice rang unexpectedly loud, and he modulated it quickly. "You saw Edward tonight?"

"Yes, he threw rocks at my window, and I told him I could not marry him. Please forgive me, Simon; I know you said I *should*, but I simply cannot. It wouldn't be fair to Edward since I love him only as a friend. Are you angry?

Your suggestion that I wed him was merely that, wasn't it—a suggestion? God did not command it?''

"No," he said, his lips quirking alarmingly, "it was just an idea of mine. How did Edward take your refusal?''

"Badly, I'm afraid. He refused to come to dinner Saturday night or to attend the ball. I have never seen him so angry."

She was surprised when he looked disturbed, and even more so when he clutched her into the embrace she never expected to feel. Moments before she'd fought envy that Lenora rested here, and now, now it was herself who gloried within his arms.

Yet, though her temples pounded at the warmth that poured through her body at his touch, there was little romance to be felt; the embrace spoke too much of protection, of desperation, for that. But she cared little—she could dwell happily here forever, no matter what strange emotions wavered through his skin.

He loosened his arms for an instant, then gripped her fiercely again. Her smile was pressed against his robe like a butterfly beneath glass. She did not care if he flattened her into a plate. "Darby," he whispered into the hair at the top of her head, "I have something very strange to request of you, and you mustn't ask questions about it. All right?''

If she opened her mouth, she would be forced to taste his robe, so she merely nodded against his chest. *Please say you have chosen to be an angel no longer, and that you want to marry me,* she begged silently. Would God allow such a thing? It didn't seem likely.

Simon drew in a swift breath, then held her at arm's length. "Promise me that you will not, under any circumstances, visit the pond. Especially not on your birthday. I intend to be around so that you don't; but just in case anything happens to separate us, you'll remember, won't you?''

Darby nodded, wide-eyed as a little girl agreeing to keep a friend's secret. She was too astonished and numb to feel disappointment at his unexpected demand.

"Good," he said, his eyes filling with sadness again.

They exchanged lingering glances, the air between them crackling with words that ached to be born. When she could bear it no longer, Darby took her leave. After he closed the door, her feet remained planted in the carpet outside his room. Finally, when her toes began to fall asleep, she turned and stumbled off to bed.

Chapter Thirteen

Simon waited on the other side of his door until he heard Darby move away, then removed his robe and threw it over the bedpost. After piling one pillow atop another, he climbed into bed and leaned against the soft stack. He knew he wouldn't be able to sleep, but he pulled the covers to his chest anyway. He had some serious thinking to do.

If he were home, he'd flip on a late-night talk show. But there was a lot to be said for a candlelit room so quiet he could hear the dust fall. There was a lot to be said about this whole time period in general. But was it enough?

Could he leave his century, his world, his career, his life, for the love of a woman? Especially for a woman like Darby, who was as exasperating as she was exhilarating?

But if he returned, how could he live knowing he'd left her? He was so far gone now, he loved everything about her: her idealism; her innocent faith (even in her angel, though he'd let her down again and again); her adorable jealousies and lack of pretense; her fierce loyalty to those she loved; the way her eyes held his, tantalizing him with hidden passions but at the same time calling him to be better than he was.

He liked himself when he was around her. She needed him; needed his rationality—all right, his sensitivity, though it unmanned him to admit it—to round the edges off her inflexible side. She made him forget his failures; somehow, she made him *better*.

But was it enough? Could he turn his back on the twentieth century and declare, "Here I stay?"

He didn't know.

It would be good to settle it, to end the escalating agony of the past weeks. In spite of his interest in the school, he was in constant mourning over their coming separation.

If only the pathway would let *her* go back with *him*. But that wasn't fair, either; then she'd have to make all the sacrifices.

First things first. He had to get her through her birthday alive, and the list of suspects was growing. First Lenora, then Edward, now Heathershaw.

He was least suspicious of Lenora but knew better than to dismiss her entirely. As for Edward, it made him cold to imagine the boy's anger at Darby's rejection; the kid wouldn't be the only thwarted boyfriend to think of murdering the girl. And Heathershaw; why was the man here, anyway? If Lenora wasn't lying and really spurned his advances, why didn't she throw him out? Was he blackmailing her because he knew something about Reece's death? Had he helped Lenora kill him? Would Heathershaw try to murder Darby because she would discover something?

Simon sighed wearily. He could lose his mind imagining the possibilities. *Nothing must happen to her.*

The days before her birthday passed in hurried confusion for Darby. The pottery had received a large order from London for Alex's nurseryware, and she became busy supervising the increased production. Aunt Gacia, into whose hands she had given the direction of the ball, plagued her with constant questions over foods, entertainments, and changes in the invitation list. Also, Darby had commissioned a new dress for the event, and there were fittings to be endured.

The school nagged at her thoughts frequently. The parents of the students were beginning to accept it, though a few still complained their children's time would be better spent learning a trade. And while Alex had not precisely endorsed it, he no longer voiced objections. That was Lenora's doing, of course.

Darby remained unsure as to her own opinion. Although she still believed the effort wasteful, she determined to wait and see before deciding. But before the three-week trial period ended, the events of one morning taught her where her loyalties lay.

Uncle Richard entered her office holding an official-looking document, which he placed on her desk. "Look here, m'girl. The signatures of Mirren's leading manufacturers, asking us to close the school."

"Oh?" She studied the paper coldly. "And what business is it of theirs what we do?"

"Ha! More than you think. Seems their workers are threatening to quit unless they get classes for their brats, too."

She felt a smile coming. "Is that so?"

Uncle Richard looked offended. "Don't know why you think 'tis amusing. Can't fly against the wind of our fellows or we'll lose business."

Standing dismissively, she said, "I don't believe that will happen, but even if it does, I'll not be told what to do in my own factory. Whatever Alex and I decide, it will be *our* decision, not theirs."

Uncle Richard glared. "Hope you won't come to regret it."

After he left, Darby was too stirred to concentrate on the stack of purchase orders awaiting her. She seized the petition and went in search of Alexander.

She was not surprised to find him in the classroom, but she *was* startled to see him helping Molly write her numbers. Simon and Lenora were also bent over students, and she felt a pang she did not entirely understand as she watched through the glass door.

At her entrance, everyone looked up, making her feel oddly shy. When she saw looks of hope and eagerness on their faces, especially Simon's and Alex's, she felt even more strange. Their expressions reminded her of children beseeching an irrational parent for justice. She had often felt as they looked, asking Uncle Richard to update the pottery.

She smiled uncomfortably and fixed her gaze on Alexander. When he joined her at the back of the room, she showed him the petition.

"Of all the crack-jawed insolence," he whispered. "I have a mind to continue the school just to spite them."

"Do you? To say truth, I'd begun to think you had made up your mind already."

He looked toward the children guiltily. "If I had, how would you feel about it?"

Indignation flared within her, then cooled. She spoke slowly, sorrow weighting her words. "That depends on *why*. Have you reached your opinion objectively, or because you want to please Lenora?"

"I'll pretend you didn't say that," he replied haughtily.

"Don't put your nose in the air with *me,*" she said, then lowered her voice when several children turned to stare. "Has Lenora spoken with you about . . . anything?"

"She speaks with me all the time. Why? Did you mean something in particular?"

Across the room, Lenora straightened, met Darby's

probing gaze, then looked from her to Alexander. Smiling, she bent over the child's paper again.

How long did the woman intend to wait?

"No," Darby said between her teeth. "Nothing . . . in particular."

Alexander grinned. "Look. Why don't you stay awhile? How can *you* be objective if you don't know what goes on here?"

She began to protest about the amount of work awaiting her, but when her eyes fell upon Simon, she changed her mind. Alexander led her to the table of the youngest children, where she heard one after another recite their letters and write. She was amazed at the varying levels of ability among them. One little girl knew her entire alphabet, while others still struggled. By the time Darby had seen the more advanced progress of the older children, she was impressed, and not only by the students. The compassion, the patience, with which Simon, Lenora and even Alex treated the youngsters took her breath away. Especially Simon. She had never loved him more than when watching him guide Clemmy's hand after the boy failed tearfully in making one of his letters.

She stayed for the greater part of an hour. As she left, the children waved and smiled goodbye. She returned their salutation in a friendly fashion, walked a few paces away from the door so they could not see her, then leaned against the wall. If she were not careful, the dreadful longing inside her would make her cry.

Without real surprise, she saw Simon emerge from the classroom. "I'm glad you came," he said, a strange, burning look in his eyes making her heart race. "What did you think?"

"The children are learning well," she said. "You and Lenora are fine teachers. Even Alex is."

"Fine enough to continue the school?"

She fastened her gaze on one of his vest buttons. "This

is not a judgment to be made lightly. I still have a few days before making my final decision, do I not?"

"Yes, but . . . have you ever felt, Darby, that some things are so important that only one answer can be made? And that you have only to make it before realizing that every event, every feeling, has been leading up to that one, perfect decision?"

Startled at the excitement she sensed in him, she looked up. "Are you—are you speaking of the school?"

"I'm talking about any decision that involves your life and your heart and . . . your soul."

"Simon." She could not disguise the hope that surged into her voice. "One of the reasons I'm doubtful about continuing the school is that I don't entirely trust Lenora to maintain her interest in it. If you, now, were to remain awhile longer . . ."

"That's not totally impossible," he said, his eyes glowing.

"Simon!" Only an odd reticence on his part kept her from jumping into his arms. "I thought you had to return to—"

"Shh. No more about this now. I . . . have to tell you something, but not until after your birthday. Then, after we talk, if you still want me to stay, we'll see."

"But there's no reason to wait until then," she said eagerly. "I have just about decided about the school anyway. In fact—"

"No, Darby. After your birthday, okay?"

She stared at him in frustration.

"Okay, Darby?" he repeated.

"Okay," she answered, rolling the unfamiliar word off her tongue and not liking it at all, though it made him laugh to hear her say it.

From that point on, she was useless to all sensible thought. Did he mean to stay? But how could he? During the next days, her curiosity and hope drove her to try speaking with him privately on several occasions, but he avoided being alone with her. One evening she even attempted to visit him in his room again, but he did not answer her knock; and when she turned the knob, she found he'd locked the door.

What if she'd misunderstood him? She couldn't bear the disappointment if she had.

It was most disturbing. Thus when she stood before her mirror on the evening of her birthday, she took only distant pleasure in her appearance. The soft blue-grey of her satin gown matched her eyes precisely; its low-cut bodice narrowed to a trim waistline (which felt strange, since it was seamed at her actual waist instead of beneath the bust as had been the fashion for years); below it, the gown flared outward to the floor. Tiny, embroidered butterflies were scattered at the hem and the cuffs of her puffed sleeves. A jeweled butterfly comb nestled into her upswept hair, which had been styled elegantly by Lenora's maid, Rena; and a few golden-brown tendrils strayed past her earrings. Dove-grey gloves, the same shade as her slippers, stretched past her elbows.

She would do, she supposed. Her heart fluttering with anxiety, she turned to open the door, then felt a rush of pleasure when she saw Alexander stood there, his hand raised to knock.

"Happy birthday, old girl," he said, and kissed her cheek. "For someone who looks amazingly like myself in skirts, you're appearing well."

She thanked him and viewed his black evening clothes with approval. "As do you. Are you ready to go down?"

"In a minute." He eased past her and pulled her farther into the room, shutting the door behind them. "I want you to be the first to know. I have something to show you."

His excitement filled her with foreboding. When he pulled a ring from his pocket, her fears became real, and her heart plummeted. He held a large ruby set in a plain gold band. It was the ring their mother had worn all her married life.

"I plan to ask for Lenora's hand tonight," Alexander said. "If she agrees, I want to announce our betrothal at the gathering."

"Oh, Alex," she moaned. Was this why the merry widow had postponed telling him of her past? Did she suspect she was so close to grasping her prize?

"I know you don't approve of Lenora, but you have come to like her better lately, haven't you? It's important that you do."

"My approval is not the issue. I fear you're rushing things, Alex. You don't know anything about her."

"What do you mean? I know all I need to know. I've known her for years." A stubborn look came into his eyes. "Your favorable opinion means much to me, but I warn you; this is one thing I intend to do, with or without your blessing."

"And you shall have it," she entreated. "Later. Just promise to wait a day longer, at least."

"Whyever should I do that? Everyone we know will be here tonight. What better time is there?"

"Please, Alex. Heed me in this."

"I listen to you in all things," he said, frowning as he returned the ring to his pocket. "But I'm not delaying because of some whim of yours. I'm going downstairs now. Do you come with me?"

"I'll be down in a moment," she said evenly, though fury was causing her earrings to shake. When he exited, she waited until he had time to leave the corridor, then stalked in a most unfeminine manner to Lenora's room, knocked commandingly at the door, and swept inside without waiting for an invitation.

"Unless you wish Rena to hear what I have to say, you'd best dismiss her," Darby said without preamble.

Lenora, garbed in a new pink confection, was seated at her dressing table while her maid adjusted a tiara over her golden curls. Seeing Darby's irate face reflected in her mirror, Lenora put her own hands to the jewelry, patted it to check for stability, then rose gracefully.

"That will be all, Rena," she said, and the maid bobbed and hurried from the room. "You are looking quite fine, Darby, though I can see something is troubling you. What have I done now?"

"It's not what you've done; it's what you have failed to do." Darby's wrath was not lessened by Lenora's well-tended beauty. Alex would find her impossible to resist tonight. "Why have you not spoken with my brother?"

Lenora's dark eyes glittered. "You mean, why haven't I told him I was an adulteress? This may be difficult for you to understand, Darby, but every time I begin to frame the words, they choke me."

"I have no difficulty understanding that at all. If you're unable to do it, say so."

"And you will tell him," Lenora said hopelessly.

"Of course. And it must be done immediately."

"Immediately? Do you mean tonight?"

"Yes, tonight." She waited a few seconds. "Well, what is it to be? Do you wish *me* to tell him?"

"No, of course not . . ."

At that moment, the door opened. "Knock, knock, knock!" sang Aunt Gacia as she entered. A beaming Uncle Richard followed on her heels. "Why, Darby, what a pleasant surprise; I didn't expect to find you here! How stunning you look. Doesn't she, Mr. Lightner?"

"She does, indeed," he said, his girth expanding the buttons of his black jacket more than it had when he last wore the suit. "Don't know which pretty flower to gaze upon—m'lovely daughter or m'lovely niece."

"And what of your lovely wife?" asked Aunt Gacia teasingly, turning and swirling the layers of chiffon that topped her multi-coloured Indian silk.

"You're the prettiest of all," he said loyally.

"Oh, Mr. Lightner!" Aunt Gacia cried, giggling. "Only listen to you; my goodness, what a sweet liar!" She grew quiet then, apparently noticing for the first time how silent the young women were. "Have we . . . interrupted something, children?"

"Darby wishes me to tell Alexander about my scandalous, unforgivable past," Lenora said flatly. "She wants me to do so this evening."

"Oh," breathed Aunt Gacia, the merriment dying from her expression. "Oh, dear."

Uncle Richard's demeanor underwent a swift transformation. In a stern voice he asked, "Why tonight? And why tell him at all?"

"Alex deserves to know the truth." Struggling against a feeling of disloyalty to her brother, she added, "He plans to ask her to be his wife."

It seemed a cool wind of joy breezed through the room.

"Tonight?" queried Uncle Richard. "I knew it was coming, but *tonight*?"

"God be praised," said Aunt Gacia. "We are saved, Mr. Lightner!"

"Perhaps not," Lenora said, hope warring with caution on her face. "I've been told Alexander is unforgiving."

"All this worry's useless," Uncle Richard said gruffly. "It would be foolishness to trouble the boy with what's gone on in the past. That's water under the bridge now, and Lenora's not to blame for any of it. You realize that, don't you, Darby-girl?"

"I understand what she did," Darby said. "But Alex must be given the chance to judge that for himself."

"Judge! Judge Lenora?" shouted Uncle Richard, growing angry again. "Everybody fancies they're a judge! Well,

I've had enough of people wagging their tongues in judgment over me and mine, and I'll not—''

"Papa," Lenora said soothingly. "Don't become upset. I'll tell Alexander, and he'll forgive me; I know he will."

Her father's face flushed. "No. Don't say a word to him until I talk with Darby here."

Darby met his gaze unflinchingly, though his colour alarmed her. "There is nothing you can say that will change my mind."

"But you—" he began.

"Why, Simon!" Lenora exclaimed effusively. "You are looking very handsome. Have you come to fetch us?"

The others turned toward the open door, where stood Simon with an attitude of polite interest. When he spied Darby, the interest grew more pronounced. She felt blushes rising to her cheeks at the look of admiration and—what was it, *relief*?—in his eyes.

Looking at him now, she knew she'd never seen a more astonishingly beautiful man. Thanks to Beckett's nimble fingers, Simon wore a black *frac,* waistcoat and trousers which fit his strong body to perfection. A white shirt and neckcloth provided dramatic contrast to the black, as did his light hair. On his feet he wore ebony shoes that had been sent all the way from London, at her insistence.

For an instant, it was as though the room's other inhabitants disappeared, and every worry about Alexander and Lenora flew from her head. *A lesser woman would faint if Simon regarded her as he does me,* she thought happily. And then worry saddled her again. What could he be planning to tell her that was so bad she might not want him to stay? Surely there was nothing so awful as that.

Simon stirred to life. "Um, yes. The guests have begun to arrive. Alexander said to hurry."

Lenora began searching for her fan while Aunt Gacia exclaimed and rushed toward the door. Pausing at the threshold, she said to her husband, "Come along, dearest. I'll need your arm."

Uncle Richard gave Darby a final glance. "We'll talk later," he said quietly. "Wait before you"—he darted a look in Simon's direction, then lowered his voice further— "wait before you speak. Just give me a moment, is all I ask." When she did not answer, he seemed to take her silence as affirmation and squeezed her hand. "There's a good girl." And hurried off to join his wife.

Lifting his eyebrows curiously, Simon offered his escort to Darby and Lenora, and the three of them descended the stairs. Uncle Richard and Aunt Gacia, in their last role as guardians, stood at the head of the receiving line; Lenora took her place next to them, followed by Alexander and Darby. Claude stood to the side, greeting the guests he knew and smiling condescendingly at the ones he did not.

As she welcomed her visitors, Darby glanced away frequently to catch Simon's eye. He seemed even more anxious than she, if that was possible, meeting her looks with tight smiles while milling around aimlessly. When the foreman of the pottery entered, appearing uncomfortable in his Sunday-best and holding his cap in his hand, Simon brightened. She was surprised to see them talking conspiratorially to one another, and even more surprised when they dashed away.

But when Simon returned almost at once, rushed to her and whispered, "I'll be gone for just a few minutes; stay inside and remember: *Don't go near the pond!*", then ran after the foreman again, she became heavily concerned. Perhaps, after all, her angel was not quite right in the head.

Darby guessed that everyone in the district was going to make an appearance at their ball; the stream of guests seemed endless. Even the local baron and his wife came. Yet there were two whose absence robbed the flavour from what promised to be deemed a successful evening. Before

she had time to truly mourn that loss, Mrs. Wallace, Evelyn,
and Edward entered. Darby could not wait until they filed
all the way down to her; she jumped out of line and pulled
Evelyn and Edward aside.

"I'm so happy you came!" she cried. Looking pointedly
at Edward, she added, "Thank you."

"We couldn't miss it," said Evelyn, who, though she
glowed appealingly in a pale green gown embroidered with
golden threads, appeared nervous. "I'm too cheered by
the prospects of having you join me in the miseries of
adulthood."

Edward directed his gaze over Darby's shoulder with
unsmiling determination. "I'm here because of my mother's tears," he said.

Darby swallowed. "I'm pleased to see you, no matter
what the reason." Forcing brightness into her voice, she
added, "Thanks to Lenora's prodding, the orchestra will
be performing several waltzes this evening. Do you think
we'll become the scandal of the village?"

Edward looked her squarely in the eye. "Yes, most likely.
Depends on how far you take it."

He was not speaking of dancing, Darby knew. She
searched her mind for something of a peaceful nature
to say but found nothing. To her relief, Evelyn clutched
Edward's arm and pushed him toward the receiving line.

"Hush, little brother. You will not embarrass me tonight;
I intend to enjoy myself. The line is breaking up over there;
why don't you go speak with Alex and leave us alone?"

"With pleasure," Edward said, and moved away stiffly.

"He has lost all kindness this week, but he'll recover,"
Evelyn commented. "In truth, I must admit I, too, was
disappointed by your refusing his offer. So was Mother.
You caused her to cry—though who or what does not?" She
looked longingly toward Alexander, who stood between
Lenora and Edward. "I always thought you and I would

be sisters, one way or another. I suppose it wasn't meant
to be."

"In my heart, we are already sisters."

"Yes, well . . . mine, too, I suppose. I just hoped among
the four of us there would be one pairing at least." With
her eyes still fixed on Alexander, Evelyn said yearningly,
"I haven't seen you in weeks. I suppose there has been no
change in that quarter?"

Darby said reluctantly, "It only grows warmer. Yet do
not abandon all hope; there are things about Lenora that
Alex doesn't yet understand."

"Truly? From the look of him, he is beyond all understanding or sensibility. You will not be surprised if I *do* try
to banish him from my mind, will you?" She made a feeble
attempt at a laugh. "I shall turn my attention to more
worthy prospects than a lump-headed . . . oh . . ."

Darby slipped her arm around her friend's waist and
offered her handkerchief. "He *is* a lump-head. A dolt. He's
not worthy of you, I know that."

Evelyn smiled and shook her head at the proffered scrap
of linen and lace. "Perhaps you are right," she said pensively, gazing again across the chattering knots of people
to Alexander, whose face was rapt as a worshiper at a shrine
as he attended Lenora and ignored Edward. "But he is
dear to me all the same. If only once he had looked at me
like that."

"I shall never forgive him for not doing so."

"Yes, you will. You love him even more than I do, and
if *I* can forgive him, so can you."

"Evelyn, you are too good for this world."

Darby looked up then and was vexed to see Uncle Richard approaching. She had no desire to speak with him.
Bundling Evelyn's arm within hers, she began making her
way through the crowd. But before she moved far, she
stopped, stunned by the sight of the pottery's school-
children lined up across the balcony. The youngsters were

clothed in matching uniforms: white shirts and black trousers for the boys; pink ruffled gowns for the girls. Their
faces were freshly scrubbed, their hair washed and combed.
Many of them held slim volumes by their sides.

The chatter in the hall began to die away as, one by one,
the guests turned their attention to the balcony. Hearing
the sudden hush, a few others wandered from the adjoin-
ing rooms. And then, to Darby's everlasting shock, Simon
appeared at one end of the line of children. A guitar
was strapped around his neck with a leather thong. While
Darby's mouth dropped, he strummed a chord, and one
of the children—Millie, she saw it was—clicked a finger
cymbal. And then the youngsters began to sing.

Their voices were sweet and true as they sang a haunting
folk song—something about a mountain flower. At its con-
clusion, before there was time for applause, Clemmy
moved down a step and recited his letters so adorably that
Darby could scarcely stop herself from rushing up the stairs
to hug him. After he finished, one child after another read
or recited a brief poem. One little girl was so frightened
she could hardly be heard, but the guests murmured
encouragingly and by the end, she was almost shouting.
And then Simon began to play chords on the guitar again,
and the children marched down the stairs and through
the kitchen while singing a farewell song. Clemmy was the
last to leave, and when he did, the audience burst into
resounding applause.

The children emerged from the kitchen to take their
bows. After that, Simon, having caught Darby's eye and
mouthing, "Remember," led them back into the kitchen
promising treats.

Darby was so delighted she could not stop laughing.
She received many compliments from her guests on the
excellent entertainment, compliments she knew were
undeserved since the program had been a secret to her.
But judging by Alex and Lenora's proud faces across the

crowded hall, the performance had been no surprise to them.

It was evident that Lenora had not spoken yet. Darby's spirits dampened just a little, and when she saw Uncle Richard again headed in her direction, they fell even further. With determination she pulled Evelyn behind a large knot of people and into the library.

"What are you doing?" asked Evelyn, who appeared in a lighter mood after hearing the children. "I feel as if we're playing hide-and-seek as we did in the old days."

"I hope you're seeking me, then," said Claude, emerging from the corner of the room half-hidden by the open door.

"Claude!" Darby heard the censure in her voice and knew Evelyn would wonder at it, but she could not help herself. "Why aren't you with the other guests?"

He looked nonplussed. "Why, I was only admiring your gifts and trying to escape Simon Garrett's caterwauling runts. What a treasure-trove you have here!" He gestured toward the space behind the door, which was piled high with decorated boxes. "Some of the larger items are unwrapped, such as this vase. Look, the card is made out to both of you, Darby; what shall you do when you marry and move away—saw it in half? Ha! At least Sir Wilfred and his wife are not such shilling-squeezers; he has given each of you walking sticks engraved with your initials." He hefted one of the sticks in his hand. "This one is yours, Darby; see the scripted *D*? How elegant, and yet how inappropriate, unless you think you need a cane at your age." He studied the mahogany object more closely, fingering a circular seam near the handle. "Say now, what is this button for? Shall I push it and find out? Egad, a blade! I suppose we must be careful of you henceforth, Warrior Darby!"

"And what have *you* given them?" asked Evelyn, who had always been straightforward in her dislike of Claude.

"I?"

"Please," Darby said. "We really didn't expect—"

"Oh, there you are!" exclaimed Uncle Richard, entering the room. "A moment of your time, my girl."

"Whatever you want, it will have to wait," Alexander said, following him. "The orchestra is starting the first dance, and several guests are demanding the birthday twins lead it."

Darby gladly moved from the room, abandoning Evelyn in her haste to flee Uncle Richard. She and Alexander threaded their way through the packed bodies in the hall, Darby pausing every now and then to allow a gentleman to sign her dance card. Finally they made their way into the conservatory, which had been cleared of all but its most decorative plants, and onto the dance floor.

The orchestra began with a waltz. How pleasant to be guided across the marble by her handsome brother, to see the circle of their friends lining the walls, watching them as they spun around and around. To think that she and Alexander were adults at last! Truly they had not been children for years, but now it was official.

Brightings was theirs. The thought led to other, darker ones.

"Have you spoken with Lenora yet?" she asked.

"There has not been the time. Are you going to scold me again about it?"

"No. Only ask her to tell you of her life with Reece before making your offer. Will you do that?"

"I shall do no such thing," he said resentfully. "Did you enjoy the entertainment? Lenora provided the children's uniforms."

"It was quite wonderful." Darby opened her mouth to say more, but then closed it. She did not want to destroy the pleasure of this dance, and besides, other couples were drifting onto the floor and they had no privacy. Her unease deepened as she looked for Simon and could not find him. Surely he was done with the children. Surely he did not disapprove of waltzing, and she would be granted at least one dance with her angel this evening.

And then she spied him in the doorway, his fair head taller than anyone's in the crowd. His eyes searched the room for her; she had no doubt he was looking for anyone else. She watched him, willing him to glance her way. And at last, he did.

So intent was she on following his progress through the twirling couples, she tromped on Alexander's feet. He exclaimed in pain, then annoyance when Simon tapped his shoulder.

"May I?" Simon asked over his protests.

"I should think not," began Alexander, but when he saw Darby's look of appeal, he relented. "Oh, very well, I suppose you deserve a dance after all your hard work. But watch her; she'll bruise your feet."

Simon stared into her eyes. "I'll more likely bruise hers," he said.

Darby made no reply; she was too lost in the feeling of his arms around her. As they swept into the swirling stream, she did not dance; she floated. He guided her expertly, and neither one of them tread on the other's toes.

"The children were charming," she said. "You've accomplished an extraordinary amount with them."

"All I did was teach them a few songs. They seem to enjoy the sound of music." He laughed inexplicably, then added, "It was mostly Lenora who taught them their letters and reading. I'm hoping the exhibition will impress some of your fellow manufacturers into giving their child labourers the same chance."

"As to that, I cannot say; but I assure you I'm convinced."

He gave her a warm look. "Do you mean . . ."

"Yes. I want to continue the school. I only worry about its direction. If you *do* decide to remain, as you have hinted you might, would you be interested in the position?"

Simon whisked her around several times, and she felt herself growing dizzy. "If you still want me after tonight, I'd be very interested."

He was referring to their upcoming talk, of course. She pushed the thought aside; it made her too edgy to contemplate. "I didn't know angels danced so well."

"I've taken a few lessons in my time," he admitted with a grin. "Have I told you how beautiful you are?"

She blushed with pleasure. "No, but perhaps you shouldn't."

"Oh? Why not?"

"Well . . . I may come to think you regard me with . . . special favor."

His hand tightened on hers. "If you don't know that by now, you're blind."

"Oh, Simon." Disturbed, she locked gazes with him, then, caring nothing for what anyone might think, pressed closer to his chest. She could hear his heart racing, pounding beneath his jacket. She looked up worriedly. "Simon? Are we in very great trouble?"

"I hope not," he said grimly. Then, seeing her fearful expression, he drew her near again and rested his cheek on the top of her head, speaking softly. "Remember that I want to talk with you after the ball. And remember— remember that no matter what happens, I love you. Everything I have ever done since we met is because I love you. Do you hear me, Darby Brightings? Do you promise to try and understand?"

She understood only one thing: *He loved her.* Although she had been sure of it for weeks, he had never put his feelings into words. She wanted to see his eyes, longed to cherish this frightening, wonderful, terrible moment with all her senses, but he gripped her too tightly. Her imagination staggered, trembled at what he meant to reveal tonight, but he loved her; *her angel loved her!*

And so far, lightning had not struck.

"Do you promise?" Simon demanded a second time.

"I promise," she said, speaking into his jacket. "I love—"

"No," he interrupted quickly. "Don't say anything more until we talk."

Feeling a little miffed, she nodded. And then, from the corner of her eye, she saw her uncle approaching. "Oh, no. Uncle Richard is trying to stop me from telling Alex about Lenora. Simon, she has not told him of her past, and my brother plans to ask her for her hand tonight!"

Simon swept her in the opposite direction from her uncle. "Do you plan to tell Alexander, then?"

"Certainly I do, if she will not."

"Oh."

His arms loosened a bit, and she leaned back and regarded his disappointment with a frown. "You disapprove. But you don't forbid me, do you?"

He moistened his lips. She sensed great conflicts warring within him, but he said only, "You should do what your heart tells you, Darby."

This served to make her feel worse, but only for an instant; her brother's happiness was too important. And still Uncle Richard pursued her, trailing like a hound; once more Simon twirled her away.

"Stay beside me," he said. "Don't leave me tonight; not for one minute."

She could not help laughing at his sudden possessiveness. "But, Simon—I'll have to dance with the gentlemen who have signed my card. And if we dance together more than once, we'll cause talk."

"We will? Oh. Well, don't leave this room, then. When it's time for supper, wait for me."

Darby agreed as the waltz concluded, and they broke apart. When the orchestra began another selection, Uncle Richard claimed her arm and demanded the next dance. Although the glassmaker's son came at the same moment to declare the second waltz was his, Uncle Richard waved him away and spun Darby onto the floor.

"Have you told him yet, m'girl?" he puffed, already winded.

"No, not that it's any concern of yours, Uncle."

"Ho, is it not? I'd like to know who is more concerned than meself. M'daughter's well-being means all to me."

Darby narrowed her eyes. "Are you certain it is not *your* well-being that concerns you?"

"You are still a child." He began turning her in wider circles, drawing near the doors to the back terrace. "What can a girl know of a father's love?"

"Here, where are we going?"

"Just outside for a bit. I need to speak with you while I still have breath in my body."

She looked across the dancers and spotted Simon standing against the wall, watching her. Shrugging helplessly, she allowed her partner to sweep her out the door. Short of causing a scene, there was nothing else she could do. But she would not have to endure her uncle long; Simon was coming toward them with high alarm in his eyes. *Why?* Did he imagine Lenora's father would harm her? *Uncle Richard?* How laughable.

Her uncle was pulling her down the steps and away from the conservatory's windows. "Truly, this is far enough," she said petulantly. "Say what you have to say now, and allow me to go back to my guests."

"Order me about, will you?" he shot, his expression turning livid. "I've never seen a woman more forgetful of her place."

"You forget *your* place!" she said vehemently, pulling against his grip, which felt like iron. "Are you mad?"

They were beneath the trees now, and he pushed her against a spruce and held her there. Seeing the fury in his eyes, she grew suddenly still and very cold.

"I've endured your orders and jibes and snobbery for

years! God knows I never knew when I might find a frog in m'bed or a spider in m'slipper! And now, to see you toss that scorn at Lenora, after all she's lived through! I'll not have you ruin it for her. Let your brother speak tonight. Let him announce it to the world! Then you may say anything, and he'll be too proud to back down!''

Over Uncle Richard's shoulder, Darby could see Simon running toward them, and someone else she could not make out behind him. Emboldened by their approach, she said, "I would never do that to him. If you truly love your daughter, you can imagine what I feel for my brother."

He seemed only to hear her refusal, not her reasoning. His face burned scarlet in rage, and he raised his fist to strike her. She watched helplessly, stricken with terror, then squeezed her eyes shut. But the blow never landed; Simon leapt upon the older man and toppled him to the ground.

Darby jumped aside. For seconds her thoughts were so jumbled that she could not sort out the tangled arms and legs flailing across the ground. Then she saw that Simon straddled Uncle Richard's chest and pounded blow after blow into his face. Her uncle had no strength to fight back; his hands were crossed over his head defensively while he groaned.

"Simon, stop!" she cried. "You are killing him!"

He did not pause. "I intend to!"

"No, no, you must not!" She looked up helplessly and saw Claude running toward them, her cane tucked beneath his arm. "Make them stop!" she begged.

Claude pulled at Simon's shoulder. "Stop!" he commanded, and shouted when he was flung aside. Looking wild, he pushed the button on Darby's walking stick and extended it behind Simon. "If you don't stop, Garrett, I'll stab you!"

"No, don't do that!" Darby squealed.

At the sound of her panic, Simon turned abruptly. Claude, perhaps seeing the movement as a threat, plunged the blade very far into his shoulder. Darby covered her mouth in horror. There was a long, taut moment while Simon turned bewildered eyes upon Claude, who looked utterly dismayed.

"Sorry, old man, didn't mean it," he said, and pulled.

As the blade exited, Simon went very pale. He crawled off Uncle Richard and sat in the grass cradling his elbow and staring at the reddening slit in his sleeve. Darby rushed to his side and extended her fingers toward the wound, then drew back. She pressed her handkerchief to it, but the cloth soon became soaked and useless.

"Thank God, thank God," Uncle Richard mumbled, and slid to the tree and propped himself against it. He brought a handkerchief to his face and blotted at the blood trickling from his nose. "The idiot was trying to kill me. Broke a tooth, he did."

"Are you all right, Simon?" whispered Darby, who was not as worried as she would be were her angel human. "Can't you heal yourself, or are you so injured you'll have to abandon this mortal body?"

How she hoped not, for she truly liked this one. Simon looked at her as if he could not understand what she was saying. She heard footsteps and turned to see Alexander and Lenora trotting toward them.

"Darby, are you hurt?" Alexander asked, kneeling beside her. After determining she was all right, he turned to Simon, noticed his injury and blanched.

"Papa!" Lenora exclaimed at almost the same time. "What has happened here?" She looked from one silent man to the other. Seeing the gaping wound in Simon's arm, she cried out, "Not again, Papa! You vowed it would never happen again!"

"What would never happen again?" asked Alexander,

looking back and forth between his sweetheart and his uncle.

"Oh, Lenora," Claude said, and sighed. "What have you done?"

"What?" Alexander demanded. "What are all of you going on about?" Into the sudden silence, Simon groaned and slumped to the grass. "Wait; our actor's bleeding like a fountain; Claude, fetch the surgeon. He's in the parlor, I think, playing cards—his name's Groat. After Simon's taken care of, I want a full explanation." When Claude dashed off, Alexander placed his hand on Darby's shoulder. "I'm sorry, old girl. It doesn't look good."

"Don't worry, he'll be all right," she said confidently, stroking a lock of hair from Simon's eyes. "He is very . . . special."

Alexander patted her back. "That's the trick; you're the stronger one of us and always have been."

Darby lifted her eyebrows at her brother's fussing and smiled faintly at Simon. When her angel did not respond but merely watched her with stunned eyes, she felt her first flash of true alarm. "You're in pain. Can you not make it stop?"

Alexander looked at her sharply. "Did you just ask him to stop his own pain? Don't go weak-headed on me now, sister."

"But you don't understand!" She touched Simon's hand thoughtlessly, then pulled back. Her fingertips were crimson with his blood. She held them before her eyes, then focused on Simon again. "Do something, won't you? Don't just lie there bleeding your life away!"

"Can you hear yourself?" Alexander tugged her shoulders, trying to urge her away. "Leave the poor fellow in peace, won't you?"

Darby jerked herself free and leaned closely to her angel's face. "Simon . . . Simon . . ."

Her tears began to mingle with the blood spreading

across his coat. Simon was breathing shakily, trying to say something. Careful not to disturb his wound, she lay her head on his chest and listened to the beating of his heart. It was very important that she hear his heart.

"Darby," he whispered. "What . . . I was going to tell you. I'm . . ." His lips trembled. "I'm not . . . an angel. Never have been . . . never . . . will be. I'm . . . sorry."

She lifted her head and met his gaze without expression, though her stomach churned with more emotions than she could name. Her heart was shattering into a thousand pieces like a defective plate. And still Simon's blood ran into the earth like scarlet rain.

Chapter Fourteen

I'm dead, decided Simon, slowly coming to awareness in a room dark enough to be a crypt. *So that's how the universe balances itself; a life for a life. Well, at least Darby didn't die.*

Or did she?

Anxiety coursed through his veins like acid. He tried to sit up, but his head barely lifted from the pillow, and even that small effort set his shoulder on fire. Feeling pain must mean he wasn't dead after all; at least he hoped so. He moved his feet beneath the sheets, murmuring in frustration.

He heard a chair creaking somewhere in the darkness, then scratching sounds and the unmistakable noise of a flame igniting. A candle glowed to life, painting the room—his bedroom at Brightings, he saw—with faint light that now grew closer. He squinted to see the identity of the shadowy figure behind it.

"Darby, thank God you're safe," he said, then blinked at the thin, rusty sound of his voice.

"What an odd thing to say when it is you who lies abed."

She placed the candle on his nightstand and pressed her hand to his forehead. "There is no fever." Pulling his blanket back a little, she checked his wound. "And no further bleeding. The surgeon said you have a strong constitution." She measured a spoonful of something into a glass of water and began stirring it. "A strong constitution is a good thing to have. Especially for a *man*."

Her words fell like icicles, and she would not meet his eyes. He watched her, his spirits lowering by the second. He noticed she no longer wore her birthday gown but a plain brown one.

"Have you been here all night?" he asked meekly. "Or is this even the same night? What day is it?"

She smiled without amusement. "It is four-thirty on the morning of June eleven. You are more concerned with the calendar than anyone I've ever known. I shall always remember that about you."

That had the ring of finality about it, but he was determined to savour his victory no matter what. "And you're alive," he said, reaching for her hand with his uninjured arm. "It's the day after your birthday, and you're *alive!*"

"Of course I am." She snatched her hand away and brought the glass to his lips, lifting the back of his head to meet it. "Here, drink this. It will make you sleep, and you need rest, as do I."

He turned his head away. "I don't want to sleep. I want to talk. What happened to Lightner after I passed out? What was Lenora saying?"

She replaced the glass on the table. "Very well, since you prevented my uncle's striking me, perhaps I owe you that much. I must say I'm grateful to you for your protection, and am sorry you were hurt because of it. We are now a household in uproar. Uncle Richard has been handed into the magistrate's keeping, and Alex has thrown Claude from the house. Lenora, you see, told all after you were brought inside and the guests left. It seems her father pushed Reece from the hotel window, and Claude saw him from the grounds."

He was silent a moment, digesting this. "So Heathershaw had been blackmailing him?"

"Claude didn't call it that. He said he never asked for money, only for a home with his beloved friends." She wrinkled her nose in distaste.

"And poor Lenora had to put up with him because she didn't want to lose her father." He grunted. "I'm amazed Gacia was able to keep the secret."

"She didn't know. She was napping at the time of the murder, and none of the others told her what really happened. Last night she became very distraught on learning her husband would have to undergo a trial." Darby's lips twisted wryly. "She recovered remarkably when I assured her she could stay with us as long as she wants."

He paused, afraid to ask; but he had to know. "And Lenora?"

Darby gave him a dispassionate look. "Lenora will stay as well. Alex did not ask her to marry him after all; one can hardly propose to a woman while her father is being arrested. But I'm certain he will. She told him everything, and he understands why she behaved as she did. My brother is more forgiving, or more in love, than I thought."

"And what about you, Darby?"

She ignored the question behind his words. "I don't know what will become of Uncle Richard, but I never want to see him again. I can tolerate many things, but not the kind of rage I saw in him last night. He frightened me. I never dreamed he could be dangerous."

"You don't know how dangerous, Darby. What if he *had* struck you, and hurt you worse than he meant? What do you think would have happened then?"

She stared. "I have no notion. That is not the kind of question I ask myself."

"Well, I'll tell you what *I* think. I think he would've dragged you to the lake and made it look like a drowning."

"How absurd you are. Uncle Richard murder me? Unthinkable." She moved toward the door. "I've told you all I know; and now that I've seen you're all right, I'm going to bed."

He moved his legs desperately. "Remember the fire I warned you about? I guess it could've been an accident, but Richard may have been behind that, too. Maybe he got word about Alexander's plans to play that prank and tried to kill both of you at once. That was before Alexander and Lenora were a couple, wasn't it? Who inherits if both of you die?"

She stared at him with disdain. "Does it make you feel better to know that my aunt and uncle do? But perhaps you will understand when I tell you I find it easier to believe you set the fire yourself."

"Why on earth would I do that?"

She turned the knob. "To convince an imbecile you were an angel, why else?"

"Wait. If you cared enough to stay until you found out I was going to be okay, surely you can spare a few more minutes to let me tell you everything."

She frowned. "Tell me everything? What, do you mean the truth? How could I judge the truthfulness of anything you say?"

"I deserve that, but when you learn—"

"I won't listen to you, Simon, or whatever your name is," she interrupted, covering her ears and walking into the hall. "I have lost all interest."

He squeezed his eyes shut and groaned pitifully. Her footsteps paused. He moaned a little louder. When he smelled the sweet scent of rosebuds nearby, he opened his eyes, saw her concerned face only inches from his, and grinned hopefully.

"I see you haven't lost *all* interest," he said.

"Oh!" she exclaimed furiously. "You are maddening!"

"You're not the first to say so. Listen to me, Darby. Remember what I said last night? I love you. I've told some lies here, but that's not one of them. Almost everything I've done has been to protect you from being killed on your birthday."

"How you make me laugh!" she exclaimed scornfully. "Are you pretending to be an angel again, an angel who can foretell the future?"

"No, I'm going to tell you who I really am. But before I do, I want you to recall that it was *you* who suggested I was an angel in the first place. Remember when you saw me disappear through the trees? Remember how it felt when *you* tried to go through?"

She paused. "I recall your saying it was a trick of the light, and now I must believe that was all it was; as for when I followed you, why, I suppose it was the wind that threw me backward. How you can blame *me* for your unholy impersonation, I know not!"

"Well, you only gave me two choices that day—angel or demon—and I decided to go with the good guys. I thought it would be easier for you to believe I was an angel than what I really am."

"Oh? And what is that, Simon? An oracle?"

He sighed. It was going to be a long day. "Sit down, Darby. You don't want to be standing when I tell you this."

On the following Saturday afternoon, Darby looked up from her account books when she heard the conservatory door slam shut. Alex and Lenora had gone for a drive, and Aunt Gacia usually slept all afternoon. The servants would not allow the door to slam, so it could be only one person.

She tossed her quill on the ledger, rushed from the parlour into the conservatory, and peered out the windows.

As she guessed, it was Simon, wearing the jacket and panta-loons that Beckett had first made for him. And he was entering the woods. With a soundless cry, she rushed out the door without bothering to close it.

He was leaving her, and who could blame him? She had greeted his fantastic story with disbelief and a thousand scathing questions. Yet who could blame *her*? One lie was more outrageous than the last. But if he hadn't lied this time . . . she might never see him again. She ran faster.

The forest closed around her, eerie yet comforting. Feeling like a desecrator in this cool, silent world, she shouted his name. And heard her own voice resonating back. She hurried onward, panting, praying that she would find him in time. If she could not remember where those trees were . . .

After she became almost ill with running, he responded to her call. Energized with relief, Darby rushed toward the sound and found him at that strange clearing near the heart of the forest. She was so happy she nearly fell into his arms. But at the last instant she collected herself and tried to greet him with dignity.

"What are you doing, Simon?" she asked, then winced at the frantic quality of her voice.

"What do you think?" His eyes were remote, as if he had already disassociated himself from her.

"Are you going home?"

"Home? Why ask that? I'm just taking a walk in the woods."

"But . . . you were planning to go between those ash trees, weren't you?"

"As a matter of fact, I was, but what do you care? According to you, nothing will happen if I do. So . . . here I go." He turned back to the trees.

"No!" she screamed.

Simon stopped and slowly faced her. A taunting little

smile lifted his lips. "No? Are you forbidding me to take a simple walk? Why?"

"Because—because . . ." Oh, he was making her angry. He was going to force her to say it, wasn't he?

"Because . . . ?" he prompted.

"Because I believe you!" she blurted, knotting her fists. "I mean, sometimes I do and sometimes I don't. But you *did* stop Uncle Richard from harming me, and I cannot think how you did unless there is some truth to your story."

"Only *some* truth?"

"Don't press, Simon; you can't expect me to swallow everything at one gulp—flying carriages and moving portraits and all of those unbelievable things."

"But you believe enough of it to think I might disappear if I walk between those trees."

"I've seen you do it before." She prodded a hollow log with the toe of her slipper. "You didn't give me enough time to become accustomed to these strange ideas. You were going to leave me without trying very hard."

His eyes softened. "I wasn't leaving for good, Darby. I only meant to find something—the family history, maybe—that would convince you I was telling the truth."

"Oh. I hope you won't do that. I don't want to know when Alex is going to die, or when I'm going to, either."

"Okay, I understand. Something else, then. Maybe my Walkman."

"Your what?"

"The heavenly music."

"No, much as I liked it, I don't want you to go back to prove anything. Something might happen to prevent your coming back."

"Nothing can stop me." He grinned, appearing to be thoroughly enjoying himself now. "So . . . you don't want me to go?"

She shook her head, then began to smile in spite of herself.

"Why not?" When she didn't answer, he stepped to her and lifted her chin. "Could it be that you love me as I love you?"

Her eyes melted into his. "That's the only sensible thing you have ever said to me."

He wrapped his arms around her, flinching a little at the painful stiffness in his shoulder. And then he kissed her, a long, searching kiss that made her helpless with longing. He pulled away, smiling into her eyes while stroking her cheek. "I'll be back soon," he said, and returned to the ash trees.

She felt as if she had fallen from a cliff. "You're not still going? Haven't I said I believe you, Simon?"

"Yes, but if I'm to live with you here, I need to transfer my cash to gold or something. I don't want to live off my wife like a parasite. It'll be hard enough as it is convincing Alexander I'll make a suitable husband for you."

She thrilled to hear him speak of marriage so casually, but a horrible premonition dampened her feelings. "You won't be living idly off our income. You've promised to run the school, remember? Unless . . . will you miss acting? I suppose"—She swallowed with difficulty—"we could move to London."

"Would you do that, Darby? Leave the pottery for me?"

Her heart clunked like an iron weight in her chest. "Well . . . you have come all this way and time for *me*. It's the least I can do."

He stepped back and kissed her joyfully. "I'm not going to ask you to do that, sweetheart. I like teaching. But apart from money, there's another reason I want to return. I can't rest, not knowing."

Darby's gaze dropped. "You wonder if Elena will be born."

"Yes, and Tay. I *must* know. Can you understand that?"

She began to tremble. "Yes. I don't want to, but I do." She threw her arms around him, causing him to shout in pain. "Oh, I'm sorry; I forgot about your shoulder." Her voice wavered, and tears made her eyes shine like crystals. "You won't come back."

"I told you; nothing can prevent me from returning to you." He kissed the tip of her nose. "It might take me a day or two, so don't wait here. And don't look like that! The sooner I go, the faster I'll return."

He tore himself away and, with a final wink, stepped beneath the trees.

Darby's hand flew to her mouth.

The space between the trees immediately darkened. Simon's hair began to ripple backward, as if a fierce gale blew from the other side. Lightning flickered across his body. He bent forward, pushing against the invisible force, walking and walking but going no farther within. She heard a terrible crack of thunder and screamed. For an instant she could not see Simon at all. And then he tumbled through the air and landed at her feet.

"Simon!" Darby knelt beside him, rubbing his hands and patting his cheek. "Can you hear me?"

His eyes opened. "What . . . happened?"

"You couldn't go through. It was like that other time when I tried to accompany you."

"I . . . see. *Well.*" With her help, he struggled to his feet and dusted his breeches. She looked away from him, not liking the disappointment she saw on his face. "I guess I'll never know what happens."

She took his hand. "Then you'll be like everyone else on earth."

A gentle light began to gleam in his eyes. "That's right; set me straight, Darby. I'm depending on you to do that from now on, since it's your fault I couldn't go back. You have to be desolate in heart, you know. I'd forgotten, but it came back to me in that wind tunnel. You've taken the sadness right out of me, and now you're stuck with a cast-away in time."

She lifted her fingers to his tumbled hair and began smoothing it. "There's a part of me that believes you've deluded yourself, Simon. Sometimes I still think you're an angel."

"Oh, no," he said, sweeping her into his arms and staring hungrily at her lips. "An angel would never do *this*, would he?"

When she could draw breath to speak, she said dreamily, "No, Simon, I don't believe an angel would."

Epilogue—1996

On the second day of his search through Witchwood, Simon Garrett found the ash trees and felt a chill that had little to do with the quiet wind ruffling the treetops. He pulled the thick letter from his back jeans pocket and recalled the awed face of Elena's solicitor as he gave it to him four months before. The letter had been handed down through the firm from father to son, father to son, for almost two centuries. The lawyer's hand had shaken as he gave Simon the sealed packet, which was addressed and dated in the same familiar handwriting that crossed the yellowed pages within: *To Simon Garrett; Los Angeles, California; January, 1996.*

At first he'd thought it a great practical joke; something Dell would do. When his agent denied it forcefully, Simon had hired a private eye to look into it. Turned out the firm of Goodehouse, Hage and Harrow of London was as respectable as they came. And now Simon's fingers trembled as he sat on a rock within spitting distance of the ash trees—*the gateway to the past?*—and read the letter again.

He skimmed through most of the pages; he'd read it so many times he'd practically memorized it. The writer knew him inside and out and revealed everything—Simon's desire to be an actor; his climb up from near-poverty; the help Elena had given him with her Brightings fortune and his resentment of it; his weakness for beautiful women; even the name of the fan, Sheila Wells, whom he never would have suspected to be so deranged—as if he was determined to convince Simon he could be only one person—*Simon himself*. And now, in the light of all that had happened, with the ash trees only yards away, he couldn't deny it. Somehow another Simon Garrett had fled into the past and found happiness there with a woman called Darby. But how could it be possible? Even the old Simon hadn't known:

Though I scarcely think about my former life anymore, sometimes I awake in the middle of the night and wonder: How could I have risked the integrity of the future for my own selfish desires? I must have changed innumerable things that should never have been changed, though I've tried to be careful. But what is the future supposed to be? If I've made it different, who is to say it will not be better—for yourself, for all the lives you'll touch?

Besides, I don't think I could have stopped myself; I'm convinced something impelled me to come. Yes, I know; you're skeptical of any hints of destiny and—dare I say it?—God; but after all these years, well . . . let me only affirm that as one grows older, one becomes more full of wonder and belief. Perhaps that's why the elderly are often called childlike. But you'll have to discover that in your own way.

I'm sixty-three years old as of this writing, and my wife is ten years younger; she's still as beautiful and full of herself as always. We have grown to cherish everything about one another—faults included. I've even learned to tolerate Darby's insistence that it's easier to believe I'm an imperfect angel than a refugee from the future; she only does it to stir me up, anyway, the minx. And though every day has not been blissful, I've known happiness, Simon, loving one woman. Our only sorrow is that we've had no children, but Alexander and Lenora's three fill our lives with joy; and now there are the grandchildren. I tell you, even the foremost desire that brought me here—the wish to assure Elena and Tay's births—fades in importance when I turn over in bed and gaze at my beloved.

In fact, sometimes I wonder if my former existence was not some grand delusion, a dream. Perhaps I was a traveling actor of the old Empire who lost his memory along the way. If so, this letter will provide a good joke for Clemmy's descendants. (How proud I am that he's established his own legal firm. In many ways he's become like a son to me.)

Now I'm beginning to ramble, when my sole purpose in writing is to help you. Selfish to the last, I guess; but only I know the pain you might be going through. If the future has reverted to what it should be—meaning, if Elena's birth was accomplished by the wedding of Alexander and Lenora, and I have no reason to doubt it, seeing their progeny—and if my warnings about Sheila Wells don't prevent your family's death, then you're probably thinking about ending your own pain. Before you do that, if your heart is desolate and abandoned, walk between the trees, Simon. Walk between them. And when you see a vibrant, grey-eyed girl, do whatever you can to protect and love her. You won't regret it.

I'm laughing at myself as I write; of course I've no idea what will happen if you follow my suggestion.

Will time loop itself into knots, over and over again? Is it possible you'll be dumped into another century this time, with equally happy results? Will the universe unravel? Somehow, I'm convinced all will be as it should no matter what you do. Therefore, listen to the dictates of your mind and heart.

With this final thought I leave you (You knew there would be a word of advice, right? It's one of the few privileges the aging enjoy. But I can't stop myself; I feel like a parent to you; no, closer than a parent, and perhaps you'll listen to me more than you ever did Mom or Dad—by the way, go see them, won't you?): I don't care how many magazines paint your face on them; fulfillment only comes in abandoning yourself to one love. Okay, you've heard it a thousand times, but truth is often found in cliches. And it is true. Try it, Simon, and find out.

Simon folded the worn pages into a rectangle and replaced them in his pocket. He shook his head, still not able to believe it. And then he stood and walked slowly toward the trees.

He knew desolation. He tasted emptiness daily. He'd tried to find solace in the fresh young bodies who offered themselves to him, but what pleasure he found was temporary at best. And now he felt an overwhelming curiosity, and hope.

He touched the sides of the trees and paused. Unless everything had been a hoax after all, he was on the verge of a very great decision and mustn't hurry himself. He swallowed and started forward, then hesitated again. Something was disturbing the silent forest, crashing through the undergrowth.

"Daddy!" called a high voice behind him. "Daddy, where are you?"

Simon looked toward the voice, then at the trees longingly. It would only take a second, and then he'd come right back. But what if something happened and he couldn't? Ropes of anxiety tightened around his chest.

"Daddy! I'm losted!"

He turned instantly, feeling the bonds unwinding. *What had he been thinking?* "I'm here, son!" he called, breaking into a run. "Over here, Tay!"

A tow-haired bundle of pumping arms and legs came into sight and launched into his arms. Simon groaned and snuggled his cheek against his son's neck, sniffing the sweet scent of him, the little-boy smell of earth and green growing things.

"What are you doing out here all alone, sprite?"

"Looking for you. Mamma wants to know if you're gonna eat supper with us or go back on the airplane."

Simon drew back and stared into the greenest, brightest eyes in the world. "I'm not going anywhere. Not unless you and your mom go with me."

Tay's face nearly split with his grin. "Then you're not mad at her no more?"

Clutching his son to him fiercely, Simon closed his eyes and rocked him from side to side. *Almost. He had almost missed this.* He didn't need a lifetime to learn.

"No more, sweetheart, no more. Let's go home."